R8-09166 KT

When Kindness Fails

Other Five Star Titles
by Elizabeth Fackler:

Patricide

When Kindness Fails

Elizabeth Fackler

Five Star • Waterville, Maine

This novel is a work of fiction. Names, characters, places, and incidents are either the product of the author's imagination, or, if real, used fictitiously.

First Edition
First Printing: August 2003

Published in 2003 in conjunction with Tekno Books and Ed Gorman.

Set in 11 pt. Plantin.

Printed in the United States on permanent paper.

Library of Congress Cataloging-in-Publication Data

Fackler, Elizabeth.
    When kindness fails / Elizabeth Fackler.—1st ed.
        p. cm.
    ISBN 0-7862-5443-2 (hc : alk. paper)
    1. Police—Texas—El Paso—Fiction. 2. El Paso (Tex.)
—Fiction. I. Title.
PS3556.A28W47 2003
    813'.54—dc21   2003052873

So I shot 'em down one by one
And left 'em 'long the rails
I use a gun
Whenever kindness fails.

Robert Earl Keene

Chapter One

Beneath the February sky of an El Paso afternoon, in the bare shade of an old cottonwood near the river, Detective Devon Gray knelt on the dry brown grass beside a woman's body. Printing neatly in his small, spiral notebook, he recorded his observations, then slid the notebook back inside his jacket pocket, stood up brushing stickers off the knees of his jeans, and waved for the coroner's crew to take the corpse.

The empty gurney clattered across the grass as he walked to the water's edge and stared at the muddy swirl of the Rio Grande. The opposite bank was in Mexico, but if either the woman or her killer had waded across, it was unlikely she would still be wearing an expensive necklace. The jewelry was an anomaly in light of her cheap dress and bare feet, although the latter were so clean she had obviously arrived wearing shoes. The single blade beneath her breast indicated her death had been quick and easy, but Devon didn't suppose what she had gone through before that was.

He turned toward the sound of Brent's approach, taking comfort from the friendly smile on the sergeant's wry face. As they both watched the coroner's crew load the body, Brent asked, "Why do you think he took her shoes?"

"Maybe they had her name inside."

Brent nodded. "I'm gonna question anyone working the restaurant last night. What're you gonna do?"

"Check missing persons. Before we find her killer, we'll

prob'ly have to figure out who she was."

He listened to Brent leave, the crunch of gravel on the dirt parking lot, then walked deeper under the trees to where the grass was crushed in a general outline of her body. Seeing the blood, a dark stain of seepage, he felt weary at the prospect of beginning again. Somewhere, sometime, he would like to believe human society was making some progress toward peace.

Samantha saw his shadow first, elongated on the concrete veranda of her second-story apartment, then Jay Lehrer stopped in the door she had left open to catch the warmth of sunset. She didn't move from where she was stretched out on her sofa with a book in her hands.

He still wore his hickory hair in a ponytail falling well past his shoulders, though his hairline was receding so his forehead looked higher, accenting the gypsy dark of his eyes. Dressed in a black shirt with three-quarter sleeves and a boat-neck over jeans and running shoes, his body was as soft and pudgy as she remembered.

He chuckled. "Are you thinking of throwing yourself under a train?"

She laid the paperback of *Anna Karenina* on the table and sat up. "What are you doing here, Jay?"

He took a step through the door. "Mind if I come in?"

Straightening the hem of her green velvet robe, which was old and rather ratty, she said, "It appears you've already done that."

"I drove straight through from L.A."

"Why?"

"Lisa called me from here," he said. "She told me not to come, but she's in trouble and I want to help if I can."

"Who's Lisa?"

"My girlfriend. Least she was 'til last week."

"What kind of trouble is she in?"

"I'm not sure."

The phone in the bedroom rang. The answering machine came on and they could hear the tape recording a message, but the volume was set so low the voice was inaudible. Jay waited until the machine shut off again, then asked, "Aren't you gonna find out who called?"

She shook her head. "That's Devon's phone."

"Who's Devon?"

"The man I live with."

Jay nodded. "I don't want to mess anything up for you, Sam. You're the only person I know in El Paso, so the first thing I did was go by the library. They told me you'd called in sick."

"I have a cold," she said. "Where is Lisa?"

"I don't know."

She sighed and stood up. "Sit down, Jay. I'll get dressed."

"You look damn good for having a cold," he said.

The phone in the bedroom rang again. The answering machine caught it on the first ring, recorded the message, then clicked off.

Jay smiled. "Devon's a popular guy. What's he do for a living?"

"He's a police detective."

Jay laughed. "I'd never suspect you of loving a cop."

She went into the bedroom and closed the door. Seeing herself in the mirror, she thought she looked terrible, and she wondered why life always sent unpleasant surprises when she felt least ready to deal with them. She put on makeup and her favorite sweater over a comfy pair of slacks in an effort to make the best of a bad situation, then rejoined Jay and offered him coffee.

They were sitting at the kitchen table waiting for the coffee to brew when Devon's phone rang again. The answering machine ran for a minute, then quit.

"Don't you ever listen?" Jay asked.

She shook her head. "Most of the messages are about his work. That's privileged information."

"Makes it easy for him to get calls he doesn't want you to know about," Jay teased.

"I'd expect you to think of that. But I wouldn't live with a man I didn't trust. It's a lesson I learned from you."

Jay grinned. "The middle of graduate school was no time to get married."

"The first year of marriage was no time to have an affair."

She stood up and walked into the living room, all the way to the stereo against the far wall where she pretended to be choosing a CD.

Jay came over to stand beside her. "What're you listening to these days?" He scanned her collection. "Country and jazz. I bet the jazz is yours and the country's Devon's. Am I right?"

"They're all mine. When Devon moved in, the only things he brought were his clothes and his answering machine for the private phone line he had installed."

"Doesn't he have a life outside work?"

She heard him approaching her open door. In the months they had lived together, she had spent so much time listening for Devon's return that she well knew the cadence of his footsteps. She met Jay's eyes, telling herself she should move away, but it was their hypnotic depth that had attracted her to him in college.

Devon stopped on the threshold. She quickly crossed the room, kissed him hello, then faced Jay with Devon at her back while she introduced them.

Jay stepped forward and offered his hand. "Pleased to meet you."

Devon accepted the handshake, though Samantha could feel he didn't share the sentiment. "Excuse me," he said. "I have to check my messages."

She watched him walk into the bedroom and close the door.

"Friendly guy," Jay quipped with a sarcastic smile.

Feeling an impending threat of loss, Devon gently closed the bedroom door. He tried to tell himself he hadn't lost anything yet, but the anger he felt at seeing them together was nothing he wanted. Using his professional discipline to keep it at bay, he rewound the tape on his answering machine. The first message was from Lieutenant Dreyfus assigning him the murder by the river, an assignment he had already received in his car. Then came a call from his sister-in-law asking if he and Sam were still coming to dinner on Sunday. The answer to that was suddenly in doubt. Last was Sergeant Brent saying the Bonneyana Boutique was closed for the night, but he would check on the necklace again first thing in the morning. Devon erased the tape and walked into the living room to see Samantha and Jay standing as he had left them.

He went into the kitchen for a beer. Twisting the cap off, he saw the full coffeepot and wondered why they hadn't gotten around to drinking any. He threw the cap in the trash, then walked back into the living room, sipping from the bottle as he assessed Samantha's ex-husband. Having heard the story of their brief union marred by Jay's affairs, Devon had accepted the paucity of Sam's description as the tip of an iceberg marking a depth of disappointment. Now he studied the man, wondering what Lehrer was doing in El Paso.

At six feet, he had two inches on Devon and carried twenty more pounds, though Jay was flabby while Devon was compactly muscular, except for a small paunch attesting to his fondness for beer. They both had brown hair and eyes, but while Devon's lanky hair fell no lower than the edge of his collar and he had disciplined himself to hide his emotions, Jay's bristly hair was tied in a ponytail that fell halfway down his back and his eyes were as darkly mesmerizing as a Rasputin's.

When Samantha sat in the rocking chair in the far corner, Devon noted she was wearing her favorite sweater, a soft yellow that brought out the gold in her shoulder-length auburn hair and the honey tone of her eyes. Jay Lehrer sat on the sofa. Both of them were watching Devon, as if they needed to hear he harbored no grudge for having found them together. He sipped his beer, then asked, "What brings you to El Paso, Jay?"

Jay cleared his throat. "My girlfriend took off last week without an explanation. Yesterday she called from here and told me to forget I'd ever known her." He glanced at Samantha, as if for encouragement, before saying, "I figured she was in trouble so I drove straight through from L.A., hoping I could help her."

"What's her name?" Devon asked.

"Lisa Escobar."

"That her maiden name?"

Jay nodded.

"She's never been married?"

"Yeah, she was once," Jay answered defensively, "but she doesn't use his name."

"Do you know his name?"

Jay shook his head.

"What makes you think she's in trouble?"

12

He shifted on the sofa, obviously uncomfortable with the abrupt pattern of questioning. "She was crying."

"Most women cry when they break up with their boyfriends."

"I guess they do," he answered testily, "but most women don't walk out to a Cadillac limousine and disappear in the night. She never said a word, not 'goodbye' or 'that's my uncle.' Nothing."

"Did you get the license number of the limo?"

Jay shook his head.

"Did it have California plates?"

"I don't know. I was so stunned by what was happening, I didn't think to look at the plates."

"When she called, did she tell you where she was?"

"No. After she hung up, I called the operator and asked that she reverse the charges to me, then I asked where the call came from. That's how I found out."

"Did she give you the number?"

"She wouldn't. Said it was an infringement of privacy."

Devon sipped his beer, sensing Sam felt guilty about something, maybe just seeing her ex-husband again. "Well, it's a big city," he told Jay. "My advice is to hire a private investigator."

"Won't the police help?"

"No crime's been committed. You could file a missing person report, but given what you've told me, nobody'll take it seriously. It appears she simply left you. Whether she did it in a Ford or a Rolls doesn't much matter." He sipped his beer again, wondering if he wasn't being unnecessarily hard on the man. More gently, he said, "Apparently you have reason to think she didn't leave voluntarily, but your suspicion isn't enough to warrant the police getting involved."

Jay gave Samantha a pleading look.

Softly she asked, "Isn't there anything you can do, Devon?"

"Not officially."

"Unofficially?" she asked with a hopeful lilt.

He wondered how far she expected him to go. Deciding if Lisa told Jay to his face their relationship was over maybe he would go back to L.A., Devon walked to the kitchen counter, set his beer down, and looked at the man. "What's your home number?"

Jay recited it eagerly.

Devon wrote it on the scratchpad near the phone. "What time did she call?"

"About eleven-thirty last night."

He lifted the receiver off the wall and punched in the number of the Emergency Investigations line at headquarters. "Detective Gray," he said into the phone. "Around eleven-thirty last night someone in El Paso called Los Angeles, 623-2819. I need the address of where that call originated." He waited, watching Samantha. She gave him a smile, her first since he had walked in the door. "Yeah," he said into the phone. "Thanks." He hung up and looked at Jay. "The Camino Real Hotel."

Jay laughed. "That was easy." He stood up. "Where is it?"

"I'll go along," Devon said, "just to make sure I haven't used my sources to interfere with a woman's right to make her own choices." He looked at Samantha. "Want to come?"

They took Devon's car, a black Lexus confiscated from a drug dealer and commandeered by the department. Samantha sat in front with Devon, Jay alone in back. As they descended Santa Fe toward the plaza, Devon glanced into his rearview to meet Jay's eyes.

"Lisa's got a kid," Jay said. "A son she left in Mexico. Her family was laying a heavy guilt trip on her for leaving him

14

behind. That may have something to do with what's happening."

"Is the kid with his father?" Devon asked.

"I don't think so. Lisa didn't tell me much about that whole situation, but I got the impression the kid was with her family."

"In Juárez?"

"Mexico City."

"Why'd she leave him behind?"

"I don't know."

Devon turned left on San Francisco, then into the circular drive in front of the Camino Real, the plushest hotel in El Paso. Just past the lobby, he turned onto the ramp leading to the basement garage. Devon parked and they all got out and walked toward the elevators. Devon pushed the button. "I think you two should wait in the bar," he said, "while I ask at the desk."

Jay looked at Samantha. She nodded.

Devon asked, "Do you have a picture of Lisa?"

Jay took out his wallet, extracted a photo, and handed it over.

Lisa Escobar was about twenty-five, with curly dark hair and the elaborate makeup typical of Mexican women, her shoulders bare over the tight bodice of what appeared to be a black satin evening gown. Maybe it was simply her solemn expression as she faced the camera, or maybe because Devon knew she had left a child behind and how that would affect most women, but he saw an unusual depth of sorrow in her eyes. Much more than the last time he had seen her. Then her eyes had been vacuous with death, and she hadn't been nearly as well dressed.

Devon slid the photo into the breast pocket of his jacket as he followed Samantha and Jay into the elevator. He pushed the button and they rode up in silence, avoiding each other's eyes. In the lobby, he led them past the sweeping staircase to the mezzanine and into the Dome Room, a cavernous space with an original Tiffany skylight above the circular bar. The walls and floor were pink marble, though the latter was covered with thick area rugs between high-backed chairs and velvet settees. Devon led the way to a corner grouping and sat down on one end of a settee. Samantha sat at the other end, looking curious as to why he had changed his mind about sending them in alone while he asked at the desk.

Jay sat down in a green velvet chair facing them across a low mahogany table. The waitress was a college kid with savvy blue eyes. After placing a carafe of mixed nuts on the table and arranging three paper napkins around it, she looked at Devon.

"What're you drinking?" he asked Samantha.

"White wine," she said.

"I'll have a Tecate," he told the waitress.

They all looked at Jay. "Heineken," he said.

She nodded and left. Devon settled back in a corner of the settee, watching Samantha and Jay exchange nervous looks. It was evident they still shared a strong bond despite having been divorced more years than married.

When the waitress had come and gone, Devon leaned forward with his elbows on his knees and told Jay, "I saw Lisa this afternoon."

Jay glanced at Samantha, then looked back uneasily. "Where?"

"Along the river a coupla miles west of here."

"Did you speak to her?"

Devon shook his head. "She wasn't alive."

Jay hid his eyes with his hand.

Devon felt Samantha's need for him to look at her, but he

stayed focused on Jay.

Finally Jay looked at her with a helpless expression, then shifted his gaze back to Devon. "How did she die?"

"Someone knifed her." He heard Samantha whimper in sympathy, striking a spark in Jay's eyes. "When I arrived on the scene, she'd been dead twelve hours."

"How do you know that?" Jay asked.

"The stage of rigor mortis."

Jay shuddered.

"Where were you," Devon asked, "at four o'clock this morning?"

"Somewhere around Blythe, I think." The pain in Jay's eyes snapped into anger. "You think I killed her?"

"I doubt you'd be here if you did."

Jay nodded. "I saw my neighbor as I was leaving home. He can verify I was in L.A. at midnight. It's a sixteen-hour drive, so there's no way I could get here by four o'clock."

"You could've flown."

"I didn't!"

"Take it easy," Devon said. "I'm just doing my job."

Jay leaned back, limp.

Devon looked at Samantha and winced at what he saw. "I'll go ask at the desk now. You all right here?"

She nodded, giving him a sad smile.

He stood up and walked away from them. When he looked back, she was leaning close to Jay, her face crumpled with concern.

Devon showed his badge at the desk. The clerk, a young man prematurely bald and smelling strongly of cologne, frowned before plastering on a phony smile.

"Do you have a Lisa Escobar registered?" Devon asked.

"I'll check." The clerk punched keys on his computer, then shook his head.

Devon showed him the photo. "Have you seen her before?"

The clerk nodded. "Mrs. Tierrasantas. She and her husband left early this morning."

"How early?"

The clerk shrugged. "I wasn't on duty."

"Did they check out, take all their stuff?"

"The maid didn't report anything left in the room."

"Can I see their registration card?"

The clerk nodded reluctantly. "Wait here."

Devon turned and looked toward the bar but was unable to see around the corner. After a minute the clerk came back and handed him the card. He laid it on the desk, took his notebook out and wrote: Sergio Tierrasantas, Chinati TX, '94 BMW, license 1-LOBO. He replaced his notebook and slid the card toward the clerk. "Thanks."

He could feel the clerk watching until he turned the corner into the bar. Jay was sitting on the sofa next to Samantha, who was holding his hand. Devon sat down across from them. "She was here with her husband," he said to their expectant faces.

"The sonofabitch," Jay whispered hoarsely. "He must've killed her!"

"Maybe," Devon said with measured calm. "Or maybe they split company and someone else did it." He paused, then asked, "Would you be willing to identify her body?"

Jay jerked back into his corner of the settee. "I can't believe we're talking about this!"

Devon lifted his can of Tecate, slid the Heineken across the table, took a sip of the Tecate and quietly set it down, then met Jay's eyes again.

Jay nodded.

Devon looked at Samantha. "Want me to call you a cab?"

"I'd like to come, if that's all right."

Devon stood up. "Let's go."

He walked across to the bar and gave the waitress a twenty, knowing their drinks cost five dollars each.

"Thanks," she said, not bothering with change.

Devon let it slide, following Samantha and Jay toward the elevators. Twenty bucks was steep for three drinks that hadn't been touched except for the one sip he had taken, but he suspected he stood to lose a lot more on this case.

Chapter Two

The morgue was in Thomason Hospital. As Devon drove east on Alameda, he wondered what Jay thought of this part of El Paso. The majority of signs were in Spanish, and the few pedestrians and most everyone else looked Mexican. Many of them probably were, though for most purposes the issue of citizenship was moot. Glancing into the rearview, he saw Jay staring at the floor, barely seeing El Paso, much less thinking about it. Samantha was looking out the window, so they were three people alone in a cop car en route to a morgue.

Far in the distance, Devon heard the warning wail of a train approaching a crossroads. No matter what he was doing, he always took comfort from the thought of a train traveling through the pass, maybe simply because of the romance of trains, or the border mythology of a town famous as a waystation for men on the run. For more than a century that whistle had echoed off the mesa to reverberate through the somnolent sun or street-wise dark, carrying the reminder that all men were simply moving through time and space to a destination that felt important but in reality was merely a place to be going.

Lisa Escobar had only two trips left. From the morgue she would be taken to a funeral home, from there to a cemetery. On both trips she would wear neither her silver and gold necklace nor her black satin evening gown.

When Devon and Jay looked at her in the chilled room of

the hospital's basement, she was naked, encased in a thin plastic bag the attendant zipped open barely low enough to reveal her head and shoulders.

"Is that Lisa?" Devon asked gently.

"Yeah," Jay whispered. He moved away to lean against the wall and hide his face in his folded arms.

Devon nodded for the attendant to put her back, then watched him rezip the bag, slide the drawer into the wall, and close the door.

Jay's shoulders were jerking with his sobs. After a few minutes, he stood up straight and used his handkerchief to wipe his eyes and blow his nose.

Samantha was waiting outside the door. She looked back and forth between them, knowing from their faces the answer they had come here to find. The three of them rode up to the lobby, then walked outside to Devon's car.

Nobody said anything as they drove west on Alameda and uphill on Santa Fe to Samantha's apartment in Sunset Heights. Parking at the curb, Devon felt as if he were the one who should get out and leave them alone.

"Where will you stay tonight?" Samantha asked Jay.

Devon watched in the rearview as Jay shrugged and said, "Guess I'll check into the Camino Real."

"Their rooms start at ninety dollars," she said. "You can get one on Mesa for thirty."

"I want to be there." He fumbled with the door handle and got out.

Devon and Samantha did too, then Devon walked a short distance away. Samantha held onto Jay's arm a moment before he opened the door of his own car. She stood where she was as he pulled a U-turn and disappeared over the crest of the hill. Finally she turned around and met Devon's eyes. He held out his hand. She took it and without speaking they walked upstairs.

The first thing she did when they were inside her apartment was open her purse and pull a twenty out of her wallet. "For the drinks," she said.

"Forget it," he said, not taking the money.

"I want to pay you back, Devon. And to thank you for being so nice to Jay."

"I'll take the thanks. But if you're gonna have a drink with your ex-husband, I'd just as soon pay for it."

She dropped the twenty back in her purse and zipped it closed, reminding him of the sound of the zipper in the morgue. "I need a shower," she said.

He waited until she had closed the bathroom door before he went into the bedroom and hung up his jacket, noting how dull his side of the closet looked compared to hers. Pulling his shirttails free of the belt holding his gun in the small of his back, he moved to the bed, then unbuttoned his shirt as he checked for messages on his answering machine.

Only Laura had called, repeating her question about dinner. When he punched in her number, his brother answered the phone.

"How you doing, bro?" Connie asked as soon as he heard Devon's voice.

"No complaints. Tell Laura I'll do my best to be there on Sunday but I can't make any promises."

"You hot on a case?" Connie teased with a laugh.

"Looks like it might take me out of town."

"Tell Samantha to come alone. She's prettier'n you anyway."

"No argument. How're the kids?"

"Misty misses you. Pesters us nearly everyday about when you're coming to see us."

"And Eric?" Having jimmied a murder case the year

before so his eighteen-year-old nephew escaped the consequences of what had all the earmarks of a set-up, Devon was still waiting to see if the kid benefited from that mercy.

"He's going to his classes," Connie said, his frivolity gone. "Guess that's all we can hope for right now."

"Is he doing his homework?"

"I don't ask. I don't want to push him, you know? Hell, I never expected him to finish high school, let alone go to college. We got you to thank for that, Devon."

"Yeah, well, thank Laura for asking us to supper, and tell her I'll let her know soon as I can." He hung up and stared at the closed bathroom door as he listened to Samantha turn off the shower. Then he sat down and punched in Darryl Brent's home number.

The sergeant picked up the phone. "Yeah?"

"I ID'ed the lady we found by the river."

Brent laughed. "That was fast. How'd you do it?"

"Her boyfriend came sniffing around and I took him to the morgue. Her name's Lisa Escobar. She was staying in the Camino Real with her husband, Sergio Tierrasantas."

"I've met Sergio. He's a charmer."

"Think he could be that good with a knife?"

"And any other weapon you care to mention."

"How'd you know to go to the Bonneyana Boutique?"

"Secretary at the morgue said the necklace was made by a Navajo named Nah Ro. They're his only local outlet."

Devon nodded. "I'm gonna ask for authorization to go into Presidio and question Tierrasantas myself."

There was a silence in which Devon knew his friend was wondering why he felt impelled to do that, but all Brent said was, "Have to take the Ranger for that jurisdiction with you."

"Joaquin's a good man to work with."

"It isn't Joaquin anymore. He resigned on account of the

governor making the Rangers hire women. One of her new recruits is stationed in Chinati now."

"What's her experience?"

"She was a clerk in the Motor Vehicle Department in Austin."

"Shit."

Brent laughed. "You still want to go?"

"I can't leave the investigation in the hands of an M.V.D. clerk."

"Especially when the subject's Sergio Tierrasantas. He's the sort of man who considers rape a political expedient."

"That should justify me going. Get your tail up to Mesilla and wake up the owners of that boutique if you have to. I'll need all the documentation I can get to pull this off."

Again Brent was silent, though his curiosity rode the wires between them. "I can't do it 'til tomorrow," he finally said. "Crossing the state line, I'll need the cooperation of the Doña Ana Sheriff's Department. You know that."

"I'm just saying don't waste any time."

"I hear you. But there's something I'm not hearing, too. I'm not gonna ask 'cause if I don't know I can't tell the lieutenant when he asks, which he surely will. You got an answer for him?"

"I'll let you know when I come up with one."

He hung up just as Samantha came out of the bathroom trailing a vapor of steam. She opened the closet and took off her robe, standing there nude for the few seconds it took to pull her nightgown over her head. The gown was an icy blue, falling loose to cover only the tops of her thighs.

Devon's mother had died when he was twelve, so except for the few years he had lived with his brother's family, and even then he'd had his own bathroom, he had never experienced sustained intimacy with a female. It still amazed him that she could so casually reveal her body, as if unaware the vessel comprising her being was a source of wonderment for him. He watched her walk to the other side of the bed and set the alarm, then climb under the covers and close her eyes against the light.

"Tired?" he asked.

She looked at him. "I feel terrible about Jay."

He nodded. "I can tell."

"Oh, Devon," she said, sitting up so the covers fell in her lap, "what I feel for him has nothing to do with us."

"I'm afraid I can't honestly say that, Sam."

She smiled sadly. "He's a good person. Probably he was too young when we got married and just wasn't ready to settle down. But he really loved Lisa, and he's hurting terribly now."

"What concerns me is you're hurting too. And what you're feeling has nothing to do with Lisa."

She studied him a moment. "I love you, Devon. No one will ever change that."

"Doesn't seem it changed your feelings for him either."

"They're different, my feelings for each of you. Jay is . . ." She paused before saying, "Jay has . . ." She stopped again.

"A hold on you."

"But it's not anything I want! You're who I want. Doesn't that count?"

"I don't know," he said, laughing in an effort to lighten their mood. "Guess we're gonna find out."

"When he first came this afternoon," she argued, "I just wanted to get rid of him. But after I learned why he's here, I decided I couldn't turn my back on a man I once loved. Even if that only meant offering you, your help, which is all I can really give Jay."

"Did he know you're living with a cop before he came to your door?"

"I hadn't spoken to him since I left California."

"Then the help he wanted had nothing to do with me."

"I'm the only person he knows in El Paso. That's why he came here."

"No. He came hoping there was enough of your love left to help him deal with the loss of his new love. You gave him exactly what he wanted: someone to hold his hand. I don't blame either one of you for that, but it makes me feel like the intruder in this triangle."

"Please don't let him come between us."

"That's not my decision. It's yours."

"I can't believe we're talking about this!"

"That's what Jay said when I asked if he'd ID the corpse." He stood up. "Maybe I oughta sleep on the couch tonight."

"Don't," she moaned.

He walked out, closing the door between them.

Sitting in the dark, he kept wishing she would come and coax him back into her bedroom. After an hour, he gave up and walked out to his car, took a black leather jacket from his trunk and put it on to conceal his gun, then drove downtown to headquarters to finish the paperwork left over from his last case. He caught a few hours sleep in the lounge and was back at his desk when the day shift came in.

At eleven o'clock the next morning, he was driving his confiscated Lexus east on I-10 toward Chinati. On the passenger seat lay a folder of papers, including a search warrant for the residence of Sergio Tierrasantas specific to the murder weapon, a formal request from El Paso's Chief of Police for Devon to act on the city's behalf in Presidio County, and a faxed authorization from the Sheriff of Presidio granting permission under the stipulation that Devon work with the Texas Ranger for that district. Also in the folder were copies of the preliminary autopsy report, a credit card receipt in Sergio's name for the necklace found on the corpse, the registration card from the Camino Real Hotel, and Jay Lehrer's photograph of Lisa.

While still at the office, Devon had asked Brent to run a general check on Lehrer with the Los Angeles Police, then he had gone home to pack an overnight bag. Sitting on the bed he hadn't slept in the night before, he called Samantha at work to tell her he probably wouldn't be back until Friday. He wanted to add a warning to stay away from Lehrer but had no rational reason, only a distrust of the man probably founded more on personal jealousy than anything else. So he had kept the conversation pointedly brief, switched his answering machine to forward his calls to headquarters, and left without changing clothes except to trade his black leather jacket for a light brown sports coat, figuring to shower in a motel in Chinati.

That had been an hour ago. As he approached the Border Patrol checkpoint at Sierra Blanca, his thoughts were gradually moving away from what he had left behind and becoming focused on what lay ahead. Once through the checkpoint, he still had three hours of solitude before he arrived in Chinati. Someone at headquarters was to call Ranger Drake and tell her he was coming, so his access was paved, but their meeting would be cold, neither of them knowing what to expect.

Devon had never worked closely with a woman. The El Paso Police had been hiring them for a few years now, but none had risen high enough that Devon couldn't keep his interaction with them minimal. This was Texas, after all, where male supremacy still reigned intact. At least it had until Anne Richards was elected governor.

Her opponent had been a dyed-in-the-wool good ol' boy. Shortly before the election, he invited some reporters for a weekend of hunting on his ranch. It had rained. As they sipped sourmash around the blazing hearth of his lodge, the aspiring governor told his guests bad weather was like being raped: if it was gonna happen, you may as well lie back and enjoy it. The joke cost him the election, and one of Anne Richards' first acts in office was to order the Texas Rangers to hire women.

At the Border Patrol checkpoint, Devon was waved through because of his government plates. He accelerated back onto the freeway, nudged the odometer up to eighty, and tried to hone his tension toward an effective edge of combat.

The Tierrasantas family had owned the town of Chinati as well as the hundred-square miles around it for nearly a century. In that situation, lawmen were considered pesky intruders interfering with the natural order. So beyond the fact that Sergio could be expected to be arrogant, Devon also knew the badges he and Ranger Drake wore would carry no more power than they could personally enforce with the strength of their will. To be saddled with a novice on such a touchy assignment, with the added liability that she was among the first female Rangers and out to prove women were up to the job, was worrisome.

Chinati lay on a plateau between the Davis and Oro Mountains, both in the six-thousand-foot range. Its business district consisted of two blocks of Victorian brick buildings, many of them boarded-up. Devon parked at the curb, got out, and stretched his back, noting the air was crystal clear, the sky an unbroken blue, and the village almost as quiet as the desert.

His view into Ranger Drake's office was hidden behind tinted windows. The Ranger insignia was painted on the door, but no hours were given and the emergency number was that of the local sheriff's office. With a diminishing hope of gaining entry, he approached and tried the knob. To his pleasant surprise, it turned in his hand.

He walked into a small room sparsely furnished with a minimum of office equipment: a fax machine, filing cabinet, and water cooler. Facing the door was an old wooden desk where a woman looked up from reading a newspaper. She was petite and close to thirty, her sleek black hair in a pixie cut with jagged bangs over bright blue eyes, her face sporting not a speck of makeup as she said with a grin, "Welcome to Chinati, Detective Gray."

"Thanks. Are you Ranger Drake?"

She walked out from behind the desk and extended her hand. "Call me Prairie."

She wore a white shirt with the silver-circled star of her badge pinned above her left breast. A colorfully-beaded belt ran through the loops of her jeans, and below that hung a gunbelt with a Colt's .45 riding her right hip. Her snug jeans were tucked into brown leather boots that bore the Ranger insignia branded just below both knees. As Devon shook her hand, noting it was as rough as a workman's, he couldn't help but laugh.

Prairie Drake laughed too, hanging onto his hand. "We've met, but I don't reckon you remember."

He shook his head.

"It was in Austin last October at that lawman's convention. The gov'nor introduced us, but I got the feeling you weren't real impressed with the notion of females joining the Rangers. I think the gov'nor got the same feeling."

Devon looked down at their hands still clasped between them.

She let go but didn't move away. "My hair was long then, pretty near down to my waist. I cut it soon as I got my badge."

"Why's that?" he asked, trying to remember her.

"Long hair gives an opponent a handle to grab you by."

"Get into many fights, do you?"

"Some," she said, walking back behind her desk. She opened a low drawer and took out a floppy brown purse with long leather fringe. Hanging its strap on her shoulder, she asked, "Can I buy you a cup of coffee?"

"Why not?"

She nodded for him to go first, then followed him out and locked the door.

"Coffee jitters my nerves so I don't keep it around," she said, already moving along the sidewalk. "Horace's Café is only a skip and a jump down the block."

"I'd just as soon have a beer," Devon called after her.

She turned back to face him. "We could go to the Range Rider on the edge of town. How's that sound?"

"Fine."

She looked at the Lexus. "That your car?"

He nodded.

"My Jeep's in the shop getting an oil change. You wanta drive?"

He unlocked and opened the passenger door, then looked at her watching from where she still stood on the sidewalk.

"I ain't had a man open my door for as long as I can remember," she said in awe.

He gestured for her to get in, noting the slender line of her thighs as she did; then he closed the door and walked around to the driver's side.

"Nice car," she said as he turned the ignition.

"The drug dealer who bought it evidently liked it."

"You don't?" she asked in amazement.

"I'd buy American, if it was my money."

She nodded. "I heard tell the El Paso Police were using

confiscated cars. The department must hold you in high regard to give you this one."

"My lieutenant drives a Mercedes. Which way we going?"

"Pull a U. It's about a mile outside of town."

He looked for traffic but there wasn't any, so he maneuvered a U-turn and headed west.

Prairie said, "I was tickled pink to hear you were coming."

"Why's that?"

"I engineered that intro from the gov, but it didn't do me any good. You looked through me like a piece of fluff you didn't need to bother blowing off."

He looked at her now.

She laughed. "Ain't any woman ever told you you're cute, Devon?"

"I don't think they used that word," he said.

She laughed again. "There was a lotta hanky-panky going on at that convention, but I didn't see you at any of the parties."

"I was involved."

"With a woman, you mean?"

He nodded.

"You still involved?"

"I'm not sure," he admitted.

"But you're not married?"

"No. Are you?"

"Reckon I'm too much woman for most men to handle."

Devon had to concede that was probably true. Ahead he saw the Range Rider Saloon, built to resemble a facsimile of a frontier barn though the structure looked new. He pulled into the gravel parking lot and killed his engine.

"You gonna open my door for me?" she asked with an impish grin.

"If you can sit still long enough for me to get around the

car," he said, amused despite himself.

When he got there, she looked up with a smile of such pure delight that he had to laugh. "Why don't you bring that folder off the back seat so we can get down to business?"

She twisted around to retrieve the folder. "You know much about Sergio Tierrasantas?"

"No."

"He's gonna be a worthy opponent," she predicted as they walked toward the saloon.

She stopped in front of the door and waited for him to open it for her, then sailed in with a seemingly irrepressible giggle. "I like being treated like a lady."

"I can well imagine you'd find it unusual," he muttered.

But she only laughed again as she led him across the empty dance floor to a booth in back. Laying the folder on the table, she sat down and asked, "Mind if I look at these papers?"

"That's what I brought 'em for."

The room was as cavernous as the barn it was designed to simulate, with high rafters and wagon wheel chandeliers. Covered with red vinyl, the bar had a brass foot rail and spittoons at each end. The waitress coming toward them wore a white cowgirl outfit: boots under a short skirt and a white fringed vest closed with one button. Since she wasn't wearing a blouse, the skimpy vest barely covered her breasts.

"What're you drinking?" Devon asked Prairie.

"Dr Pepper," she said with freshly ignited delight. "You gonna order for me?"

He told the waitress, "I'll have a draft and the lady wants a Dr Pepper."

The waitress looked askance at Prairie, who laughed and said, "Hi, Suzy."

Suzy nodded. "Be right back," she said, leaving them alone.

"We're gonna be an item around town," Prairie said. "The big city cop and the local Texas Ranger. Hell, we'll prob'ly make the papers."

"Let's hope it's 'cause we solve the case."

"Yeah, we'll do that too," Prairie said, opening the folder.

Devon watched her study the documents, then looked up at Suzy bringing their drinks. After she had left again, Prairie said, "We got a problem here, Devon."

He sipped his beer, hoping the alcohol would ease the kinks of tension in his spine. "What's that?"

"The sheriff didn't sign your authorization, only his deputy."

"Dreyfus accepted it. That's good enough for me."

"He's your lieutenant, right?"

Devon nodded.

"Reckon we can go with it, but I'm just warning you, Rufus ain't gonna like it."

"The sheriff's name is Rufus?"

"Rufus Bowlin, yeah. He's a mean sonofabitch."

Devon sipped his beer.

"When you figure on questioning Sergio?" she asked.

"Why not right now?"

"It's a two-hour drive to the ranch house."

"We oughta get started then."

She pulled her Dr Pepper close and sucked on the straw, keeping her eyes to herself.

"Have you ever investigated a homicide?" he asked.

She shook her head. "This is my first case."

"Your first homicide?"

"My first anything."

"Shit," he muttered, looking away.

"I was the top shooter in my marksmanship class."

He met her eyes, bright blue in the gloom. "I generally

solve my cases without using a gun."

"This ain't the city, Devon. And Sergio Tierrasantas ain't no alley rat apt to fall apart under a hard interrogation. His family's been the power around here for nigh on a hundred years, and he went to Harvard Law School. He's smooth, and he's smart, and he's used to getting his way. If he thinks we're any kinda serious threat, he's got an army of *vaqueros* who'll kill and bury us someplace where nobody but his cows ever go. So don't be discounting my abilities with a gun."

"Killing a cop's capital murder. Not even a Tierrasantas can get away with it."

"All our bosses will know is we went out there and didn't come back. There won't be no *corpus delicti* and there won't be enough evidence to indict, let alone convict. 'Sides, if it comes to that, it won't matter a whole helluva lot to us 'cause we'll be dead." She smiled around the straw in her Dr Pepper, then took a noisy sip.

"How well do you know Sergio?" he asked.

"We went to school together, all the way from kindergarten through high school. Then we were both at UT Austin at the same time, though he majored in Western Civ and I was in Criminal Justice. There ain't a lot of people out here, so the social classes mingle pretty freely and we both went to the same parties growing up. I never dated him though he asked me a coupla times. The girls who did either called in sick the next day or came to school wearing heavy makeup and dark glasses."

"Know his wife?"

"Met her once or twice, is all. General consensus was they got married 'cause her father's ranch abutted his across the international line. In the five years they lived together, she was brought to the hospital twice 'cause she either fell down the stairs or got bucked off a horse. The first time she had

34

bruises worthy of the loser in a heavyweight fight, the second time she had multiple lacerations that appeared to be made by the blade of a knife, though nobody I know ever heard of a staircase or horse either one using a knife." She sucked Dr Pepper through her straw. "Sergio Tierrasantas is a sadist with the mind of a legal genius. If the Marquis de Sade had never lived, what he called fun, we'd call Sergioistic. You got the picture, Devon?"

He nodded.

She turned the page to the preliminary autopsy report.

The outside door opened, throwing a sliver of sunlight across the floor to their booth. Devon squinted at the silhouette of a man coming in, then the door closed and it took a second for his eyes to readjust enough to see that the man was walking straight toward them.

"Looks like we have company," he said softly.

Prairie looked up. "Oh hell," she muttered with disgust. "It's Carl."

"Who's Carl?"

"Used to be my boyfriend. Now he's just an ass with poop in his pants."

Chapter Three

Carl stopped a few feet away and glared at Devon, then at Prairie.

"What'cha want, Carl?" she asked.

"Just to say hey," he answered with a belated smile.

"Hey," she said, returning her gaze to the autopsy report.

"Ain't ya gonna introduce me to your friend?" Carl asked.

Prairie slowly raised her head, glanced at Devon, then said, "This here's Detective Devon Gray, Carl. We're working, so why don't you get lost?"

Carl extended his hand instead. "Carl Lowdy," he said.

Devon stood up and shook hands, then stayed on his feet, holding the man's eyes. Carl was a few inches shorter, blond with a solid barrel body, but though his face bore several scars probably earned in brawls, he backed down from Devon's direct stare.

"Pleased to meet'cha," Carl muttered.

"Same here," Devon lied.

Carl looked at Prairie. "You gonna be at Cynthia's party tomorrow night?"

"Reckon I'll be busy," she answered with overblown patience.

Carl stared at her a moment, then nodded at Devon and walked over to the bar. Devon sat back down.

"You don't need to stand up for the likes of him," Prairie said.

"I don't need you to tell me how to handle myself," Devon replied.

Prairie shrugged. "Says here the victim was killed with a knife having a four-inch blade. That's too big to fit in most pockets."

"Unless it's a switchblade."

"Also says the blade went in just below her wishbone at the exact right angle to penetrate her heart, but there wasn't nary a bruise on her arms or neck. That means she didn't fight her killer, which prob'ly means she knew and trusted him."

"Probably."

"Makes me doubt it was Sergio, though. He gets his kicks roughing up women. I can't see him taking much satisfaction in killing her clean."

Nudged with a worry he couldn't quite name, Devon rubbed his chin and realized he hadn't shaved since yesterday morning. "Maybe I'll grab some supper and a shower before we drive out there."

"We can do it at my place," Prairie answered. "I'll fix something to eat while you're washing up and save us some time."

They picked up her Jeep at the garage and Devon followed her from there. She lived five miles east of town in a weathered gray cabin with a veranda. Off to the side was a corral holding an Appaloosa and a pinto in front of a small stable. The yard was a barren expanse of dust. As Devon took his overnight bag from his backseat, he heard the horses nickering a welcome to Prairie.

"Hey, *caballos,*" she called, waving as she crossed the yard to her front door. She unlocked it and disappeared inside.

Distant mountains circled her home. Except for the two vehicles and power lines running from the road, Devon didn't guess the place would have looked much different a hundred years ago. The horses were watching him, their ears turned forward with curiosity, the mare white-faced with a black-and-white harlequin coat, the gelding gunmetal gray with black spots on its rump. Devon carried his small valise across the yard, up the stairs to the veranda, and inside.

A stone fireplace filled the wall to his left. Facing the hearth was an overstuffed sofa covered with an old Navajo blanket. A coffee table with a barbed-wire sculpture of a bucking bronco was between the sofa and fireplace. Through an open door on his right he could see the foot of a brass bed. In front of him was a knotty pine breakfast bar with two wooden stools, and beyond that Prairie was cooking in a cubby-hole kitchen.

"The bath's through the bedroom," she said without stopping work.

Devon walked into her bedroom, noting the brass bed frame was tarnished with a patina of age. On the nightstand was a lamp fashioned out of ocotillo stalks and a shade printed with the Lone Star flag of Texas. Beneath it a chocolate brown phone sat on a black answering machine. A chiffonnier was the only closet, a gun case holding half a dozen rifles the only other furniture.

The bathroom was small, the shower tiled in blue, the linen closet open shelves crowded with neat stacks of colorful towels and sheets. The room was so compact he could barely turn around, so he set his valise just outside, hung his jacket and shirt on the knob, and left the door open while he looked for an outlet to plug in his shaver. There was only one, in the light fixture over the mirror. He had to unplug her hairdryer, which was laying on a stack of *Field and Stream* on the back of the commode. Just before he turned on his shaver, he heard the crackle of something frying in grease.

After his shower, the aroma from the kitchen was surprisingly enticing. Leaving his jacket on the back of her sofa, he carried his valise out to his car, noting the horses were now eating a pile of hay she had thrown on the ground.

When he walked back inside, Prairie chirped, "Just about ready. You want another beer?"

"What else've you got?" He sat down at the breakfast bar, which she had set with two plates and silverware arranged on yellow paper napkins. On the stove, chicken-fried steaks sizzled beside crusty-brown home fries.

She opened the refrigerator and surveyed its interior. "Coke, Dr Pepper, o.j., milk?"

"Coke," he said.

She opened a can and set it in front of him, then went back to the stove. "I don't drink beer much myself. But I keep it for company."

Sipping his Coke, he looked around the spotless kitchen and shiny wood floor of the living room. "I wouldn't have expected you to be so domestic."

"I ain't," she answered, shifting the potatoes in the skillet with a long-handled fork. "Oh, I can cook a mean steak or fry eggs easy-over, but Cynthia keeps my house. She comes by every morning to clean up and feed my horses if I'm not around."

"The same Cynthia giving the party tomorrow tonight?"

Prairie nodded. "She's about my best friend."

"A best friend's good to have."

"Who's yours?" she asked, forking the steaks onto the plates.

"Guess it's my brother."

"One of them's good to have, too." She chased the potatoes out of the skillet, set it back on the stove and the plates on the counter, sat down beside him, and dug in.

He watched her a moment, then cut into the steak and

tasted a bite. "Good," he said around it.

"Thanks," she mumbled, not looking up.

He kept glancing at her during the meal, but guessed she considered eating serious business because she didn't raise her head until her plate was empty. Then she carried it and her silverware into the kitchen, rinsed them under the faucet, and left them in the sink. Only half-finished with his meal, Devon smiled at her as she lifted her Dr Pepper off the counter and took a sip while she leaned against the refrigerator.

"It'll be dark 'fore we get there," she said. "What if Sergio ain't home?"

"I've got a search warrant for the premises."

"Yeah, I saw it. But it'd take a week to search that house and all the outbuildings."

"We'll do what we can."

"It's a helluva ride for nothing. You got any objection to me calling and asking if he'll be there?"

"That'd give him warning to hide the knife, if he hasn't already."

"I won't mention you're coming along. It'll sound like a social visit."

"That something you do often?"

"My predecessor told me it's a good idea to keep in touch so folks know who they'll be dealing with when they're in trouble."

"All right," Devon said. "Go ahead and call."

She left her Dr Pepper on the counter and walked into the bedroom. He finished his meal, hearing her punch in Sergio's number and noting she hadn't needed to look it up.

"*Bueno*," she said into the phone. "*Soy* Prairie Drake. *¿Coma estás,* Estrella?"

Devon sat still, listening to her say, "*Sí. Quiero hablar con*

Sergio." After a moment, she said, *"Gracias."* He picked up his plate, carried it and his silverware into the kitchen, and rinsed and left them in the sink as she had. Then he heard her say, "Hey, Sergio. How you doing?"

Devon carried his Coke over to the open front door and stood looking out at her horses. He heard Prairie ask, "You gonna be around?" After a minute, she said, "Nah, I just need to go by Cipriano's and thought I'd check in with you." She listened, then said, "Yeah, he found some wire cut alongside Coyote Canyon." She laughed softly. "I ain't saying you cut it, Sergio. Why would you, after all the trouble your old man went to getting Cipriano to keep his sheep off your range?" She listened, then said, "That's the only reason." Listened again and said, "I'm fixing to leave now." After another pause, she said, *"Hasta."*

Devon turned around and watched her come out of the bedroom carrying a black denim jacket.

"Ready?" she asked.

After stopping at his car to get the folder of documentation, he joined her in her Jeep. It was a green four-wheel-drive Cherokee with a rifle rack behind the seats holding a .44 Winchester with a high-power scope. She waved at her horses as she drove out of the yard.

As she turned onto Highway 90 going west, he wondered at her sudden silence. It stretched out so long he finally asked if she was nervous. She glanced at him before saying, "I'm always nervous when I go out there. Sergio usually manages to make me feel damn uncomfortable before I leave."

"How?"

"You'll see."

They didn't speak again until she turned south on Farm-to-Market Road 2810 and they had traveled a few miles along the two-lane blacktop. In a field on the right was a handmade billboard proclaiming: IN TEXAS THE COPS *ARE* THE ROBBERS! Devon laughed, then looked at Prairie.

"Carl painted that soon as I got my badge," she said with mild disgust. "That's his pasture there."

Devon turned around to look at the pasture fast disappearing behind them. Half a dozen pinto horses grazed on the sparse grass. "Those his horses?"

"Yeah. He gave me Bandit, my pinto. If I didn't love the mare so much, I'd give her back just to keep from being beholden to him. But I've got her bred now, and he's told me the stud I chose ain't worth a damn and he'd abort her if I did, so I'm keeping her least 'til she foals."

"What's wrong with the stud?"

"He ain't a pinto, is all. But he's got good lines and won a coupla trophies as a cutting horse, so I ain't all that concerned about color. Handsome is as handsome does in my book."

Remembering her description of him, he asked, "What does that say about cute?"

"Cute's what women like to cuddle in bed."

They shared a smile, then fell silent again. For the next hour, the only sounds between them were the occasional squawks of the police radio mounted under her dashboard and the repetitious whir of the tires. The whir changed to a rolling crunch when they left the blacktop and the road became gravel. Ahead, the silhouette of the Chinati Mountains expanded like a fungus above the horizon. After another few miles, she turned left onto a dirt road and drove by a sign proclaiming they were entering the private property of the Tierrasantas Ranch.

The chaparral around them softened in the thick light of sunset, then turned dusky rose before fading into a lavender that kept slipping in barely perceptible increments until the earth was blanketed with a slate blue only slightly dimmer than the sky. A few minutes later, Prairie turned on her highbeams and suddenly they were traveling through a tunnel of light traversing a dark wilderness.

Abruptly, she said, "Don't reckon you consider me much of a partner on this job."

He studied her pertly pretty face in the flattering glow of the dash as he considered his answer. Finally he said, "I won't deny I'd rather be going in with your predecessor, but from what I've seen so far, you handle yourself all right."

She flashed him a smile of gratitude that was quickly gone. "Can't honestly say I blame you. Sergio's the kinda man who makes being a woman a real liability."

"As long as he stops short of violence, he can only do that if you let him."

"I can handle the violence."

He let his gaze slide over her slender body. "I don't want to diminish your confidence, Prairie, but have you ever been in a fight with a man?"

"I put Carl in the hospital when he took exception to my breaking off with him." She smiled. "Course I had to use brass knuckles to do it, but when you only weigh a hundred and ten, you gotta give yourself an edge."

He nodded. "You have your brass knuckles with you now?"

"I always keep 'em in my jacket pocket, but I won't have cause to use 'em." She sighed deeply. "I hope you've seen your share of blue movies, Devon, 'cause unless Sergio's changed tactics, he'll have one going when we walk in."

"Don't look at it."

"I try not to, but it's a tactic male officers don't ever have to face down. I don't think a man can appreciate how humiliating it is to see your entire sex depicted as nothing

43

more'n a victim to be hurt."

"It's not your entire sex. You walking in wearing a badge is proof of that."

She flashed him another smile that didn't reach her eyes. "The last time I visited Sergio, he had a snuff movie going. It's damn hard to stand there and shoot the shit while one whole wall's lit up with the image of a woman having her throat cut."

He winced. "Snuff movies are illegal. You could have arrested him for being in possession of one."

"Yeah, but it's a misdemeanor so the most he'd get is thirty days, and being a Tierrasantas, he wouldn't serve a minute of it. All I'd accomplish is making him an enemy. That's a piss poor position for anyone in this county. He's about our only employer and nobody bucks his orders. If it got around that I'd lost his good will, I'd be pretty near useless as a lawman."

"Well, if we can pin this murder on him, he'll be giving his orders from prison."

"I don't think that's something I'll live to see."

Five minutes later the lights of the compound lit the horizon ahead of them. Half an hour after that, Prairie drove through the gate into the yard.

When Samantha arrived home that night, Jay Lehrer was sitting on the wooden bench outside her door, arousing within her a strong sense of *deja vu*. When she and Jay had been married, they had a wooden bench outside their front door, and because his hours at the computer firm were erratic, she had often come home to find him basking in the sunset while waiting for her to get off work.

Trying to suppress the memory of how happy she had felt then to find him home, she reminded herself of the disappointment she ultimately took from their marriage, then chided herself because she needed reminding. Reluctantly inviting him in, she asked, "Have you learned any more about Lisa?"

He shook his head. "I left several messages at headquarters for Devon, but he didn't return my calls. Finally I got tired of hanging in my hotel room, so I came over here."

"He's gone to Chinati to question her ex-husband."

"Leaving you alone with yours."

Though she felt uncomfortable, she said, "Sit down, Jay. I'll go change."

Closing the bedroom door, she turned around and stared at the bed, remembering she had slept alone the night before. It disturbed her that Jay's mere arrival had driven a wedge between her and Devon. Within hours of Jay showing up, Devon had withdrawn into the armored shell of his autonomy that she had worked so long and hard to crack. Now after a night of silence, he was out of touch for another night, leaving her, as Jay had said, alone with her ex-husband.

Samantha quickly changed from her work clothes into a blue cotton sweater, jeans, and running shoes. She freshened her makeup and brushed her hair, telling herself it was silly to feel nervous.

When she rejoined Jay, he was looking out the open front door with a beer in his hand. "Hope you don't mind that I helped myself," he said with a teasing smile.

She shook her head. In the kitchen, she opened the refrigerator for a Diet Coke.

"Is this Devon's Budweiser?"

She nodded, opening her Coke.

"I prefer imports myself."

"If you feel impelled to criticize him, surely you could come up with something more important than his taste in beer."

"Surely I could." Jay's smile was conciliatory. "But I'm not trying to do that."

She decided she was blaming him for something that wasn't his fault. "I'm sorry. Devon and I quarreled last night, and I guess I'm feeling out of sorts because of it."

"What was your quarrel about?"

"I'd rather not discuss it."

"Okay. How about if I take you to dinner?"

"I don't think I should."

"Is Devon the jealous type?"

"Just the opposite. He usually gives me more space than I want."

"Doesn't sound to me like you're real happy with him, Sam."

"You don't seem particularly upset over Lisa's death."

A wave of sorrow darkened the fun in his eyes, making her regret her words.

"I'm sorry," she said. "I had no right to say that."

"I don't mind, Sam. Even though we haven't seen each other for a while, I still consider you my best friend. As for Lisa . . ." He shrugged. "I guess when she left without bothering to say goodbye, I emotionally closed the door on her out of self-defense."

"Yet you still came all this way to help her," Samantha suggested gently.

Jay sipped his beer. When he looked up, his dark eyes were sparkling with fun again. "I don't have anywhere to go but back to my hotel. Why not let me take you to dinner?"

The Tierrasantas home was a hacienda in the old style, a walled courtyard around the adobe house with a portal along the front of the first floor and a veranda on the second. A century of cultivation had rendered the interior of the courtyard as crowded with vegetation as if the home were in the tropics, though the plants were towering cactus and delicately-leafed desert willows. Illuminated by an amber lantern that had probably burned kerosene before being wired, the ornately-carved double door was opened by a maid almost the instant Devon and Prairie stood before it. Since they hadn't yet rung the bell, he could only surmise the maid had been watching for their arrival.

"*Buenas tardes,*" she said. "*Pasan ustedes.*"

"*Buenas tardes,* Estrella," Prairie replied.

They followed her across the terra cotta tiles of the foyer and hall to a room at the far end. Estrella pushed a button set in the adobe wall, then silently turned away. Devon watched her disappear in the dark shadows beneath a spiral staircase. Looking back at the door just as it opened, he heard the sound of film running through a projector.

Sergio Tierrasantas was in his late twenties. His straight black hair was worn rather long, and his sharp eyes were dark beneath brows so gracefully shaped they seemed sculptured. He wore sandals without socks, yellow linen trousers with no belt, and a white, ribbed, scooped-neck T-shirt. A gold necklace glimmered against his dark skin as he gave his visitors a sardonic smile.

"Hey, Boots," he said, letting his gaze slide down then up Prairie's figure with a familiarity bordering on impertinence. The glimmer of a challenge played in his eyes when he shifted his gaze to the man at her side.

"Evenin', Sergio," she said. "This is Detective Devon Gray of the El Paso Police. Devon, Sergio Tierrasantas."

Neither man extended his hand. When Sergio saw his intended slight fail because Devon hadn't initiated a gesture that wouldn't be received, his smile became more wily. "Please come in," he said, taking a step back and gesturing for them to enter his theater.

The room was long and narrow, lit only by a corner lamp with a rose satin shade and the light from the film projected onto a screen against the far wall. On the screen was the grainy image of a crying girl being tied to a bed by two men using wire to secure her wrists and ankles to the bedposts.

Devon crossed to the projector and turned it off. In the abrupt silence, he met Sergio's eyes and said, "I find that offensive."

"Why?"

"It trivializes suffering."

Sergio's eyebrows rose with appreciation above the sarcasm of his smile. "I thought it particularly apropos, since Boots came here to discuss the cutting of wire."

"That's what I wanted to talk to Cipriano about," she said. "Not you."

Sergio flicked his gaze at her but continued to study Devon. "May I offer cognac or some other refreshment to compensate for having offended you?"

Devon shook his head. "This isn't a social visit, Mr. Tierrasantas."

"I'm beginning to understand that. Would you like to sit down?"

Again Devon shook his head. "When was the last time you saw your wife?"

"I don't have a wife."

"Lisa Escobar."

"Ah, my ex-wife. I saw her in El Paso only a few days ago. Has she filed a complaint against me?"

"For what?"

"The vagaries of women are infamous."

"Whether or not she had cause, she wasn't able to file a complaint because she was murdered."

Sergio lost his suave demeanor. It returned in the flash of a sympathetic smile. "And it's your job to discover who killed her. Yes, I understand now why you're here. Please, won't you sit down?"

Devon shook his head. "Where were you on Tuesday night?"

"Ah, you're attempting to establish if I have an alibi. Well, as it happens I do. I arrived home about noon on Tuesday and haven't left since. My staff will corroborate that."

"Can I ask them myself?"

"I employ fifteen people in the house and on the grounds, not to mention several dozen *vaqueros*. Do you wish to speak with all of them?"

"Just the ones who saw you Tuesday night."

Sergio returned to the door and pressed a button. "I'll bet Lisa was killed with a knife." He smiled slyly. "She always did have bad luck around sharp instruments."

"You should know," Prairie said. "She was admitted to the hospital in Chinati with knife wounds inflicted by you."

"No, Boots." His smile was supercilious. "We used a razor blade to avoid leaving any really terrible scars. And my inflictions, as you call them, were to accommodate her requests."

"She wanted you to cut her with a razor?" Prairie scoffed.

"I'm sure it isn't to your taste, but we enjoyed making love with our bellies slick with blood. The time she went to the hospital, we'd been drinking and the cuts went deeper than we'd intended. But I meant her no harm. After all, it was I who drove her to the hospital."

The door opened and Estrella stood in the brighter light of the hall. Sergio spoke softly to her in Spanish. She glanced at Devon, then nodded and closed the door.

Sergio crossed the room to open a rosewood cabinet inlaid with an intricate floral pattern of lighter wood. "Are you certain you wouldn't like a drink?"

"Yes," Devon said, watching him pour brandy into a snifter.

He turned around and sipped at the brandy, then sat in a nearby leather chair and crossed his legs. But his conciliatory smile died when Devon asked, "Do you own a knife with a four-inch blade?"

Chapter Four

"I shouldn't be surprised if I do," Sergio answered. "There are no doubt many knives in the kitchen and even more in the stables. Would you like me to have them collected for you?"

Devon shook his head. "Did you pick up Lisa in a limousine in Los Angeles before bringing her to El Paso?"

"What a charming thought. But no, I didn't."

"How did she get to El Paso?"

"I'm afraid I didn't ask. If that's a problem you're having with the scenario, I'm sincerely sorry I can't help you."

"Who arranged your visit there?"

"She called and asked me to meet her."

"When did she call?" Devon took his notebook out.

Sergio swirled the brandy in his snifter. "I believe it was last Sunday." He shrugged, meeting Devon's eyes again. "I hadn't any plans to speak of, so I complied with her request."

Devon wrote: *Called S.T. at home, Sunday.* "What did she say about why she wanted to see you?"

"She said she missed me," Sergio answered with a smug smile.

"Nothing about her son?"

"No. Ricardo isn't mine, you know."

"Who's his father?"

"Lisa's first lover."

"Do you know his name?"

"It's a family secret, kept even from me."

"Where is the boy?"

"With her parents in Mexico City."

"Why wasn't he with her?"

"Lisa's family didn't consider her a good mother." Sergio chuckled. "So they enrolled Ricardo in a boarding school where I'm sure he's receiving the best of mothering."

"What are her parents' names?"

"Umberto and Feliciana Escobar. They have an apartment on the Paseo de la Reforma, quite near the angel."

As Devon wrote in his notebook, a soft buzzer sounded.

"Ah, my alibi," Sergio said, rising to open the door.

Estrella stood there with an exceptionally pretty teenage girl, also Hispanic and dressed simply in inexpensive clothes.

Sergio introduced everyone and explained to his servants that the detective needed to ask them some questions.

Estrella studied Devon warily. The girl, Elita, kept her eyes on the floor.

Using his street Spanish, Devon quickly established from Estrella that Sergio had arrived home at noon on Tuesday and spent the afternoon in his office. At eight she served him supper in the dining room, then he came to his theater and asked for Elita. After sending the girl in, Estrella had gone to bed and hadn't seen her employer again until six the next morning when she served him breakfast.

Devon thanked her and turned to the girl, whose fear was evident. Gently he asked, still in Spanish, "Did you spend Tuesday evening with Mr. Tierrasantas?"

She nodded.

"What time did you leave him?"

"At dawn," she mumbled, her gaze again on the floor.

To ease her discomfort, Devon put his notebook away before asking, "Did you spend the night in his bed?"

"*Sí,*" she whispered.

"Are you certain he didn't leave during the night?"

Elita glanced at Sergio, then hid her eyes again.

" '*Sta bien,*" he said with humor. "*Contesta el hombre.*"

Devon had to strain to catch her words when she whispered, "I hurt so badly, I couldn't sleep. *El patrón* was beside me all night."

"*Gracias,*" Devon said. "You can go."

Estrella led the girl out and closed the door.

Sergio laughed. "Are you satisfied, Detective?"

"I think they'll say anything you asked 'em to."

"Nevertheless, I do have an alibi for all of Tuesday night, so I'm afraid you'll have to find someone else to accuse of this murder."

"Do you own a black Cadillac limousine?"

Sergio chuckled, rising to replenish his drink. "No, I don't."

"Do you know anyone who does?"

"A dozen people, maybe more." He swirled the fresh brandy in his glass. "Would you like their names and addresses?"

"How about Lisa's family. Do they own one?"

"I believe her uncle does."

"What's his name?"

"Estefen Escobar."

Devon took out his notebook and wrote down the name. "Where does he live?"

"Juárez." Sergio smiled. "Perhaps he's your culprit."

"Would he have reason to kill her?"

"I had the impression he was especially fond of her."

"Do you know his address?"

"Not his home, but he has a business in the ProNaf. It's called Escobar Imports and Exports, so shouldn't be too difficult to locate, even for an officer of the law."

Devon ignored the aside. "When and where did you last see Lisa?"

"I left her in the Camino Real on Tuesday morning."

"What time?"

"Around eight."

He wrote it down. "Did she check out with you?"

"No."

"Did she seem upset or unhappy about anything?"

"She was always moody."

"Did you have sex with her there?"

"Of course."

"Did the two of you go to Mesilla together?"

Sergio smiled with naughty delight. "Was she wearing her necklace when she died?"

"What necklace?"

"The one I bought her in Mesilla. Surely that's where your questions are leading."

"Did you buy her a necklace?"

"Yes, a Navajo piece she'd commissioned. I thought it rather silly, myself. Was she wearing it when she died?"

Devon nodded.

"I find that touching," Sergio said. "You know, it's not surprising she was killed with a knife. As I said before, she was always unlucky around blades yet attracted to men who enjoyed using them."

Jay Lehrer was craving Szechwan food, so Samantha took him to Uncle Bao's. The restaurant was crowded and they had to wait in the bar for over an hour because Jay had demanded a corner booth. When they were finally called, the hostess led them past the mammoth mural of running horses in the main dining room to the congested air of the smoking section. Samantha had never eaten in that room before. She found the smoke nauseating, and her view of nothing more than the wall behind Jay left her at the mercy of his eyes.

Watching him clean his plate and finish hers, even gleaning every grain of rice from the bowl, she cringed at how he scarfed the food down as if he hadn't eaten all day. Then she thought maybe he hadn't. She tried to forgive him in an effort to be kind, though she couldn't remember ever going to a Chinese restaurant without taking leftovers home.

Arriving back at her apartment building, she initially stopped beside his car parked on the street. He insisted on walking her to her door, so she drove around to the garage beneath her building. As they climbed the stairs to the patio, he clutched her arm and mumbled, "Damn, I'm dizzy. Guess I had too much to drink."

Since he had polished off five double scotches and an after-dinner brandy, she couldn't disagree. Believing it irresponsible to send a drunk onto the streets alone, she reluctantly suggested, "Why don't you come in for coffee?"

"Thanks, Sam." He laid his arm across her shoulders as they climbed the stairs to her apartment.

She unlocked the door and stepped out from under his arm to turn on a lamp. "Have a seat," she said, dropping her purse in a chair on her way to the kitchen. As she filled the coffeepot, she looked across the counter and saw him sprawled on the sofa, his dark eyes surveying the room.

"I don't know, Sam," he said as she scooped coffee out of the can, "it strikes me you're like a woman Devon's keeping on the side, his main love being his work. If you hadn't told me he's living here, I never would've guessed it. There's nothing visible to prove his presence."

She turned away to put the pot together, thinking she *had* accommodated Devon into her life while he hadn't made many changes other than hanging his clothes in her closet and sharing her bed every night, which counted for a lot when she remembered Jay's infidelities. She rejoined him in the living room, intending to sit in the chair in the corner.

He patted the sofa. "Come sit by me."

She sat at the far end. "Still feeling dizzy?"

"No, I feel fine. Well, almost fine." He frowned. "It's odd how I can pass hours without thinking of Lisa, then out of nowhere I remember she's dead." He leaned forward, hugging himself as he moaned, "Murder's so irrevocable, Sam."

She slid closer and murmured, "A terrible thing."

He turned to press his face against her breasts as he sobbed like a child. She rocked him in a lulling rhythm until he fell silent.

"Sam?" he petitioned, his voice muffled against her sweater, "do you think any good can come of Lisa's death?"

She searched for something more than platitudes about the wisdom gained from loss, but all the examples she could offer came from surviving the demise of their marriage and didn't seem appropriate.

He raised his face, his lashes wet. "Do you think maybe, because her death brought us together again, you could give me another chance to make you happy?"

"I'll get the coffee," she said. But when she tried to stand up, he held her beside him.

"Think about it, Sam. If not for me, Devon might never have found out who she was. Don't you think there's a reason for my having come?"

"You helped him," she conceded.

"What about us?"

She shook her head.

"Help me, Sam," he pleaded, his grip tight on her arms. "Shelter me from the violence raging right outside that door."

She tried to loosen his grip. "You're hurting me, Jay."

"Love is what you want, isn't it?"

"Not yours." She tried to pry his hand off her arm.

"I understand," he crooned, dragging her onto the floor. "If you say yes, you'll be disloyal to Devon. Isn't that right, Sam?"

Her denial was muffled by his hand on her mouth.

"Quit fighting me!" He grinned as he unbuttoned her jeans. "You'll love it in a minute."

She flailed with her fists, kicked with her knees, but he outweighed her by a hundred pounds and her resistance failed. Barely managing to breathe beneath the weight of his palm, she gagged as he pummeled her like a mallet pounding the floor. Finally he withdrew without having come and staggered toward the bathroom.

Frantically she fumbled for her panties and jeans, had barely found them when he returned. She held them in a crumpled wad in front of her as she skittered away from him, then watched through a blur of tears as he stalked out the door without looking back. She crawled across and locked both the deadbolt and chain. Sliding to the floor, she curled herself into a ball and cried.

Like needles projecting threads of safety through a threatening wilderness, Prairie's headlights illuminated only the road. When the radio squawked from under the dash—a highway patrol report of a stranded vehicle ten miles north of Casa Piedra—she reached down and switched it off, leaving her and Devon with only the hum of the tires on the graded dirt until they were off Sergio's land and crunching over gravel on the county road.

After turning north on the smooth blacktop of 2810, she accelerated to sixty before asking, "What's your next move?"

"Go home and see if I can't lure Estefen Escobar into my jurisdiction."

"Are you thinking he did it?"

"I try not to decide anything until I have all the facts."

"Doesn't sound like you think Sergio did it, though."

"I haven't formed an opinion on that either."

"Why didn't you use your search warrant?"

"Didn't have reasonable cause in light of his alibi."

"But you don't believe his alibi?"

"Do you?"

"Kinda. I know he could get those women to lie for him, but Elita was so embarrassed it felt like she was telling the truth."

"Maybe she was, about everything except the night it happened."

Prairie sighed, then suddenly laughed. "You were great, the way you just walked over and turned off his projector. I wish I'd thought of doing that."

"You will next time."

"If I can figure out where the switch is." She laughed again. "And the way you looked him in the eye and said you found the film offensive. That was damn courageous."

"You think it takes courage to voice your opinion?"

"Yeah. I mean, I think those films are offensive, but I've never been able to tell Sergio that."

"Well, it also takes courage to walk into where you know you'll be offended but it's your job to be there."

This time her smile was appreciative.

"If you can't find the switch," he said, "you can pull the plug."

She nodded. "I'll remember that."

When she drove into her yard, she cut the engine so her Jeep coasted to a stop in the moonlight. They sat comfortably for a moment, then she asked, "You driving back tonight?"

Although he had dreaded meeting her, he now found himself postponing telling her goodbye. "I'll check into a motel and drive back first thing in the morning." He hesitated. "Unless you'll let me buy you breakfast before I go."

"If I can buy you a beer tonight."

"Deal. But let's not go to the Range Rider again. We might run into Carl and I've had enough confrontation for one evening."

She laughed softly. "How about my porch swing? That's about as non-confrontational as it gets."

Though he doubted that, he smiled and said, "Sounds perfect."

They walked across the soft dust of her yard, listening to the horses nicker a welcome. Devon sat on one end of the swing while Prairie went inside. He leaned back with his feet on the railing, enjoying the starry sky and newly-risen moon coating the distant mountains as if with mother-of-pearl.

Prairie came back with two bottles of Lone Star, handed him one and sat down at the other end of the swing. They sipped their beers in silence, then he asked, "What made you want to be a Ranger?"

"I thought it'd be fun."

"Is it?"

"Sometimes. I like wearing a gun. I guess you think that's odd."

"I wear a gun."

"Not on your hip like I do. And you keep your badge in your pocket."

"That's the difference in our beats."

"Reckon." She sipped her beer. "I guess I just always thought being a lawman would be more interesting than pretty near any other job."

"Where're your parents?"

"My dad was killed in Vietnam when my mom was pregnant with me. She died giving birth. There wasn't a hospital here then, and she hemorrhaged during delivery. They were both just kids. I've already lived almost twice as long as they did."

"Who brought you up?"

"My granddad. He was an old cowboy who didn't know nothing about raising a girl. Reckon that's why I'm kind of a half-breed." She laughed, pleased with herself. "He did well by me though. Put me through college and all. Died of a heart attack the month I graduated. After that it just felt too sad being here, so I stayed in Austin and got a job in the licensing division of motor vehicles. I was a supervisor, wore high heels and makeup to work. Can you believe that?"

"Hard to imagine," he murmured, amused.

"It was boring as hell! I'd majored in criminal justice in college, thinking maybe I'd go to law school, but the tuition was too steep and my grades not good enough to get a scholarship. So I thought to become a lawman. I applied to the Austin P.D. first but they turned me down, saying I was too scrawny to throw my weight around. When I heard Gov'nor Richards had ordered the Rangers to accept women, I applied, not expecting nothing to happen." She took a swig of beer. "Joaquín Jackson was so disgusted with the Rangers hiring women, he retired and I got his job. Reckon you know he was about the best Ranger ever was, so it's a bittersweet victory, knowing I was the cause of his resignation."

"Some men find it hard to change with the times."

She faced him on the swing. "Do you think a woman can be a good lawman?"

He considered his answer. "On some assignments, a woman might be better."

"But overall, you don't think we're up to it, do you?"

He shook his head. "Most criminals are men and it takes one to deal with 'em. I'm not talking about physical strength but understanding what drives a man."

"You don't think a woman can do that?"

"No," he said gently.

"I admire the hell outta you, Devon. How can I admire what I don't understand?"

"It's my experience a person most admires what they're least capable of achieving."

She opened her mouth but nothing came out. Finally she said, "Oh, you're tough."

"If that bothers you, you're better off keeping your distance."

She shook her head. "Who do you most admire?"

"People like your grandfather, raising kids who make the world a better place."

She laughed, snuggling close. He lifted his arm and let it rest on her shoulders as they admired the moonlit world. After a while she asked, "Why don't you stay here tonight, Devon?"

"I don't think that's a good idea."

"There's only one motel in town, and Ol' Man Borough goes to bed pretty early. If you check in now, you'll wake him up."

"If he didn't want that to happen, he wouldn't run a motel."

"I could make you a bed on the couch, if that's what you want."

"It isn't."

She set her beer on the floor, then straddled his lap and asked coyly, "What *do* you want, Devon?"

"Not to hurt you when I go home tomorrow."

"Back to the woman you're maybe still involved with?"

He nodded.

"I don't care. All that matters is now."

He leaned back away from her. "What do you want for breakfast?"

"A strawberry waffle with a mountain of whipped cream! What do you want?"

"*Huevos rancheros* with the eggs runny and the chili hot."

"I can cook 'em like that."

"Do you know a restaurant that makes 'em like that?"

"Yeah. Felipe's on the east edge of town."

He stood up, lifting her with him. She gripped his hips with her legs while he kissed her, then he set her down and walked to his car, calling back over his shoulder, "Meet me there at six."

Chapter Five

At a corner table in Felipe's Café, Devon couldn't help smiling as he watched Prairie spoon whipped cream into her mouth. She closed her eyes, savoring the flavor, and when she opened them again he caught himself thinking they were the same indigo blue as the sky outside the window. Still pink from the chill of dawn, her cheeks matched the nascent sunrise on the horizon, and though her mood was frivolous with a delight apparently inspired merely by sharing his company, he knew if he had spent the night in her bed they would not now be enjoying this lightness between them.

During the years that his romantic adventures had been nothing more than one-night stands, he had stayed until morning only once. When he awoke to share the woman's disappointment as she realized their passion had no more lasting effect than the ease gained from drinking half a dozen beers in a bar, he vowed never again to sleep with a woman he didn't expect to see again. Since he wasn't likely to see Prairie unless another case brought them together, he knew it was best they remain colleagues with no lingering disappointments to interfere with their work.

Her plans, however, didn't dovetail with his. Cutting a chunk off her waffle, she announced, "Think I'll ride along to El Paso."

"Why?"

"All of west Texas is my jurisdiction." She took the bite

into her mouth and met his eyes as she chewed.

"I've got plenty of help in El Paso."

She swallowed. "Yeah, but I figure it'll benefit me to work with you; then if I ever have to investigate a homicide on my own, I'll have learned a few tricks." She smiled. "I won't get in your way, Devon."

He concentrated on cutting a triangle of tortilla loaded with runny eggs and red chili, suspecting her desire to spend more time with him had little to do with increasing her professional competence. On the other hand, cooperation between jurisdictions was valuable to cultivate, and he couldn't reasonably deny her a training opportunity. "All right," he said, lifting his fork to his mouth. He met her eyes as the hot chili ignited his tongue.

She laughed. "I already packed a bag and asked Cynthia to take care of my horses. There's just one tiny problem."

"What's that?"

"I hate motels. Do you think you could maybe put me up?"

"Sam and I only have one bedroom."

"That's cool," she said, not missing a beat. But her voice was softer when she asked, "Her name's Sam?"

"Samantha." He cut another triangle of *huevos rancheros*. "I guess you could stay with my brother. He's married with kids, but there's a guestroom upstairs with its own bath, and his house is only a coupla miles from Sam's apartment."

"Sounds fine," she said.

He finished his breakfast, then sipped his coffee as he watched a sheriff's car park in the lot. A tall, thin man in a brown uniform got out and walked toward the café. Devon set his cup down as the officer came through the door.

Prairie turned around to see what he was looking at. "It's Hank Gentry," she whispered. "Bowlin's deputy."

His sandy blond hair falling to brush against his darkly-mirrored sunglasses, Gentry stopped by their booth and asked in the cold tone of business, "Devon Gray?"

Devon nodded, disliking the opening steps of this maneuver.

"Sheriff Bowlin asked that I bring you down to his office. You wanta come in my car or yours?"

"Mine," Devon said. "What's this about?"

"The sheriff'll explain." Looking at their empty plates, Gentry asked, "You ready?"

"Soon as I pay the bill," Devon said, standing up.

The county courthouse was a red brick building on the town square. After parking in back, Gentry led them down wooden steps to what appeared to be a waiting room in the basement, through a swinging half-door at the far end to the office of an absent secretary, and across to another door, its frosted-glass pane painted with black letters: SHERIFF RUFUS BOWLIN. Gentry knocked, then opened the door and gestured for Devon and Prairie to go in.

Sheriff Bowlin sat behind his desk, his steel gray hair in a crewcut above his long, thin face. He frowned at Prairie and said, "This ain't Ranger business."

"I'm assisting Detective Gray in his investigation," she retorted, "so I reckon it is."

Bowlin shifted his glare to Devon. "Your investigation's illegal. Without proper authorization, what you've been doing is impersonating a peace officer."

"I have authorization," Devon said, "signed by your deputy."

"He ain't got the power to sign such a document."

"Why didn't you sign it then?"

"I din't know nothing about it 'til I learned Mr. Tierrasantas was being harassed by someone claiming to be

65

from the El Paso Police. Common courtesy demands you take me with you when you question any of my constit'ency."

Thinking Tierrasantas must be worried if he had felt threatened enough to call the sheriff, Devon said, "The authorization specifically ordered me to work with Ranger Drake."

"It shouldn't've. So what you're claiming to be authorization ain't nothing but a piece of paper. And I don't know you from Clint Eastwood."

Devon took his shield and police ID from the inside pocket of his jacket and tossed the wallet to fall open in front of the sheriff.

Bowlin barely glanced at it. "Far as I know, that could be a forgery."

"Call El Paso and find out."

"You got a gun?"

Devon nodded.

"Got a permit to carry a concealed weapon?"

"It's inherent in the badge."

"Like I said, I don't know that your badge is authentic. I'm gonna have to hold you 'til I find out."

"You're shooting kinda low, Rufus," Prairie said. "You know damn well who Detective Gray is."

"No, I don't. And I ain't gonna take the word of no rookie Ranger for it neither." He looked back at Devon. "You best give me your gun."

Reluctantly Devon pulled the .38 out of its holster in the back of his belt and laid it next to his identification.

"For the moment, Mr. Gray," the sheriff said, "you're under arrest."

"What!?!" Dreyfus bellowed into the phone, feeling the color rise in his already florid face.

"You heard me, Lieutenant," Bowlin drawled. "He's cooling his heels in one of my cells right now."

"He's in the middle of a murder investigation!"

" 'Cept he din't have authority to poke his nose into my county and upset my citizens with his high-handed methods."

"We requested authorization and got it. If there's a problem in your office, it's no concern of mine. But the detention of one of my detectives sure as hell is. I want him released!"

"I un'erstand how you feel," Bowlin said in his maddeningly slow drawl, "but he stepped on the toes of Sergio Tierrasantas. In case you don't know it, Mr. Tierrasantas pretty near owns this county, and I don't cotton to no city-slicker cop riling my constit'ency. Next time you wanta investigate a crime in my jur'sdiction, I suggest you go through proper protocol."

"The crime didn't occur in your jurisdiction! As for protocol, all we needed was the same cooperation we've given you many times, Sheriff."

"I wouldn't accept an underling's signature as granting me permission. I wouldn't accept nobody's but that b'longing to the Chief of Police. You owe me the same courtesy."

"I apologize for assuming your deputy signed in your absence. Time is of the essence in a murder investigation, and Detective Gray thought it imperative to question the victim's ex-husband immediately. We don't weigh political clout when assessing the culpability of a suspect."

"Are you implying Mr. Tierrasantas committed this murder?"

Dreyfus took a deep breath. "No. But he was the last person known to have seen the victim alive."

"Un-huh. Mr. Tierrasantas also has an air-tight alibi for the time in question, a fact I could've ascertained without causing this whole rigmarole. What I'm trying to impress on you is that there was a better way to handle this."

"If Mr. Tierrasantas has already been questioned, then Detective Gray no longer has any need to be there. On the contrary, we need him here to continue the investigation."

"I can't spring him 'til he's brought 'fore our justice of the peace on Monday morning."

"If you don't release him," Dreyfus growled, "I'll have your badge."

"The on'y man able to run me out of office is Sergio Tierrasantas. So I suggest you assign your case to another detective and let me handle justice in my county."

Dreyfus slammed down the phone, then buzzed his secretary. "Get me the Texas Ranger in Chinati! Now!"

The cell was eight-by-four with no window, three brick walls, and one of iron bars. Suspended on chains, the metal bunk was bare, lacking the grace of either a mattress or pillow. Devon assumed he would be issued those amenities if forced to stay the night, but for now he sat on the hard surface staring at the hundred-year-old bricks in front of him. If he looked the other way, he could see the far side of the corridor, the pattern of its texture different only because rusted iron bars intervened.

The air was stale, the meager light supplied by a fluorescent tube running the length of the corridor, and a filthy seatless commode squatted so close to the bunk he figured he would have to sleep with his head toward the bars to avoid dreaming of sewers, all of which made the prospect of a night in Sheriff Bowlin's basement jail less than pleasant.

As if his anger were a kite in the wind, Devon mentally

wound it in slowly so the string wouldn't break and his anger whip into rage. The sprockets of that imaginary reel turned on rational explanations of why he was locked in a cell. He didn't doubt his arrest had been instigated by Sergio, but that pleased him by proving Tierrasantas felt threatened. Devon's anger sprang from the sheriff's kowtowing to a murder suspect. By having a deputy sign the authorization so it could be yanked at whim, Bowlin had aligned himself with Sergio from the start.

In Devon's opinion, crooked cops were the most craven of criminals. Peace officers who betrayed the public trust, hiding their deviant behavior behind a badge, crippled the force by making citizens discredit the only power between them and chaos. But Presidio wasn't his beat. All he could do was wait out his confinement and go home, leaving the county to fend for itself.

Because he had been granted deference on the presumption he might actually be a fellow officer, he hadn't been deprived of his personal possessions. He still had his watch and whatever amusement he could conjure by going through the contents of his pockets. Other than his keys and spare change, he had only a clean handkerchief, succinctly devoid of interest, and his wallet. Inside that were his driver's license, Chevron and Visa cards, two hundred dollars in cash, and a picture of his brother and nephew he had used on a case and never gotten around to putting back inside the shoe box where the family photos were kept.

He studied his brother caught in the golden glow of an autumn afternoon on the front porch of their father's house. The old man had bequeathed it solely to Devon, and though he still held title, it was Connie's now, a gift Devon had offered in an attempt to help his ex-convict brother make good. Connie was doing all right, and Eric seemed to be

69

holding his own after coming close, at the age of seventeen, to being arrested for the shooting of his girlfriend's father, who had been enraged after catching them in bed. The weapon Eric used was a shotgun conveniently left primed in her closet, which made Devon suspect the whole thing had been set up. Her brother, Teddy, took the fall, believing Elise pulled the trigger, but Devon had put Teddy in prison for committing a second murder to cover the first.

Seeing the habitual sneer Eric wore in those days, he knew he had been right to think no jury would have cut the kid slack. And remembering that the sneer was mostly gone now, replaced by the ingenuous face of a boy not good at hiding his feelings, Devon felt reassured that he had been right to spare his nephew a jailhouse education. One condition of his mercy had been that Elise sever her relationship with Eric. As far as Devon knew, that condition was being met, maybe only because she had moved out of state. He put his wallet back and looked at his watch. A mere hour had passed.

Devon was rarely idle. Usually it happened when he had to wait through courtroom protocol to testify against someone he had arrested, but even then he wasn't alone. Now he understood how after a few days a prisoner often warmed up to the arresting officer merely because he was a link to the outside world. Understood, too, that old cliché about freedom being one of those things you didn't appreciate until it was gone, knowing lost time, among other things, was irretrievable.

Like the trust he thought he had built with Samantha. Because a ghost of her past had walked through her door, a relationship he had considered strong was suddenly shaky. He would lay odds Jay Lehrer had taken her to dinner last night. The thought of what might have happened after made Devon stand up and pace the meager confines of his cell.

★ ★ ★ ★ ★

Samantha looked up from the reference desk to see Jay come in off the street. She turned away, searching for someone nearby who might be able to help her. But the only other employee in sight, Tom Hernandez, was clear across the room assisting a patron with the on-line catalog. The security guard was no where to be seen.

Jay sauntered over and stopped in front of her. "Morning, Sam," he said cheerfully. "Thought maybe you'd let me take you to lunch."

In the length of her stunned silence, Tom came back to the desk, looked curiously at Jay, then sat down and busied himself with paperwork.

"Guess I had too many drinks last night," Jay said with a devious smile. "On top of being out of my mind with grief, I lost control. Hope I wasn't too rough on you."

Feeling the pinprick of Tom's attention, Samantha stood up and led Jay toward the door. "I want you to go away," she whispered.

"You do?" he asked in a crestfallen tone.

She led him outside where a hard wind blew her hair into her mouth as she asked, "Did you really expect me to go to lunch with you after last night?"

His expression was baffled. "What do you mean, Sam?"

She pulled her hair out, wet. "You raped me!"

He smiled as if at the imagination of a whimsical child. "That wasn't rape. It was two old friends filling each other's needs on a lonely night."

"It was a brutal act of rape!" she cried, making a man walking by turn his head to stare back at them. She felt herself blushing, as if she were the guilty one.

Jay gave her a wounded smile. "You don't believe that." His expression became conniving. "If you did, you would've

71

been on the phone first thing telling Devon all about it. Have you talked to him yet?"

She shook her head.

Jay chuckled. "Of course not, 'cause he won't believe it any more'n I do. He'll think his girlfriend cheated on him when he was out of town. Isn't that right, Sam?"

"Go away!" she whispered desperately.

He raised his hands as if under arrest. "I'll go, but I'm concerned about you, so I'll call tonight to see if you haven't rearranged your thinking. If you don't answer the phone, I'll have to explain to Devon exactly what happened and how worried I am that you're not seeing it straight."

"Please don't tell him, Jay."

He smiled. "Talk to you later then." Turning his back, he ambled away.

She ran upstairs to her office where she closed and locked the door. Crying at her desk, she told herself if she hadn't let Jay take her to dinner, none of this would be happening. The irony was she hadn't even wanted to go. Though she knew her silence was akin to a lie, all she wanted now was to keep what happened a secret from Devon.

Prairie walked into the sheriff's office and slapped an Order of Extradition on his desk. Rufus frowned, seeing the governor's signature at the bottom of the fax. He leaned back and drawled in an unsuccessful effort to disguise his anger, "I heard tell you and Anne Richards're friends."

"That's right," Prairie said. "When I told her what you're trying to pull, she expedited this Order and assigned me personal to escort Detective Gray back to El Paso. So why don't you give me his stuff while your go-fer lets him out?"

Deputy Gentry was standing in the door Prairie had banged open and not bothered to slam shut. Rufus nodded at him, then told Prairie, "After you've been on the job a mite longer, li'l miss, you're gonna discover law enforcement's a matter of cooperation. Texas Ranger or not, nobody does it alone. I won't forget this."

"Me neither," she answered.

He continued to fix her with a hostile glare. Finally he pushed himself up and trundled across to retrieve the badge and gun from the top drawer of his file cabinet. Handing them to Prairie, he snarled, "Get him outta my county quick as you can."

In the hall she met Devon accompanied by the deputy. Devon gave her a smile, but Gentry's face was clouded with an unspoken threat Prairie wasted no time leaving behind. Making an abrupt turn into a stairwell going up, she handed Devon his gun and the wallet holding his police ID.

He slid the wallet into the inside pocket of his jacket, then surprised her by flipping the .38's cylinder open and checking the rounds. Using both hands to snap it into his holster as they climbed the stairs, he asked, "You still coming to El Paso?"

"Have to now." She grinned, showing him the extradition. "Gov'nor's orders."

"How'd you manage that?"

"At one time my granddad was head wrangler on Anne Richards' ranch. I don't s'pose there's ever been a gov'nor of Texas who ain't been a lover of horses."

Devon laughed as he opened the door to the bright sun outside.

"Let me get my stuff," Prairie said, running toward her Jeep.

Leaving Chinati on 90 West in his Lexus, he had gone only a few miles before he turned south on 2810.

"Where we going?" she asked.

"To pay a call on Sergio."

"Holy shit, Devon! Don't you reckon we oughta make tracks outta this county?"

"Can't leave tracks on asphalt."

"But you know the sheriff's gonna call Sergio and tell him you're loose."

"I figure it'll take him a while to get up the nerve to do that. With any luck, we'll beat his call there."

"Then what?"

"Impress on Sergio his power isn't as great as he thinks it is."

"Does that mean you've come around to thinking he killed Lisa?"

"If not, he overreacted to our visit last night. He didn't strike me as a man who overreacts."

"Are you gonna arrest him?"

"Rule One of working homicide, Prairie: To arrest a suspect you have to place him at the scene, discover a motive, and connect him to the weapon. We can't do any of that with Sergio."

"So why're we going there?"

"To rattle his cage and see what falls out."

"If the sheriff shows up, I'm not sure I can make this extradition stick, Devon."

"Sure you can. All it takes is balls."

"Yeah, well, I don't have any, you know."

"I do," he said.

Estrella opened the door. To Prairie's inquiries in Spanish, the maid answered that her *patrón* was at the stables. Saying she knew the way, Prairie led Devon around the house toward a long adobe building surrounded by a dozen corrals, each holding a single horse.

"Arabians," she said. "You like 'em?"

"They're pretty," he conceded, noting they were fine-boned with small, delicate hooves compared to Prairie's horses.

"Too high-strung," she said. "And slight to my eye. Oh, Arabians have stamina, I'll give 'em that, but I like the round-apple butts on quarter horses."

"You look at their butts?"

"You judge a horse's strength by its haunches. You look at the legs, too, if you're interested in speed, and the forehead and eyes, trying to assess if it has any intelligence in its bee-bee brain. The rest of it's just a matter of aesthetics. Arabians are pretty but that's about all. Like I said, they're too nervous to make good cutting horses, too arrogant to work cattle, and I'd never trust 'em with a child. Now a quarter horse'll do anything you ask, from roping an ornery bull to giving a five-year-old kid a gentle ride."

They entered a wide lane between the corrals leading to the stable door. "So raising Arabians is a rich man's hobby?"

"Pretty much. Sergio keeps a herd of brood mares in a pasture. These here are all prize stallions."

"What're they worth?"

"Fifteen, twenty thousand a piece." She laughed at his surprise. "Carl wants to breed a strain of pinto Arabians. They're rare, and he thinks he'll get rich if he can do it, but Sergio's lowest fee is five thousand, so Carl's been trying to convince him to donate the stud on consignment. The problem is the issue'll only be half-Arabian, and if it ain't a pinto, it won't be worth more'n your standard grade, so Sergio can't bring himself to take the risk, though all he'd be risking is his stallion's semen."

Entering the stable, Devon stopped in amazement. Its floors were white marble, the stalls polished mahogany.

"Nice quarters," he muttered.

"These critters live better'n most folks," Prairie agreed.

At the far end of the barn, Tierrasantas was admiring a black stallion held by a groom. Turning at the sound of their voices, he spoke curtly to his employee, then walked forward to meet them.

"Good morning, Boots," he said pleasantly, though his eyes glittered with anger. "Detective Gray."

"Morning," Prairie said softly.

"Your ploy didn't work," Devon said.

"Which ploy was that?" Sergio asked as if bored.

"Didn't it cross your mind that trying to put me out of action would only increase my suspicion of your guilt?"

"Since my conscience is clear, the suspicions of a petty official aren't worth my concern."

"Then why tell the sheriff to arrest me?"

"Did he do that?" Sergio laughed softly. "Have you escaped jail, then? Am I harboring a fugitive merely by allowing you on my property?"

Prairie piped up, "His release was more legal'n his arrest."

Sergio smiled at her, then looked back at Devon. "I can understand how suffering the fate of a criminal would make you angry, Detective. But I haven't spoken with the sheriff for several days, so if you're blaming me for what happened, I'm afraid you're mistaken."

"Who else has the power to coerce him?"

"Estefen Escobar."

"What interest does he have in Presidio?"

"He's executor of Lisa's trust fund, which includes her share of the Escobar ranch just below the border. They import cattle through Ojinaga, and Sheriff Bowlin owns the holding pens where the cattle wait out quarantine. All that's a matter of public record, so if you'd do your homework you wouldn't need to inquire."

"I knew that," Prairie said. " 'Cept the part about the trust fund."

Devon glanced at her, then asked Sergio, "Will it go to Lisa's son now?"

"I assume so."

"Will Escobar be executor of that, too?"

"Ah, you've stumbled onto a possible motive, haven't you, Detective?"

"I was led to one."

Sergio chuckled. "Estefen called me last night. When I told him of your interrogation, he wasn't nearly as amused as I was."

"Why were you amused?"

"I found your visit quite titillating, especially the way you turned off my film. Few people are bold enough to oppose me. And then your questioning of little Elita added a piquancy to my evening."

"Apparently not one you care to repeat."

"What makes you say that?"

"You were angry when you saw us a moment ago."

"How observant you are. Yes, I was, but not with you. I've given orders to preserve my privacy, and you shouldn't have been allowed in without being announced. That was the source of my anger." He smiled as they heard a plane coming in low for a landing. "That's probably Estefen now. He told me he'd be here for lunch. Would you care to join us?"

"I'd like to meet him."

"Good," Sergio answered with a crafty smile. "Shall we go to the house?"

As the three of them walked along the lane between corrals, he said, "I have the distinct impression, Detective Gray, you don't believe I want Lisa's killer caught. I assure you I do, but I can understand why you don't believe me."

"Why wouldn't I?"

"Because you've mistakenly latched onto the idea that I did it. However, as long as you pursue the false trail of suspecting me, you're blinding yourself to other possibilities. Would you concede that might be true?"

"It might."

"Will you allow me to prove my innocence?"

"That's why I'm here."

Sergio opened a back door into the house and gestured for them to precede him, then led them along the wide central hall to a door on their right. Again he opened it and gestured for them to go first.

The room was a library with floor-to-ceiling books and a spindly desk with its back to a wall of shuttered windows. Facing the desk in the center of the room was a Victorian settee between floor lamps sporting silk-fringed shades at each end. "Please, sit down," Sergio said, walking behind the desk.

Prairie sat on the settee, smoothing its purple horsehair with her palm, while Devon stayed on his feet. Sergio smiled as he reached under the desk.

Hearing the soft hum of machinery, Devon sensed the ceiling move. He looked up to watch a panel slide back to reveal a mirror reflecting the view into a formal parlor next door. The trick was possible because the intervening wall didn't quite reach the top, though when the panel was closed it created the illusion of a barrier.

"A device of my father's," Sergio said.

"Clever," Devon admitted.

"Yes, he was. He also had that parlor designed to amplify sound, so you'll have no difficulty overhearing what Estefen has to say." Sergio smiled. "Come, come, Detective. Don't look so censorious. You're thinking I'm disloyal to betray my ex-wife's uncle."

"It crossed my mind."

"But I've never liked him, and since the financial remunerations consequent to that marriage have already been accrued to my accounts, I don't need him. So because of that, and because however many flaws Lisa may have possessed she didn't deserve to be murdered, I'm willing to lay on the altar of justice whatever Estefen has come here to say."

"Even if it implicates you?"

"There's no way it could. You may not approve of my sexual proclivities, but I do not kill people I love." He walked out from behind the desk and crossed to the door, then turned around. "I think you're cosmopolitan enough to concede that love wears many guises but is no less genuine for the idiosyncrasy of its expression. And no matter how perverted those guises may seem to the unjaded eye, when it crosses the line and becomes murder, it ceases to be love in anyone's definition. Don't you agree?"

Devon nodded.

Sergio walked out, closing the door with a quiet click.

"Don't he give you the creeps?" Prairie whispered.

The door to the next room opened. In the reflection of the mirrored ceiling, they watched Sergio enter, followed not by Estefen Escobar but Carl Lowdy.

Chapter Six

"I saw his Lexus," Carl said.

"Yes, he and Boots are in the stable," Sergio replied.

"What're they doing there?"

"Admiring my horses, I imagine." He poured a snifter of brandy, then swirled it in the glass as he faced Carl. "Cognac?"

Carl shook his head. "She pulled rank with the gov'nor and got some kinda order releasing him in her custody. That's what Hank told me."

"So your scheme not only didn't work, it united them with legal shackles, at least as long as he's in Presidio."

"I just relayed the message. But now you've seen 'em together, what d'ya think?"

"I think their mutual regard is professional and you're mistaking a bed sheet for a ghost."

"You ain't been around all the times she's talked like he's the goddamned Lone Ranger."

Sergio sipped his brandy. "Which you definitely are not."

"I was good enough 'fore she went off to college."

He smiled. "I've always maintained the education of women is dangerous."

"She'll change her tune."

"Come, come. Once a woman decides a man is beneath her, he can howl like a dog and it won't make any difference.

You should move on. In the dark, you know, all women are equal."

"I like leaving the light on."

Sergio laughed. "I wouldn't have expected that of you, Carl."

"Just 'cause I wasn't born with a silver spoon don't mean I ain't no more'n an ignorant cowpoke. In least one respect, I'm better'n you."

"And what might that be?"

"I don't see all women as being the same."

"And Boots is a princess in your eyes, isn't she."

"That's right."

"Even though she broke your nose. What had you done to inspire such wrath from a princess, Carl? In the passion of that fight, weren't you trying to make her a whore?"

"I oughta break *your* nose for using that word in any way connected to her."

"But then you won't get the use of my stud, and your ambitions will come to naught."

Carl frowned. "Are you saying we got a deal?"

"I could let you breed Gargaleote to one of your mares. His name is Portuguese for soldier of fortune, so it seems apropos, don't you think?"

"What's in it for you?"

"I don't choose to say."

"But you're forcing the situation, so it's one or the other for me."

"Yes, I am."

Thinking with his mouth open, Carl clenched his hands into fists. "Can you arrange it so I talk to her 'fore I go?"

"If she's willing. Why don't you wait out front?"

A telephone rang in the room. Sergio picked it up and said, *"Bueno."* He swirled his brandy as he listened. *"Sí, entiendo.*" He hung up and smiled at Carl. "My lunch date just canceled and I feel the need of a siesta. Did you say you were leaving?"

He watched Carl walk out and close the door, then drained the brandy from his snifter and left the glass behind. A moment later he entered the library.

"I was mistaken about the plane," he told Devon. "It must have been my foreman returning from checking the stock. Estefen just called and said he can't make it." He shifted his gaze to Prairie. "Will you have the mercy to talk to Carl? He's moonstruck to see you."

She looked at Devon.

"Go on if you want. I'll be out in a minute."

She slipped quietly through the door.

Devon studied Sergio. "I'd ask what you want from Carl if I thought you'd give me an answer."

"It's a private arrangement."

"Sounded like a dirty one to me."

Sergio smiled. "I imagine all transactions between mere mortals seem soiled when you have the reputation of a Lone Ranger."

"Was Escobar ever coming, or was that the conversation you wanted me to hear?"

"You're welcome to call and ask. There's a phone on the desk behind you."

Devon shook his head. "I'll be in El Paso by dark."

"Have a safe trip," Sergio said.

Devon walked down the hall and out the front door. The patio was empty except for a boy cutting back a patch of prickly pear with a machete.

"Did you see a woman come out a minute ago?" Devon asked.

"*Sí,*" the boy answered. "She left with Señor Carl, but I

don't think she wanted to go."

Tom Hernandez leaned across the table in the dining room of the Plaza Hotel and whispered, "Is that man stalking you, Sam?"

"Who?" she answered, trying to sound unconcerned.

A quietly religious man, Tom was more than a colleague; he was one of her best friends. His round, pink face creased with concern, he said, "The man in the library this morning. He's at a table across from us and hasn't taken his eyes off you since he sat down."

When she glanced at Jay, he gave her a playful smile, making her shudder. "That's Jay Lehrer, my ex-husband."

"Am I wrong to think you're having a problem with him?"

She shook her head. "Last night he took me to dinner. He had a lot to drink, so I invited him in for coffee." She stopped and squeezed her eyes shut in an effort not to cry.

"Wasn't Devon home?"

She opened her eyes to see Tom had guessed what she couldn't bring herself to say. "He's out of town."

"When will he be back?"

"Tonight. Or tomorrow."

"What will you do about Jay Lehrer in the meantime?"

"What can I do?"

"Call the police and have him arrested."

She shook her head, and her tears escaped and ran down her cheeks.

He watched her brush them away, then leaned close again. "If you were raped, Sam," he said softly, "Devon would want you to press charges."

She fumbled in her purse for a tissue. "You don't understand," she said, wiping her nose. "Jay's girlfriend was murdered. Anyone would be knocked off balance by that."

"Murdered? By whom?"

She shrugged. "That's why Devon's in Chinati, investigating the case."

"Have you talked to him? Told him what happened?"

"I don't know how to reach him."

"Call his lieutenant. He'll know."

She shook her head. "If any other woman went to the police complaining that her ex-husband took her to dinner and got out of hand afterwards, then came to her workplace and apologized—and he did apologize, Tom, you heard him —they'd think he was trying to reconcile the marriage, which isn't a police matter."

"Rape is."

"By going to them I'll only compromise Devon. Back him into the corner of defending me and escalate this whole situation into something even uglier than it already is." She shook her head. "All I can do is hope Jay goes away before Devon comes home."

"Do you think that's likely?"

Again she looked at Jay. This time his smile was pleading. She looked back at Tom. "Maybe I'm blowing the whole thing out of proportion. Jay was so drunk last night, he probably didn't realize what he was doing. I mean, his girlfriend *was* murdered."

"That's what worries me the most."

"If he had anything to do with it, he wouldn't be here. Even Devon said that."

"Maybe Devon was wrong."

"I don't think so. Jay wasn't the best of husbands, but he wasn't ever violent."

"Why don't you come stay with me tonight?"

"I can't let Devon come home to an empty apartment."

"Leave a message on his answering machine telling him where you are."

She shook her head. "I can't stop thinking I encouraged Jay out of some sense that I could help him, that it was the right thing to do. Maybe it still is."

"You can't be serious," Tom scoffed.

"Okay, maybe I'm grasping at straws. But the only way I can get a handle on what happened is to tell myself I won't be a victim if I take responsibility for allowing it to happen. Doesn't that make sense?"

"Not if it isn't true."

"But if it is true and I admit it, I'll be more in control next time."

He looked toward Jay's table. "He's leaving."

She sighed. "Maybe that's the last I'll see of him."

"You should take precautions to be certain it is."

Devon floored his Lexus in pursuit of Prairie. He figured Carl probably drove a pickup incapable of much speed, but even traveling sixty miles an hour along the dirt road, Devon couldn't catch sight of any dust ahead of him. Fishtailing off the dirt onto the gravel, he remembered the sign he had seen in the pasture: IN TEXAS THE COPS *ARE* THE ROBBERS. Prairie had told him that pasture belonged to Carl. Figuring his house might be nearby, Devon sped toward the highway.

By the time he hit the blacktop stretch of 2810, the pavement was empty. The only difference between the views from his windshield and his rearview mirror was the wind-driven dust in his wake. Carl should be stirring up an equal amount, but there wasn't a trace of another vehicle anywhere. That probably meant he had taken a back road Devon had no way of finding. Operating on the instinct that a man driven to punish a woman might do it in the bed she had scorned, Devon continued on course.

He allowed himself the pleasure of hating Tierrasantas with the lethal wrath of a provoked bull, knowing Sergio had masterminded Prairie's abduction. If Carl killed her, Devon swore that before anyone stopped him he would kill Sergio in such a way that the arrogant sonofabitch knew exactly what was happening and by whose will. For long moments, Devon assuaged his dread with visions of revenge. When he realized what he was doing, he reined himself back, honing his rage into a confined thrust of intent. Success meant Prairie alive. To achieve that he had to maintain control, not charge blindly at the first red cape in front of him.

Highway 90 was in sight when he spotted a bullet-riddled mailbox with no name, only a number. He shimmied off the asphalt onto a dirt lane leading to what he hoped was the home of Carl Lowdy.

Easing off the accelerator, he killed his engine so he coasted into the yard. A brown dog on a chain yapped an alarm in front of a faded blue house trailer with a rusted red pickup parked off to the side. Devon slid into the dust on his knees and pulled his gun as he heard the trailer door open.

Between his car door and the edge of the windshield, he saw Carl in the trailer's shadowed interior aiming a double-barreled shotgun. Both barrels fired, their pellets ricocheting off the hood of the Lexus. Devon stood up and sent a single bullet to its mark. Carl lurched back and fell inside.

Devon cautiously approached the trailer. Carl was sprawled just beyond the door, his shotgun thrown over his head by the force of his fall, the front of his shirt bloody. Devon reached down and felt for a pulse. There wasn't one. He stood up and scanned the room, thinking if he had been here before all this came down he could have guessed Carl was on the edge. The walls were papered with posters of women in submissive postures, the kitchen reeked with an accumulation of rotting garbage, and enough guns were scattered around to arm a band of rebels.

"Prairie?"

He entered the hall, his gun in his hand. To his left was a minuscule bathroom, the shower mildewed and the toilet unflushed. Another few steps and he was in the bedroom.

On the wall above the bed were photographs of Prairie. Some were from newspaper stories about her being sworn in as the first woman Ranger, others snapshots of her as a teen-ager with long hair, evidently mementoes from when she had been Carl's girlfriend.

Nearly hidden in the bed's filthy sheets was a Colt's .45, making Devon fear the worst. He looked at a narrow closet, its latch closed with a padlock.

"Devon?" she called from inside.

He allowed himself a second of relief, then said, "Stand back. I'm gonna shoot the lock."

Flattening himself against the wall, he took aim and fired. The hasp fell open, but was hot. He shook his hand and tried again, keeping a grip long enough to open the door.

Huddled as far back in the closet as she could get, Prairie slowly stood up. "Where's Carl?"

"Dead."

She stepped forward, put her arms around Devon's neck, and pressed herself close. Feeling her tremble, he held her tight. She sighed deeply, then broke free and stood on her own.

"He got my gun," she said. "I didn't expect him to try nothing so I wasn't ready, but losing control of your weapon is about the worst mistake a lawman can make. There ain't no way I'll ever be able to justify putting you at risk by letting it happen."

"I'm okay," he said. "Are you?"

She nodded, saw her pistol, picked it up and checked the rounds, then slid it into her holster. Still holding his .38, he held out his left hand. She took it and followed him into the living room. Stepping over Carl's body, she said, "Good shot, Devon."

When he faced her in the yard, her smile was gently teasing. "I think you can put your gun away now."

He snapped it into its holster in the small of his back, looked at the dusty brown dog watching him, then at his car, the hood pocked with shot pellets, the door still standing open. Wanting nothing more than to put Presidio County behind him, he went back inside the trailer, found the phone next to the sofa, and punched in 911.

When the female dispatcher answered, he said, "This is Detective Devon Gray of the El Paso Police. There's been a shooting at the home of Carl Lowdy on State Road 2810. We don't need an ambulance, the man's dead, but we'll need the sheriff out here to make a report."

"Can you give me a better address, Detective Gray?" she asked.

"I'm sure the sheriff knows where it is." He hung up and punched in the number for headquarters. "This is Detective Gray. Let me talk to Dreyfus."

The lieutenant came on the line. "Devon! Where are you?"

"Still in Presidio. I've just shot a man in the line of duty."

Dreyfus caught his breath. "Is he dead?"

"Yes."

After a moment, Dreyfus said, "I'll put an internal affairs lawyer on the next flight to Chinati. We'll stand behind you."

"Appreciate it," Devon said.

"Don't suppose the man you shot was Lisa Escobar's killer?"

"I haven't made that connection."

Again Dreyfus hesitated before asking, "You didn't shoot Tierrasantas?"

"No. But if he was in front of me right now, I might."

"Hold on, Devon. I don't know what you're into over there, but keep your cool."

"Yeah."

"We got a copy of the governor's extradition, so we'll have you home tonight."

"Thanks."

He hung up and joined Prairie on the steps to the front door. Sitting beside her with Carl at their backs, he slid his arm around her waist as they watched a dust devil coalesce and whirl across the desert in front of them before it dissipated into nothing as suddenly as it had begun.

Softly she asked, "Was Carl the first man you've killed?"

He nodded.

She leaned her head on his shoulder. "Don't guess it sits easy even knowing he deserved it."

"Not as easy as if it'd been Sergio."

"We walked right into it, didn't we."

"Yes."

"Sergio's prob'ly watching one of his nasty movies, fondling Elita while he waits to hear from Carl." She snorted. "Doesn't make me feel real important to know I was traded for a wad of horse cum."

"That wasn't why Carl did it."

"Nah, he was crazy jealous, but not 'cause he loved me. He tried for a deputy sheriff's job but couldn't pass the civil service test. That's what he really hated: that I aced mine and got a Ranger's badge."

"Makes sense, as far as it goes."

"What do you mean?"

"The more important question is why Sergio wants you out of his way."

Hearing the wail of a siren still a long distance down Highway 90, they listened to the sound waffling across the heat waves rising off the land.

Prairie said, "Maybe it had something to do with me saying Cipriano's sheep fence was cut."

"A range war between cattle and sheep men sounds like something out of the history books."

"It ain't that. Coyote Canyon starts within a hundred yards of Sergio's landing strip and leads straight to the Rio Grande. Doesn't that sound like a natural-born highway for smugglers?"

"Could be."

"Thing of it is, no wire was cut. I made that up as an excuse to be out Sergio's way. He sure bolted at the suggestion, though, didn't he?"

Devon nodded, listening to the siren warble as the car slowed to take the turn onto 2810. "I'd say you hit a sore spot, Prairie."

"You think it might be connected to Lisa's murder?"

"Do you?"

"Hard to figure, ain't it. I mean, if Sergio's running contraband through Coyote Canyon, the last thing he'd want is to land smack in the middle of a murder investigation. I'm not saying he wouldn't kill Lisa if it fit his purpose, but he wouldn't leave her body to be found by a police force he doesn't own."

The siren was loud now, making the brown dog howl on its chain. "You think Rufus has a piece of the Coyote Canyon action?"

"Not much happens 'round here he doesn't nibble on one way or another."

"Then we're better off not mentioning it," Devon said, "if we want to get out of his county tonight."

When Samantha arrived home from work, her living room was still disarrayed from the night before. The coffee table was pushed against the stereo cabinet, the sofa pillow that had been used to elevate her hips was on the floor, and one of her sneakers lay abandoned in the middle of the room.

Quickly she closed and locked the front door, then set about re-establishing order to the appearance of her home. Discovering the pillow was stained with a shiny crust of semen, she threw it in the garbage. She put the coffee table where it belonged, and looked in vain for the missing shoe. Not finding it, she secreted the solitary sneaker in the back of her closet behind a stack of boxed shoes she had been mistaken in buying, as if what had happened could be dismissed as equally insignificant. Then she vacuumed with a vengeance and dusted everything with lemon-scented Pledge.

When she had finished with the living room, she went into the kitchen and ran the dishwasher, though the only things in it were the cups she had set out for her and Jay. She placed the scorched, cracked coffee carafe in the trash with the pillow, and would have carried them down to the Dumpster if she'd had the courage to open her door.

After reassuring herself that both the deadbolt and chain were securely in place, she went into the bedroom and changed the sheets. To her knowledge, Jay hadn't touched anything in this room, but she dusted and vacuumed it, too. When she finished, she looked through the open bathroom door.

She vaguely remembered him going in there, and too vividly she remembered douching, then standing under the hot water for what seemed like hours, trying to wash away what had happened. Now she scoured the bathroom, from the commode and the floor to the tiles above the tub. Finished, she stripped herself naked, belatedly realizing she had done all that in her work clothes. She stuffed them in the hamper, stepped into the shower and let the heat stream over her body. Finally she shampooed and lathered herself with soap, rinsed it all off, and stood another long time watching the suds funnel down the drain.

She turned off the water and pulled the curtain aside to stare through the open door as if she were seeing an alien world. The bed she had shared with Devon seemed a strange artifact from an ancient past, the clock and lamp like furnishings of a lost normality.

From her bureau, she selected the bottoms of a pair of white silk pajamas, then moved to the closet and put on the pastel flowered robe Devon had given her for Valentine's Day. Tying the sash tightly around her waist, she walked across her now pristine living room to the kitchen. Inside the refrigerator was an unopened bottle of Chardonnay.

Clumsy with the corkscrew, she used a knife to push the cork down the neck of the bottle. She drank the first glass without stopping and was pouring another when the doorbell rang.

She overflowed the glass and had to pull a paper towel from the roll to wipe up the spill. Telling herself she could handle whatever else happened, she walked to her door and peered through the peephole.

Jay stood outside, dressed in a navy blue jacket over a white shirt. He rang the bell again as she watched through the distortion of the magnifying glass.

"Samantha," he called. "Please let me in."

"Go away!" she whispered.

"Come on, Sam. You're not one of those women who see their own fear in the face of a man who wants to love them. Are you?"

His words struck her with dread. Did she still love Jay in some dark recess of her heart, and had her denial of that fact caused him to treat her with so much anger?

"Devon asked me to give you a message," he said.

"Devon?"

"I can't hear you, Sam! Open the door."

She turned the deadbolt and opened the door the scant crack the chain allowed. "Why would he give you a message for me?"

"He said he's been trying to call but apparently your phone's unplugged."

She glanced toward the bedroom, wondering if she had accidentally disconnected the phone in her frantic vacuuming.

"Sam," Jay pleaded softly, "please let me in."

She shook her head.

"Don't you want to hear Devon's message?"

"Yes."

He smiled. "He found Lisa's killer in Chinati. Arrested him and put him in jail."

Samantha felt a rush of relief. She had been right to think Jay was incapable of murder, so her defense of him was justified. He *had* been drunk, out of his mind with grief.

"Devon'll be home in an hour," he petitioned. "Won't you let me talk to you before he gets here? There're things I need to say when we're alone."

"Like what?" she whispered.

"You gonna make me say 'em through the door?"

She nodded.

"Okay, basically it's this: I've never loved anyone but you. Lisa was just a cure for my loneliness. I was hoping maybe Devon filled the same need in your life."

"Don't, Jay."

"Don't tell the truth? I can't help it, Sam. It's my nature. You know that. Remember when I was having those affairs when we were married, how I never lied? When you confronted me, I told the truth, didn't I?"

She shut her eyes against the pain of those memories.

"We only have a few minutes," he coaxed. "Won't you let me in?"

The neighbor, Alicia Resendiz, opened her door and peered out. "Is anything wrong?"

"Hello," Jay said lightly. "I'm Sam's ex-husband and we're just talking over old times."

Alicia gave Samantha a knowing smile of camaraderie, but Sam had often suspected her of making a play for Devon, so in response to what she saw as a devious woman's mock concern, she said tartly, "Everything's fine, thanks." Then she unhooked the chain and let Jay in.

Chapter Seven

He sauntered into the kitchen and laughed. "Couldn't get the cork out?"

"No," she said, assuaging her fear with the reassurance that Devon would be home soon.

Jay examined the corkscrew. "You always were clumsy."

She threw the soggy towel in the trash and returned the bottle to the refrigerator, then leaned against the closed door. "When did you talk to Devon?"

"He called me at the hotel a while ago. Said the case was closed so I could go home, but I think he was trying to get rid of me. You think he might try to do that, Sam?"

"Not unless you told him what happened."

Jay shook his head. "I think he's worried we're rekindling our love." He tossed the corkscrew in the air and caught it.

She stared at the stainless steel point protruding from his fist.

"You afraid of me, Sam?"

She tried to brush past him, but he caught and pulled her back, touching the hollow of her throat with the point of the screw. "Where you going?"

"Please don't hurt me, Jay."

"Since you let me in, you must want me here."

"I don't." She looked with longing at the door.

"Devon's not coming. Not for a while yet." He ran the point lightly down the opening of her robe, smiling as she winced. "Say please again, so we can make love like we did last night."

Her ragged breath staggered her words. "That . . . was not . . . love."

"Then let's do it right." He covered her mouth with one hand, the corkscrew in his other, and pushed her into the bedroom and onto the bed, where he untied the sash and opened her robe. "Did Devon buy you this?"

"Yes," she whispered, her breasts bare beneath him. She searched his eyes for some remnant of the man she had known, but their darkly mesmerizing beauty was erratic now.

He straddled her hips and pressed the corkscrew against the pulse in her throat so the point pricked her skin with each beat of her heart. "You should've known I'd be back," he said, " 'cause I only took one shoe."

"What do you mean?"

"Ask Devon. Being a detective, he'll figure it out." He pressed the corkscrew between her breasts, then etched a line down her belly to her navel, grinning at her sharp intake of breath. "The dude who killed Lisa. Devon said he's a sadist."

"That wasn't a lie? That he arrested her killer?"

"I don't lie, Sam. Don't you know me by now?"

"It's been so long, Jay."

He nodded. "I got so fucked up without you, I lost my job. Was fired so I couldn't even collect unemployment. For a while I still had the royalties on the programs I'd written, but Lisa was an expensive lady. I sold my rights and spent all that money on her. When it was gone, she left me." He touched the point to the tip of Sam's nose. "Don't you think that was dirty pool?"

"Yes," she whispered.

He frowned. "I keep seeing her dead. Her feet were so soft, it hurts to remember them bare among all those stickers."

"What happened was awful, Jay."

"Our life got really strange, Sam. PG&E cut off the power when I couldn't pay the bill, so we didn't have any light. We got so used to the dark, I wouldn't let Lisa go out 'cause the street lights were too bright, you know?" He positioned the corkscrew in her navel and pushed in the point. "I thought she'd disappear and then I wouldn't have anyone to play paper dolls with."

"Paper dolls?" she whimpered.

"Yeah, you know," he laughed as he lifted the screw, "lady dolls with holes and men dolls with pokers. You put 'em together and tell stories. Lisa was real good at it. When she left me, I didn't have anyone to play with."

"I'll play with you, Jay. Let's go into the living room and cut some out of magazines."

He smiled. "I've graduated since then, Sam."

It was past one when Devon parked in front of his brother's house in the gentrified neighborhood of Kern Place. He led Prairie up to the front door and used his key to let them in. Turning on a lamp in the living room, he told her to wait, then walked through the dimly-lit hall and knocked on his brother's bedroom door. "Connie?"

"Yeah," he answered, his voice muffled as he roused himself from sleep.

Devon walked back into the living room and gave Prairie a smile. When Connie came in, running a hand through his dark shoulder-length hair, he stopped stock still seeing a pretty Texas Ranger wearing a gun in the middle of his living room. She stared too, taking in his muscular bare chest above low-slung jeans and the tattoo BORN TO LOSE flaunted on his biceps.

Again Devon smiled, this time at her obvious surprise

that he had such a disreputable-looking brother. He introduced them and explained that she needed a place to stay the night.

Connie laughed, nonchalantly at ease. "No problem, bro. You gonna come back in the morning?"

"I'll be here for breakfast, if that's all right."

"Sure. Tomorrow's Saturday and the kids'll be glad to see you."

Devon gave Prairie another smile on his way out.

As he meandered the streets toward Sunset Heights, he felt weary to the point of exhaustion. Rufus Bowlin hadn't been happy to honor the Order of Extradition in the first place, and Devon having killed one of his constituents in the meantime didn't improve the sheriff's mood, but the internal affairs lawyer sent from El Paso had prevailed. The lawyer convinced Bowlin that Prairie's corroboration of the shooting as a justified act meant the extradition was still valid, and that Devon was merely returning to his own jurisdiction until a formal inquiry could be held. Along with a veiled threat implying failure to honor the governor's order would carry serious consequences, the lawyer's argument allowed Bowlin to let Devon go without losing face.

All that had taken hours to accomplish, however, and Devon and Prairie spent more long hours driving to El Paso. Neither of them said much. Appreciating her ability to keep her own counsel and let him keep his, he had let his thoughts return to the murder of Lisa Escobar.

Sergio had been right about one thing: Devon had become sidetracked by honing in on her ex-husband. That her killer would leave behind a necklace recently purchased with his own credit card was unlikely, and as Prairie had said, if Sergio had killed Lisa, he wouldn't have left her body in a public place. In all probability, she had been killed by a stranger, which widened the field of suspects but not enough to include the entire male population of El Paso.

What Devon had to do was account for the hours between when Lisa called Jay in Los Angeles and when she died. A woman as striking as she was would have been noticed, and he decided to question the taxi drivers working the Camino Real after midnight. Maybe she had gone out for a drink. If he could discover where, someone in the bar might remember her and, more to the point, who she left with.

What he was looking for was a man who liked to play games with knives. Such men didn't typically kill their partners the first time out. Like a junkie needing an escalating rush to get off, they slowly spiraled to the flash point of murder, leaving a trail of accomplices behind. Accomplices, victims, or co-dependents, depending on who was calling it. To Devon, a woman who allowed a man to commit minor transgressions on her body was an accomplice in whatever destruction he eventually dealt. That theory wasn't part of the legal definition, but it was intrinsic to his definition of moral complicity.

As he parked his car in front of Sam's apartment, he heard the mournful whistle of a train approaching downtown. The last time he had heard that forlorn melody muted across the miles, he had been en route to the morgue with Samantha and Jay. Now, looking downhill toward the Camino Real, he remembered standing nearby watching them say goodnight, and he had to admit that giving her time to sort out her feelings had been part of why he had gone to Chinati.

Using his key to let himself in, he was struck by the lingering lemon scent of furniture polish. He opened a window before closing the door, then turned on a lamp. The living room was immaculate, as was the kitchen, though a full glass of white wine had been left on the counter. Sensing something amiss, he moved quietly to open the closed bedroom door.

She was asleep under the covers, the light from the living room not enough to wake her. On the floor lay the robe he had given her for Valentine's Day. He crossed the room and looked down at her lying on her side facing away from him. Her regular breathing told him she was deeply asleep, so he picked up the robe and laid it across the foot of the bed, then walked into the bathroom and closed the door.

This room, too, had been scoured spotless. He guessed she was tired after spending her evening cleaning house, and he tried to dismiss his misgivings as coming from their quarrel. Evidently she had gone out of her way to make amends by proving she could be domestic when she wanted. She had probably been disappointed when he was so late getting back and had a few drinks to take the sting out of it.

He took a blanket from the linen closet and returned to the living room. Since he hadn't shared Sam's bed their last night together, he didn't feel he could simply resume possession without discussing all the ramifications of what had been said. As he shook out the blanket, he saw the sofa pillow was gone, and again he felt nudged with a suspicion that something wasn't right. The pillow was new. He remembered how pleased Sam had been when she came home with the exact shade of yellow she wanted. Telling himself she had probably spilled something on it and put it in the laundry, he walked back into the bedroom.

She was so soundly asleep even his second intrusion didn't wake her, though always before the mere sound of his key in the lock was enough. Yet the even rhythm of her breathing suggested no cause for alarm. Probably it was simply that she'd had too much to drink. Maybe the wine in the kitchen had been rejected when she realized she'd had enough, and at that point she had been too tired to put it away.

He saw the corkscrew half-hidden under the bed. When he picked it up, it felt sticky. Probably she had spilled the wine opening it, though Samantha wasn't usually that clumsy.

He leaned across for the pillow she wasn't using, watching her face for any flicker of reaction. There was none. Quietly he closed the bedroom door, then tossed the pillow on the sofa as he carried the corkscrew into the kitchen.

When he rinsed it under the faucet, the water running down the drain was pink. So she had cut herself opening the wine. Knowing she usually came close to fainting at the sight of blood, he figured she had wrapped her finger in a paper towel and gone to bed. Carrying the corkscrew? Maybe. Dropping it with aversion as she climbed under the covers? Possibly.

He laid the corkscrew in the drainboard, dumped the wine in the sink and opened the dishwasher to put the glass inside. Only two cups and a knife were there, so he thought she must have eaten out. Maybe she'd had a few drinks at dinner, and that explained her clumsiness.

Opening the refrigerator, he saw the nearly full bottle with its floating cork. He tried to imagine the scenario of her struggling with the corkscrew, giving up and pushing the cork down with a knife, then filling a glass and putting the bottle in the fridge and the knife in the dishwasher. After all that, why would she pick up the corkscrew and cut herself? Maybe she was trying to determine how it was broken.

Deciding this wasn't a case and there was no need to work it out when he was so tired he could barely think, he returned to the living room and sat on the sofa. The breeze through the open window felt pleasantly cool. He leaned back and closed his eyes, almost falling asleep. His brief respite was broken by a soft knock on the door. He stood up and opened it to see

Alicia Resendiz standing there dressed to the nines, apparently having just returned from a date.

She smiled awkwardly. "I saw your car on the street. Hope I didn't wake you."

He shook his head. "Want to come in?"

"No, thanks. I was just wondering if Samantha's all right."

"She's asleep."

Alicia nodded. "Her ex-husband was here earlier. I thought they were having an argument, but when I opened my door to ask if there was a problem, she said everything was okay and let him in, so I figured it wasn't any of my business. Still in all, it didn't seem right somehow, so I thought I'd check and make sure she's okay."

"She's fine," Devon said. "Thanks."

Alicia gave him an embarrassed smile, as if she had committed a faux pas by telling him Samantha's ex-husband had visited while he was gone. He watched her unlock her apartment and disappear inside, then he closed the door and sat again on the sofa, looking around.

Samantha had definitely cleaned house, but not for him. And far from being worried about their argument, she had evidently enjoyed herself so much with Jay she'd had too many drinks and was now sleeping them off. She had even worn the robe he'd given her while she was entertaining her ex-husband. He wondered if the corkscrew hadn't ended up in the bedroom because they had been drinking in bed, and if Jay hadn't left the full glass in the kitchen on his way out the door.

None of that set right with Devon. In the months they had been living together, this was the first time he had left her alone overnight. Of course it was also the first time her ex-husband was in town, but after extending himself to help the man, Devon resented even more that Sam had taken advantage of his absence to play him for a fool.

With a growing conviction that he had been right to sleep on the sofa, he undressed, then vigorously punched the pillow before stretching out. Despite his anger, he fell quickly asleep, surrendering to the fatigue of what had been one of the longest days of his life.

When he awoke in the morning, Samantha was sitting across the room watching him.

She was wearing her green velvet robe, and her feet were bare, incongruously reminding him of Lisa Escobar's feet on the prickly grass by the river. He sat up, combed his hair with his fingers and ran his palm over the bristles of his whiskers, thinking he was in no shape for a confrontation. Wearing only his undershorts, he kept the blanket over his lap as if he were cold. A chill breeze *was* coming through the window behind him, lifting the drapes and letting them fall. He sniffed, hoping to pick up the fragrance of fresh coffee, but apparently she hadn't made any.

"How you doing?" he asked.

"What time did you get home?"

"Nearly two."

"Was your trip successful?"

He smiled ruefully. "It was close to an unmitigated disaster."

She stared at him. "You didn't arrest anyone in Chinati?"

He shook his head.

She looked away.

He waited, hoping she would tell him about her evening without being asked. When she didn't, he said, "Think you could make us some coffee?"

"The coffeepot's broken."

He nodded slowly. "I'm due at my brother's for breakfast anyway. Guess I can wait."

They watched each other warily.

Giving her another chance to volunteer the fact that she had seen Jay, he said, "I noticed you cleaned house."

She shrugged.

"Did you see Jay while I was gone?"

"Why do you ask?"

"I was just wondering if he's still in town."

"I haven't seen him," she said.

He kept his voice lightly teasing. "Stayed home alone and had too much to drink?"

She met his eyes. "What makes you say that?"

"I found the corkscrew on the bedroom floor."

She looked away again.

After a moment, he asked, "Mind if I shower, or do you want to go first?"

"I've already showered." Still not looking at him.

"Good," he said, " 'cause I feel grungy enough to grow mold."

She didn't even smile at his joke.

Gathering his clothes, he left the blanket behind and walked into the bedroom. She had not only made the bed, she'd changed the sheets. A pink corner poked out though he distinctly remembered they had been blue the night before. Noting it was barely seven, which meant he'd had less than five hours of sleep, he unlaced his belt, laid it and his holstered gun on the bed, then went into the bathroom and dumped his clothes in the hamper. It seemed unusually full. When he walked back into the living room after his shower, Samantha hadn't moved. "You want to go to the Rincon for breakfast?"

She looked up with tears in her eyes. "I thought you were going to your brother's."

"I'll call and tell him I can't make it."

"Will you let me get dressed?"

"If you go out in your robe, you're apt to be mistaken for an Alzheimer's patient."

Again she neither smiled nor laughed at his joke. "I'll just be a minute," she said, hurrying into the bedroom.

Deciding she evidently regretted whatever she had done with Jay, Devon called his brother from the wall phone in the kitchen.

"Hey," Connie greeted him with a laugh.

"I'm taking Sam out to breakfast. Tell Prairie I'll be there in an hour."

"No problem, bro. We're all enjoying her company. She's a spitfire, ain't she?"

"Yeah, she is."

"When I led her upstairs last night and told her that used to be your room, you'd've thought I was ushering a teeny-bopper into Mick Jagger's boudoir."

Devon smiled despite himself.

"Damn sexy boots she's got." Connie snickered. "Does she make it with 'em on, or ain't you found that out yet?"

"You gonna keep your hands off her 'til I show up?" Devon asked, only half-joking.

"It's not me you gotta worry about. When Eric met her this morning, his jaw dropped to his knees. Since then he's been more of a charmer than I thought he had in him, but you know playing a gentleman's the opening act of a rake."

"I'm sure Prairie can handle him. See you later." He hung up and called Dreyfus at home. "Devon Gray," he said when the lieutenant came on the line.

"Glad you called," Dreyfus said. "You doing okay?"

"Fair. When's the inquiry likely to be held?"

"Internal affairs needs time to prepare your defense."

"It's cut and dried."

"Nothing's cut and dried when lawyers're involved, but you should skate without much more'n a lot of hollering. Usual procedure, though, is to put an officer on leave 'til the decision comes down. How do you feel about a vacation?"

"I'd rather keep working on finding Lisa's killer."

"Good. Garcia's in California and Snyder's in the hospital with an emergency appendectomy, so we're shorthanded. But keep a low profile, Devon. With Tierrasantas involved, the press is on a feeding frenzy. Think you can crack the case without dragging his name in any deeper?"

"Depends on how deep he's in it."

"You think he might be our perp?"

Devon watched Samantha come out of the bedroom wearing jeans and a maroon sweater under a blue blazer. "As of right now, I'm short on leads."

"What's your next move?"

"Her uncle, Estefen Escobar, runs an import-export in the ProNaf. Think we could get him over here?"

"Someone has to pick up the body. Want me to start protocol with the *comandante* in Juárez?"

"Yeah, and let me know when Escobar's coming. I'll meet him at the morgue."

"Be sure'n keep me informed, Devon. This could explode into an international incident, so don't leave me out of one iota of what you're doing."

"I won't." He hung up and smiled at Samantha. "Ready?"

Demolishing his plate of *huevos rancheros* at Rincon de Cortez, Devon watched Samantha pick at her omelet. He cleaned his plate with the last scrap of tortilla, then leaned back and looked at her so intently she was forced to meet his eyes.

"What's happening in your head, Sam?" he asked gently.

She shrugged, looking across the parking lot to the tawny hills above the Sun Bowl.

"I know you saw Jay last night."

Her eyes darted back to his.

He smiled, using his professional skills at softening up a witness. "Alicia came to the door after I got home and told me she thought you were having a problem with him, but when she asked, you said everything was okay." He watched a confused turmoil ignite behind her eyes. "Why did you lie to me?"

She looked away again, folding her arms across her breasts as if she were cold.

"I think I deserve an answer."

"I wish I had one to give you, Devon."

"You slept with him, didn't you."

She kept quiet.

"All I need is a yes or no, Sam. Your reasons are irrelevant."

"Are they?"

"From my point of view."

"Then yes, to use your metaphor: I slept with him twice while you were gone."

He sipped his coffee to camouflage his anger, watching the cup as he set it back down.

"I didn't want it to happen!" she whispered. "I didn't even want to let him in."

He met her eyes. "Why did you?"

"Last night he said you'd called from Chinati and given him a message for me."

"Why would I relay a message through him?"

"You wouldn't." The panic in her eyes hardened into accusation. "But you didn't call me, did you, Devon?"

"I was busy."

She nodded, but her hand shook when she lifted her cup, spilling her coffee so she set it back down.

"What's got you so spooked, Sam? If you want to go back to him, I won't stand in your way."

She dabbed at the spill with her napkin. "I don't want anything to do with him, but he doesn't think my feelings are any more relevant than you do."

He watched her crumple the wet napkin in her fist. "Are you saying he raped you?" Hearing how combative he sounded, he softened his voice, "Tell me the truth, Sam."

"Yes!" Then she contradicted herself when what he needed was certainty. "Maybe the first time I allowed it to happen, maybe because of our quarrel, and because Jay seemed to need me when you never do. But last night he held the corkscrew to my throat and forced me into the bedroom, then used the point to mark me." She managed a bitter smile. "I don't suppose you'd like to see it?"

He shook his head. "Because he left marks you hadn't counted on doesn't give you grounds to cry rape."

"Do you think I wanted him to do that?"

"I met a man yesterday who cut his wife with a razor 'cause they enjoyed feeling blood between 'em."

She paled. "I'm not like that, Devon. You know I'm not like that."

He shrugged. "It looks to me like you had too much to drink and things got a little rougher than you anticipated. Now because you're wearing evidence, you say you were forced. The rape squad deals with similar stories all the time."

She let out a gust of air. "I was actually afraid you'd avenge my honor."

"I can't see that you have any."

108

She jerked as if he had slapped her, then hid her face and cried.

Feeling the needle-prick of the other customers' attention, he turned over the bill and read the amount while reaching for his wallet.

"You're making a scene, Samantha," he said dryly. "Let's go."

She was still crying when she ducked inside his car. He walked around and got in behind the wheel. Exiting onto the street, he turned left toward the Sun Bowl. In the middle of its empty parking lot, he stopped and killed his engine, then sat staring at the cold stadium lights.

"Devon?" she whimpered. "I didn't mean for this to happen."

He met her eyes. "Regret isn't enough, Sam."

"He asked me to dinner. That seemed harmless, but all through it I was miserable, counting the minutes until I could get away from him. He had a lot to drink, so when he brought me home I invited him in for a cup of coffee. Once we were inside he started crying, saying he could forget about Lisa for stretches of time, but then he'd remember. I tried to comfort him. Maybe he misinterpreted what I was feeling, but it was only simple compassion for someone who's suffering. The next morning I told myself that's what happened: he'd misjudged my feelings. So last night, after he told me you'd called, I let him in again."

"Why did you lie to me?"

"Because I knew this was how you'd react! I was only trying to help him. Even when he was doing that with the corkscrew and I was terrified, I felt sorry for him. He's devastated by Lisa's death! He told me it hurts him to remember her bare feet among all those stickers. My God, Devon, anyone would feel compassion for what he's going through!

How can you hold it against me?"

"Her bare feet?"

"What?"

"Is that what he said?"

She shook her head.

"Think, Sam! Is that what he said?"

"That it hurt him to remember her bare feet among all those stickers?"

"I didn't tell him she wasn't wearing shoes."

"My God," she whispered.

He turned the key and gunned his engine. Accelerating out of the lot to follow Sun Bowl Drive downtown, he lowered his window, slapped the light on his roof, and flipped the switch to activate his siren so he could run hot as he entered Sunset Heights.

Sam was crying, but he didn't take his eyes off the road till he came abreast of her building. Slamming on his brakes so his car bounced broadside against the curb, he reached across and threw open her door. "Get out."

She lurched onto the sidewalk, her face incredulous as she staggered backward when he slammed the door.

Still running hot, he cut a U-turn and sped back down the hill to the Camino Real. He double-parked in the driveway, his siren dying when he shut off the engine, but he left the light revolving and his door open as he jogged inside.

In front of the desk, he flashed his badge at the startled clerk and asked for Jay Lehrer's room number.

"He checked out this morning," she said.

"Did he say where he was going?"

She shook her head. "But he did mention returning his rental car to the airport."

Devon stared at her so long she took a step away. "Thanks," he said, belatedly giving her a weak smile.

Back in his Lexus, he took the emergency light off his roof and turned the ignition. Telling himself to stay cool so he could take care of business, he drove north on Mesa toward his brother's house to pick up Prairie.

Chapter Eight

The family was sitting around the dining room table when Devon walked in. He met Prairie's eyes, silently communicating his desire to leave.

"I'll just be a minute," she said, then hurried upstairs.

Connie sat at one end of the table with Laura on his lap, her long dark braid tied with a red ribbon to match her smock dress. Getting her pregnant had been Connie's response to her going back to school. Devon had paid the tuition on an accounting course she was still attending, though it was unlikely she would leave her new baby to work a job. But the threat of that happening had motivated Connie to keep a steady paycheck coming in, and he had already been promoted to supervisor of the loading dock at a small manufacturing company, so Devon considered the money well-spent. If Eric could keep himself out of trouble, the family might experience more than transitory happiness for a change.

Laura asked, "Want some coffee, Devon?"

He shook his head. "Don't have time."

"Please," Misty pleaded. She was fourteen, her short black hair tousled and her face pleasingly free of makeup so early in the day. "We haven't seen you since forever."

"Prairie was just telling us about her horses," Eric chimed in. His lanky dark hair was longer than Misty's, his face clean-shaven except for a tiny dark triangle beneath his lower lip.

Devon shrugged with regret. "Can't do it."

"Tough case?" Connie asked.

Devon nodded, hearing Prairie's boots on the stairs. When she appeared wearing her gunbelt and badge, he smiled, and again responding to his unspoken communication, she laughed.

Devon looked at his brother. Connie winked, having recognized that more than a professional partnership was evolving between Devon and Prairie. But Laura looked sad when she asked, "Will we see you for Sunday supper?"

"I'll let you know," he said, suspecting everyone except Prairie was thinking of Samantha.

"Your family's peaches," Prairie said when they were descending the hill toward the freeway.

Devon didn't answer, reproaching himself for his less than sympathetic reaction to Sam's claim of being raped. But that nudge of self-recrimination only served to increase his anger, so when he hit the wide open on-ramp, he kicked the Lexus up to eighty, propelling it into the fast lane.

"Where we going?" Prairie asked, fastening her seat belt.

"The airport."

His brief enjoyment of the nip and tuck of high-speed maneuvers ended abruptly when he exited onto Airway Boulevard and got stuck behind an ancient Chrysler driven by an old lady. Frustrated by his inability to pass or hurry her, he slapped his emergency light on his roof and activated his siren. The old lady slowed down so suddenly he had to brake to avoid a collision before she scooted out of his way. Mumbling a curse, he shot through a red light, leaving an eruption of horns in his wake.

"What the hell you doing?" Prairie yelled.

"Getting to the airport," he muttered.

"The way you're going about it is what I call an abuse of power."

As he entered the congestion in front of the terminal, the cars ahead cleared the lane in obedience to his siren. Spotting an empty space at the curb, he whipped through a crevice to claim it, then left his light revolving on his roof as he headed for the closest door into the terminal.

Prairie ran to catch up. "What're we doing?"

"Canvassing car rental agencies."

"Who're we looking for?"

"Jay Lehrer. From L.A."

"L-E-H-R-E-R?"

"Yeah. I'll talk to security."

The director was out, so Devon asked that he be paged, then watched Prairie at the counter of Super Star Rent-A-Car. When the clerk checked his computer and shook his head, Prairie moved to the counter of Alamo.

"Detective Gray?" The head of airport security was a beefy man with a boil on his neck. By the time Devon had explained the situation, Prairie was walking toward them with a cocky grin.

"Alamo," she said as soon as she was close. "Took it out at two-fifteen Wednesday morning and ain't brought it back."

Devon led her and the director over to Alamo, showed the clerk his badge and told her to delay Lehrer with paperwork when he showed up and to call security. She listened with wide eyes.

"He's dangerous," Devon warned. "If he gets away from you, watch to see if he goes into the terminal or outside." He looked at the security boss. "If he goes in, stop him from getting on a plane, but don't try to do it alone."

The man nodded.

"If he takes a taxi," Devon told the clerk, "get the company and number of the cab."

"I understand," she answered.

Devon looked at Prairie. "Let's go."

He took the light off the roof of his Lexus as he slid behind the wheel, tossed the light into the backseat, and picked up the mike to his radio.

"Detective Gray," he told the dispatcher. "I want an APB on Jay Lehrer." He paused to read the paper Prairie held up. "Driving a '94 white Ford Fiesta, license EP34AL. Approach with caution, but don't let him get away."

"Was that J-A-Y L-E-H-R-E-R,'94 white Fiesta, EASY-PAUL-3-4-ALSO-LOVE?" she asked.

"Roger."

"Approach caution? Detention stat?"

"You got it."

He hooked the mike and eased away from the curb.

"Who is he?" Prairie asked.

"The killer of Lisa Escobar."

"How do you know that?"

"Take my word for it."

The radio crackled, then Dreyfus shouted, "Devon?"

He picked up the mike. "Yeah."

"Our friend from Juárez has an appointment at three o'clock. You still gonna meet him?"

"You bet."

"Come by my office and fill me in on this APB first."

"All right."

Static erupted then faded behind the dispatcher announcing the APB to all units. When the radio was quiet again, Prairie asked, "You gonna fill *me* in, Devon, or d'ya think I'm just a flunky following orders?"

"Texas Rangers are independent agents taking orders only from their superior and the governor."

"I don't need you to tell me that."

"You want me to take you back to the terminal so you can catch a plane home?"

"No. I want you to tell me how you found out Jay Lehrer killed Lisa."

Knowing he would eventually have to explain it to someone harder to talk to than Prairie, he tried to formulate an opening sentence as he looked for a quiet place. From Airway, he turned east on Montana and drove to the lot of the Cielo Vista Golf Course. After parking to face the brown winter grass, he glanced in his rearview at the row of green Chevy Suburbans in front of the Border Patrol Headquarters across the street, then shut off his engine and looked at Prairie watching him expectantly.

The cold wind he had felt chilling his back that morning had returned, dropping the temperature into the low fifties, bowing the trees surrounding the course, and flaunting the pennants marking the goals of the game as he tried to find an opening move.

Prairie said softly, "Let's start with Lehrer. Who is he?"

"Lisa's last boyfriend." He took a deep breath. "And Samantha's ex-husband."

"Oh," Prairie said.

"He showed up at Sam's apartment saying Lisa had called him from here. He also said he thought she was in trouble and he wanted to help her. I checked the source of the call and learned it originated from the Camino Real, so the three of us drove down there. When Jay showed me a photo of Lisa, I recognized her as the victim of the murder I'd been assigned that afternoon."

"You didn't suspect him of killing her?"

"Sure I did, but he had all the right answers." He watched the pennants flap in the wind. "Said he'd driven straight through from L.A., which would've put him in Blythe about the time Lisa died. I didn't check to see if he was driving a rental car because he seemed truly hurt by her death."

"So you dismissed your suspicion?"

He nodded. "Lisa had been registered at the hotel with Tierrasantas, so I went to Presidio."

"Leaving Samantha with Jay."

Aware of the anger strong in his voice, he said, "To hear her tell it, she was as taken in by his act as I was."

Gently, Prairie said, "You're gonna have to be more specific, Devon."

He forced himself to meet her eyes. "Both nights I was gone, she fucked him. This morning she gave me a song and dance about how he misread her feelings and took her farther than she wanted to go. At the end of her . . . apology . . . she repeated something he'd said about Lisa's bare feet. I hadn't told Jay she wasn't wearing shoes, so there's only one way he could've known."

"Where's Samantha now?"

"Home, I guess."

"Don't you think she needs protection?"

"Against a man she welcomed with open arms?"

"You said she was taken in by his act."

"Her reasons don't matter to me."

"She's in danger, Devon. If this had happened to any other woman, you wouldn't fail to see that."

He kept quiet, watching the flags flutter above the withered grass of the field.

"Seems to me," Prairie said, "any killer who'd calmly hand over a photo of his victim to a detective is playing cat and mouse. Don't you think what he did to Samantha was aimed at pulling you into his game?"

"None of what came down between them had anything to do with me."

"Maybe not from her side of it, but as long as your anger keeps you away from her, you're giving her to him."

"I'm not giving him anything! We had no connection before he showed up on her doorstep."

"You're the detective assigned to the murder he committed."

He met her eyes, fighting within himself to allow her argument credence.

"I know this ain't easy, Devon, but you gotta set your feelings aside. If you wanta catch Jay, Samantha's your bait."

"I won't use her like that."

"Ain't your choice but his, and he's already made it."

He pounded the heel of his hand against the steering wheel in frustrated denial.

"Let *me* stay with her," she suggested. "You try'n catch him every way you know how, and when he shows up at her place again, I'll call you." After a minute, she added, "If you get me there in time."

Samantha heard the two sets of footsteps approach her door. Expecting them to go on by, she felt prickled with fear when they stopped and someone rang the bell. Slowly she pulled herself up from where she had been sitting since she arrived home. Peering through the peephole, she felt a rush of relief to see Devon with a woman wearing a badge.

Then she realized her relief was unfounded because he hadn't used his key. Yet the presence of the female officer meant he had accepted her claim of rape, and she opened her door dreading the examination she suspected lay ahead.

She saw no forgiveness in his eyes, only an impersonal desire to be fair. After closing and relocking her door, she stood with her back to it as they shared an awkward moment of silence.

Finally Devon said, "This is Ranger Drake. She'll stay with you until we arrest Lehrer."

Samantha glanced at the slight, dark-haired woman wearing a gun and knee-high boots sporting the Ranger insignia. "Why is this a case for the Texas Rangers?"

"If I assign someone from the department, you'll have to make a report. I'm trying to spare you that."

"Spare me? Or yourself?"

"I can take you to the hospital right now and have you examined in the presence of an officer. Is that what you want?"

She shook her head.

"So it's acceptable to you that Ranger Drake stays here?"

She nodded, chilled by his tone.

He turned to the Ranger. "You know how to reach me."

Both women watched him leave without a backward glance.

Prairie reset the deadbolt and fastened the chain, then looked around. The apartment was exceptionally clean and tastefully decorated, a large painting of mostly blue sky dominating one wall, the furniture territorial New Mexican, the stereo and television top quality. Through the door she could see just a corner of a bed covered with what appeared to be dark blue silk. Uncomfortably, she looked at Samantha, who was even prettier than she had imagined.

Samantha walked into the kitchen and put the teakettle on. "Won't you sit down? You make me nervous standing there."

"Why's that?"

"I suppose it's your gun."

Prairie nodded and sat on the edge of the sofa.

Placing a flowered teapot on the counter, Samantha asked, "How did you get involved in this case?"

"I was with Devon in Presidio."

"He told me things hadn't gone well there, but he didn't go into any specifics."

"The sheriff arrested him 'cause his authorization wasn't strictly legal. I had to get an Order of Extradition from the gov'nor to spring him from jail."

"Devon was in jail?"

"Only a few hours. But on our way outta the county, he had a run-in with a local citizen and his lieutenant had to send an internal affairs lawyer to make the extradition stick."

Samantha smiled sadly. "After all that, he comes home to this."

"It's thrown him for a loop."

Samantha sat down at the kitchen table, as far from Prairie as she could get and still be in the same room. "How much do you know about us?"

"I know you're living together."

"We were. I don't think we are anymore."

"Most men have trouble dealing with situations like this. I think it's even harder on cops 'cause they feel they're s'posed to keep their loved ones safe."

"Devon doesn't believe I was raped."

"I know," Prairie said gently.

Samantha raised her chin higher. "Apparently he's told you all about it."

Prairie shook her head. "I had to pry out what little I got. Right now he's mad, mostly at himself for letting it happen, but once he catches Lehrer, he'll calm down and see things different."

The kettle whistled. Samantha stood up and took it off the fire. "Do you want some tea?"

"Yeah, thanks," Prairie said, though she didn't.

Devon shared the elevator at headquarters with two uniformed patrolmen. One of them said, "My house is a mess 'cause my maid was raped last week and didn't come."

"She must not have enjoyed it then," the other quipped.

Devon winced as the door opened and he left them behind.

At his desk, he opened the morgue admittance report on Lisa Escobar. Her only personal effects were a necklace and pink dress. The absence of underwear suggested rape, a supposition supported by the preliminary autopsy report noting contusions on her vulva and inner thighs. Given that she had spent her last few days with Sergio Tierrasantas, the bruises could be no more than souvenirs of rough sex. Vital semen had been taken from her vagina, however, and the normal life span of sperm was forty-eight hours. If the DNA matched Sergio's, nothing was proved; if it matched Jay's, it was evidence he'd had sex with Lisa within a time span contradicting his statement that he hadn't seen her since she left L.A.

Devon was hoping he could make a case without involving Samantha. Lehrer had no doubt left evidence in her apartment, but to use it would require her testimony. Remembering how the corkscrew had been sticky, probably with Lehrer's sweat as well as Sam's blood, Devon had to admit Prairie was right. If he hadn't initially shut his eyes to what he didn't want to know, he would have seen from the start that the corkscrew was a weapon left by an assailant.

Berating himself for having destroyed evidence, he emptied the envelope containing Lisa's personal effects. The labels had been cut off the dress, making it impossible to trace. Even if he managed to find the discount store selling that particular item, there wouldn't be any record of who had purchased it. The necklace was different.

Among the documentation was the receipt proving Tierrasantas had paid for the necklace with his American Express card the day prior to Lisa's death. With tax, it had cost over three thousand dollars, but a thousand had been paid almost a year ago. Next to the deduction were the words: ON ORDER.

Devon called the Bonneyana Boutique in Mesilla and asked to speak with the manager. She told him Lisa had custom-ordered the necklace with specific instructions of what she wanted the artist to depict.

"Those pieces are called storytellers," she said, "because each piece does exactly that. Nah Ro includes a few motifs in all his pieces: a hogan, a corral, and an outhouse." She giggled. "But the rest of the figures are created according to the customer's specifications."

Devon thanked her and hung up, then spread the necklace flat, trying to decipher the tale told with gold figures above a silver background. At the far left were the outhouse, corral, and hogan. In front of the hogan stick-figures of two boys were running in play. Then they were young men, one astride a horse looking down at the other, who had his arm around a woman's waist. In the next scene, the couple had a girl child between them as they looked up at the brother on his horse. Then the girl was on the horse behind her uncle. Then she stood alone holding a baby. In the next scene, the uncle was riding away with the baby under his arm. The last scene showed the girl walking toward an airplane.

The story of incest was obvious to Devon, the simplicity of the art poignant in its polished depiction of a tragedy as old as time. He slid the dress and necklace inside the envelope, carried it down to the evidence room and checked it back in, then rode the elevator down to the garage.

After driving south on Piedras, he turned east on Alameda toward the morgue.

Lieutenant Dreyfus had taken Escobar into an employee lounge in the basement of Thomason Hospital. The two men were studies in opposites: Dreyfus stocky with a florid face; Escobar tall and willowy, his slick black hair accenting the pallor of his complexion. Devon had no way of knowing if Escobar was pale because he avoided sunlight or because of the ghoulish chore that had brought him north of the border. But as Dreyfus introduced them, Devon knew he didn't like Estefen Escobar, and from the wariness in Escobar's eyes, the aversion was mutual.

"We need a relative to identify the body," Devon began.

"Your lieutenant has told me," Escobar replied. "Shall we do it then?"

"After I ask you a few questions. When was the last time you saw your niece?"

"Not for several months."

"That's a lie."

Escobar's black eyes simmered with anger.

"You picked her up in California last week."

"Perhaps you are mistaken."

"Jay Lehrer told me she left with her uncle. Wasn't that you, or was it another?"

"I am the only uncle Lisa has."

"Had. She was murdered by one of your successors."

Escobar looked at Dreyfus. "Is this man in charge of the investigation?"

Dreyfus nodded.

"In México," Escobar told Devon, "our police officers are more polite."

"Maybe because you butter their bread."

123

"Isn't your bread buttered, Detective, by the people you serve?"

"I don't serve criminals."

Escobar's eyes glittered like a fighting cock's. "Is your point to suggest I had something to do with Lisa's death?"

"Indirectly."

"What is he trying to say?" Escobar demanded of Dreyfus. "I don't understand this man's intent."

"I rarely understand it myself," Dreyfus drawled. "But Detective Gray has the best conviction rate in Homicide, so I give him free rein."

Escobar glared at Devon.

"Did you pick her up in L.A. last week?" he repeated.

"Since whether I did or not has nothing to do with her death, I don't feel it's any of your business."

"Murder makes everything connected to it my business."

Escobar capitulated with a shallow sigh. "I was attending a conference in L.A. when Lisa called my hotel and asked that I come get her."

"Why?"

"She wished to go home, and thought to catch a ride on my plane."

"Why did she want to go home?"

"Why does anyone?"

"We're not discussing philosophy. I want to know what she said."

The glitter in Escobar's eyes hardened. "She said she'd grown weary of Los Angeles."

"Nothing about the man she was living with?"

"Only that she no longer cared to be with him."

"So you gave her a ride to Juárez?"

"Yes."

"From there she called Tierrasantas and arranged to meet him here?"

"Probably. It seems your first impulse was to accuse him of this crime. Since that didn't work, are you now accusing me?"

"Did you want her dead?"

"On the contrary. I was happy to have her in my home."

"I bet you were."

"Why am I picking up a snide insinuation from your remarks?"

"Who told you of Lisa's death?"

"The *comandante* came to my home just this morning."

"Sergio told me you knew yesterday."

"Yes, all right. Jay Lehrer called and told me."

"What'd he say?"

"That she had been murdered and her body was in the county morgue. He seemed to be gloating."

"Had you ever spoken to him before?"

"I met him once in Los Angeles."

"Only once?"

"Yes. I didn't like the man."

"Why not?"

"He's a lot like you: impudent without cause."

"I have cause, it's just that I can't arrest you for a crime committed in Mexico."

"What crime are you implying I committed?"

"In this country it's called molesting a minor."

Escobar lifted his lip in a silent snarl.

"Do you deny Lisa had your child?"

"No, but what you're suggesting was rape in reality was the seduction of a girl marvelously developed for her age, and what happened between us was consensual."

"What happened to her child wasn't. You took the boy

away from her, didn't you?"

"Though splendidly equipped to be a mistress, she wasn't ready for motherhood."

"You should've thought of that before making her a mother."

"I fail to see the relevance of this discussion to your duties, Detective."

"Let's go look at her. Maybe it'll come clear to you."

Again Escobar glanced at Dreyfus, but the lieutenant only moved to open the door.

Devon followed them into the morgue. The room was dark until he switched on the overhead light, then the chilled space was harshly bright. Dreyfus walked across to open the door of the locker and pull out the drawer. Devon crowded Escobar from behind, herding him into position as Dreyfus unzipped the body bag to reveal Lisa's still pretty face.

Chapter Nine

"Is that your niece?" Devon asked.

Escobar nodded.

"What's her name?"

"Lisa Escobar."

"Your brother's daughter?"

"Yes."

"Who brought her to this?"

Escobar met his eyes. "I don't know."

"You did," Devon said.

"If you're accusing me of murder, I demand the presence of my attorney."

"Did you know she was knifed? The blade was thrust in just under her left breast at an upward angle to pierce her heart. How does that make you feel?"

Escobar shrugged. "It's unfortunate, but not my doing."

"You're wrong. She graduated from your school to a long line of men who hurt her. Because you taught her that's what men do, she kept mistaking cruelty for love until she found one who killed her. You may not have wielded the knife, but you're as guilty as whoever did."

"That's an interesting theory, Detective, but I doubt it would carry credence in any court."

"It carries credence in one. You'll find that out in hell."

Escobar laughed.

Devon made the mistake of looking at the face of a woman

who had suffered all her life for the pleasure of men. The brittle sound of her uncle's laughter snapped his control and sent the full force of his fist into the snidely amused mouth.

Escobar staggered backward, no longer even smiling as he sat down hard on the linoleum floor.

Devon started after Escobar, but Dreyfus grabbed hold of his arm and shouted, "Stop it, Devon!"

He shook Dreyfus off and took a step away. "Crawl back in your hole," he told the man on the floor, "and keep your filthy fun in the dark it deserves." His hand still clenched in a fist, he walked out.

Escobar shouted after him, "That was an unprovoked assault! You can be sure I'll press charges!"

He kept yelling threats that echoed down the hall until the elevator door shut Devon in a solitude loud only with his own rage.

He knew he had to catch hold of his anger or he wouldn't have a chance of holding it back when he found Lehrer. With the shooting in Presidio now compounded by his assault on Escobar, Devon was skirting the precipice of being suspended. If that happened, he would lose his legal sanction to interfere with Jay, and whatever came down when they met, Devon would be acting out of personal vengeance and crossing a line he had spent his life striving to avoid: failure to separate the emotional need of the moment from what was right.

By the time he slid behind the wheel of his confiscated Lexus, he was a cop again, not an angry man out of control. He was driving west on Alameda toward Sunset Heights, intending to check in on Samantha and Prairie, when he received a call on his radio that the car rented by Jay Lehrer had been found in a parking lot near the Santa Fe Bridge.

Sergeant Brent was standing beside the white Ford Fiesta

parked near the red brick building with *ROPA USADA* painted on its walls. Devon motioned him over and asked him to get in, then backed the Lexus into a space with a clear view of the Ford and Brent's empty squad car nearby.

"It's locked, I suppose," Devon said.

Brent nodded. "Attendant said it came in at ten o'clock this morning and the guy paid for twenty-four hours."

"Did he happen to notice which way he left?"

"Said he didn't pay any attention, but most of his customers park here and walk over to Juárez."

"Yeah, well, Jay Lehrer isn't typical."

"You want it towed?"

Devon shook his head. "I want a stakeout posted in case he comes back." He smiled at his friend. "You can assign a rookie if you want, but don't leave 'til he gets here."

"All right."

"If Lehrer shows, have the rookie tail him while calling for backup. Tell him not to try'n make an arrest by himself."

"Okay, but it's apt to be a she. Lowest man on the totem pole's Sharon Quell."

Devon looked away, thinking of Sharon, or maybe even Prairie, at the mercy of the likes of Jay Lehrer. "What do you think of women in law enforcement, Darryl?"

"Sign of the times."

"Not that you asked, but I don't like it."

Brent chuckled. "I was the first black on the force. A lot of veterans didn't like it when I was hired either."

"A man's capacity for the job has to do with his character and physical prowess, not his race."

"Women say their capacity has to do with those things rather than their gender."

"They're wrong though. Since the beginning of history, men have used sex to subdue women. I don't know why they want to take the risk, but I'll bet a month's pay the first female officer who's gang-raped turns in her badge on her way to the hospital."

"Men can be raped."

"You ever hear of it happening to a cop?"

"Saw a TV show about it once."

"Yeah, well, TV's about as relevant as Disneyland. You want to know why nobody'll ever rape a cop?"

"A male cop, you mean?" Brent teased.

"It won't happen 'cause the cop'd go back and blow the fucker's head off."

Slowly, Brent said, "By taking revenge, the male cop would lose his badge as fast as the female, so I can't see much difference, myself."

Devon took a deep breath, willing his heart to stop beating like a fast freight. "I came close to doing that this morning."

Brent's smile vanished. "Losing your badge?"

Devon nodded. "I floored a man 'cause I don't like him."

Brent made a clucking sound. "Guess we've all crossed that line one time or another."

"I hadn't." Feeling he owed his friend an explanation, he forced himself to say, "The man we're looking for raped Samantha. At least that's the way she tells it."

After a moment, Brent said, "Don't let him do it to you."

Devon met his eyes.

"If you blow him away, you'll kill yourself along with him."

Devon nodded. "Appreciate it."

Brent opened the door to get out, looking back over his shoulder. "If you need someplace to sleep, there's a spare room in my condo. I'll leave word with the super to let you in."

Devon nodded.

Brent started toward his squad car, then came back to stand by Devon's window. "Have you seen L.A.'s answer to the inquiry we sent?"

Devon shook his head.

"I haven't either, but it should be on your desk by now." He walked away again.

"Thanks," Devon called after him.

Brent waved without looking back.

Devon sat at his desk to read the fax from L.A. He had requested it as a routine step in his initial investigation, but if he'd read it before going to Chinati, he wouldn't have gone.

The L.A.P.D. had questioned Jay Lehrer about the rape-murder of one of his neighbors, then released him because his live-in girlfriend gave him an alibi. Her name was Lisa Escobar. Looking at the date, Devon calculated it must have been the same day Lisa asked her uncle for a ride home.

Devon called the detective handling the case in L.A. His name was Paul Stone. After Devon told him Lehrer was in El Paso, Stone asked eagerly, "Have you picked him up?"

"Not yet. But I've got an APB out on him in connection with the murder of Lisa Escobar."

"Shit. I knew the fucker was guilty, but we didn't have enough to hold him."

"What did you have?"

"The victim filed a sexual harassment suit and got him fired, so we figured that was a good enough motive. After he skipped town, we got a search warrant for his apartment and found the victim's shoes under his pillow. One of them had her blood on it."

Devon saw Dreyfus enter the far end of the room and glare at him. "Lisa's shoes were missing."

"Was she wearing a cheap pink dress?" Stone asked.

"Yeah." He watched Dreyfus stride toward him.

"So was ours. We'll file extradition if you nab him."

Devon handed the fax to Dreyfus. "If we take him alive."

Stone laughed. "Dead or alive's all the same in Texas? Sounds like a sane way to run a P.D. Let me know when the fucker's dead."

"I'll do that." He hung up and told Dreyfus, "After Lehrer left L.A., they got a search warrant and found the victim's shoes under his pillow."

Dreyfus looked up from the report. "I think I'll let the media know this guy's in town. Have you seen him?"

Devon nodded.

"Get together with the artist and see if you can come up with a sketch."

"Think I can get a photo."

"From L.A.?"

Devon shook his head.

Dreyfus frowned. "You want to clue me in?"

Devon looked around the empty room, then met his lieutenant's eyes. "Lehrer's Samantha's ex-husband. When I was in Chinati, he hurt her."

Dreyfus stared at him.

"Ranger Drake's staying with her in case Lehrer comes back."

Color rose up the lieutenant's already florid neck. "I oughta yank you off this case."

"Who you gonna put on it?"

"Maybe nobody'd be better'n a cop with blood in his eyes."

"You know me better'n that."

"I'm warning you, Devon, if you step out of line to the least degree I may not be able to save your badge. You've already got the shooting in Chinati and the assault on

Escobar. Another incident'll mark you as a rogue cop out of control."

"I'm in control."

"Stay that way."

He turned to leave, then wheeled back. "And keep me informed! How do you think I'd look if it got out my department was using the services of a Texas Ranger and I didn't even know it?"

"Figured it was unofficial."

"Protocol's established for good reason. Use it!"

Devon watched him leave, then picked up the phone and called Samantha.

When she answered, her voice was like a melody of good things lost. Knowing he should apologize, he asked instead, "How you doing?"

"I'm all right. Are you coming soon?"

"On my way. Is there anything you need?"

"A coffeepot."

"Anything else?"

"You. Is there any chance of that?" The silence hummed so long, she sighed and said, "It'll be good to see you, Devon, for however long."

"I can only stay a few minutes."

He took Piedras to I-10 North, caught the Mesa exit and pulled into the parking lot of Wal-Mart. It was Saturday afternoon and the store was crowded. Standing in line at a register, he saw the pink dress first, then the long ponytail hanging down Jay Lehrer's back.

Devon stashed the boxed coffeepot in a bin of rubber balls and reached for his gun as Lehrer paid the cashier. Jay was walking toward the door when Devon approached from behind. A woman saw his gun and gasped. Lehrer looked over his shoulder and did the unexpected. Rather than pushing through the crowd in front of him, he ran deeper into the store. Devon pivoted back through the check-out counters in pursuit.

"Freeze," he yelled, firing into the ceiling.

Customers dived with frantic screams and shouts of dismay as Devon sprinted through the sporting goods to see Lehrer disappear behind a display of tennis rackets on sale. Colliding with a teenager at the end of the aisle, Devon took hold of the boy's shoulders and set him aside, watching Lehrer run past a rack of frilly baby clothes, heading for the corner.

Devon ran past a woman holding a toddler on the floor. Sliding on the waxed linoleum, he saw Lehrer beyond a counter stacked with bolts of material. Devon raised his gun in both hands, took a stance, and fired at Lehrer pushing against an emergency exit.

The alarm bell rang, permeating the store with its deafening siren as Lehrer disappeared in a blinding flash of sunlight. Devon was out the door a minute later, but Lehrer was gone.

Devon looked the length of the store in both directions. The alley was empty. He ran to the edge of the arroyo behind the store, scanning the area for any telltale dust kicked up. Seeing none, he jumped the five-foot cliff into the arroyo, then saw where Lehrer's feet had left divots, marking an easy trail to follow through the sand. Devon shadowed the tracks to where Lehrer had left a trough in the wake of his scrambling ascent. When Devon crested the bank of the arroyo, he was alone behind K-Bob's.

For a few steps, Lehrer's feet had dropped a trail of sand, enough to point Devon in the right direction. But when he turned the corner of the restaurant, no one was there. He ran to the lot in front and saw no one among the cars. Surveying the distance, he saw a blue Sun Metro bus pulling away from the curb.

Devon ran for his Lexus, hearing sirens all around. Squad cars were braking to a stop in front of Wal-Mart as he floored his accelerator and shimmied out of the lot. Slapping his light on his roof to run hot, he nosed into the traffic on Mesa. The civilians got out of his way as he sped after the bus.

When it edged close to the curb to give him room to pass, he swerved in front of it and slammed on his brakes. The bus driver did the same, stopping only inches from impact. The driver had the door open by the time Devon reached it. He ran up the steps, his gun in his hand, and scanned the rows of startled faces. Jay Lehrer's wasn't among them. Devon looked at the driver. "Did you pick up anyone in front of K-Bob's?"

The driver shook his head. "Let a lady out."

"Did you see a man running in the vicinity?"

"Yeah, I did. He dodged across the traffic in the middle of the block."

"Thanks," Devon said, descending the steps.

He checked for traffic, his siren still wailing, then gunned his engine to jump the center divider. Heading back toward Wal-Mart, he reached for his radio. "All units: APB suspect seen crossing Mesa in front of K-Bob's heading north. Six feet, two hundred pounds, blue shirt, brown ponytail. Net the area now."

He turned off Mesa into Coronado Terrace, cruised Flemish Circle, Le Conte, and Dianjou before backtracking to Sands Drive and Sunny Road. Then he caught the freeway and drove as far as the first crossover without seeing Lehrer. Returning to Mesa, he shut off his siren and coasted to a stop amid the squad cars in front of Wal-Mart.

A skinny, blond rookie stood staring into the store. Devon

beeped his horn, making the kid jump before casually saun-
tering over.

"Got a report of a shooting inside, Detective," Patrolman
Winnett said with self-importance. "Fortunately no one was
hurt."

"I was the shooter. Did you hear my APB for a net?"

Winnett shook his head.

Devon looked at the half-dozen squad cars in front of him.
"How many units we got in this section?"

"Just what you see right here."

"They're all inside I suppose, using their pencils instead of
their brains."

"Questioning witnesses, yes, sir."

"Shit!" Devon pounded his steering wheel. "Go in there
and tell 'em the suspect got away 'cause nobody was listening
to their goddamn radio!"

Knowing he had been left outside to do exactly that, a cha-
grined Winnett jogged into the store.

Devon's radio crackled as a prelude to Dreyfus yelling,
"Devon! Can you hear me?"

He picked up the receiver and muttered, "Yeah."

"There's been a shooting at the westside Wal-Mart.
Where are you?"

"In the parking lot. It was me shooting at Lehrer."

A pause filled with static, then Dreyfus: "You opened fire
in a crowded store?"

"I aimed at the ceiling. No one was hurt."

"Jesus Christ, Devon! Did you get your net?"

"No! They're all inside investigating the shooting."

"What do you expect when someone opens fire in a
Wal-Mart on a Saturday afternoon?"

"I expect 'em to leave a man listening to their radios."

"Jesus Christ."

"You got anything more helpful to offer?"

"That attitude's gonna sink your boat, Devon. You're already bailing water."

"Take my badge and you'll be giving free rein to the scum."

"A police department's more'n one man!"

"The rest of your department's inside questioning witnesses. I'm the only one on the street."

"Keep this up and your leave's apt to be permanent."

Devon kept quiet.

"You hear me, Devon?"

"Yeah."

"I want you in my office now."

"I'll be there in an hour."

He switched off his radio so he couldn't hear the lieutenant's reply, took the emergency light off his roof and tossed it into the back as he drove slowly out of the parking lot, still scanning the terrain for anything moving. Halfway down Mesa, he stopped at K-Mart for another coffeepot.

Samantha opened her door, giving him a hopeful smile that reminded him of better times. But all she said was, "It'll be great to have coffee again."

He handed her the boxed pot, then looked at Prairie sitting in the corner. Her smile was a gently teasing acknowledgment that they were caught in a tense situation.

"We found Jay's car," he told them, "so he's on foot unless he got another one."

"Maybe he left town," Samantha said.

"I saw him in Wal-Mart half an hour ago."

Both women stared until he shrugged and said, "He got away."

Prairie winced with sympathy for what he wasn't saying, the details of his pursuit, the anger and frustration of failure.

"I ran a check through L.A.," he told Samantha. "He's wanted there for a murder with a similar M.O.: he dresses his victim in pink before he rapes and kills her."

Still hugging the boxed coffeepot, Samantha slowly sank onto a stool at the breakfast bar. "I can't believe it," she whispered.

"That he's capable of murder, or rape?"

Prairie stood up. "Think I'll catch a breath of air." She walked out and quietly closed the door.

Devon watched her go, then looked back at Samantha. "I don't suppose you still have the pillow?"

"Which pillow?"

"The yellow one off the sofa."

"I threw it out."

"Why?"

"It was dirty."

"With what?"

"Don't, Devon," she moaned.

"I'm not trying to torment you, Sam. I just thought we might be able to match the DNA taken out of Lisa Escobar."

She shivered. "I threw it away."

"In the Dumpster?"

She nodded. "But don't bother to look. Yesterday was trash day."

They stared at each other, then he shrugged. "We couldn't have used it without involving you. So far I've been able to avoid doing that officially."

"Not unofficially?"

"Dreyfus knows."

"What did you tell him?"

"Only that Jay's your ex-husband, and while I was gone he hurt you."

"You didn't say I was raped?"

138

"He knew what I meant."

"But you couldn't bring yourself to say it, could you, Devon? Can you now? Admit I was raped?"

"All I know is I don't feel in good company being one of your lovers."

She blinked back tears. "And what you feel is much more important than what I feel, isn't it."

He sighed. "We can talk about this another time. What I need from you now is a photo."

"Of Jay?"

"No, the King of Kubla Khan. Who the hell else are we talking about?"

"You don't have to be so sarcastic!"

"Spoken by the queen of sarcasm."

She laughed, and he smiled, both of them recognizing the tenuous thread of a bridge blowing between them.

"I'll have to dig it out," she said. "It's buried in the remnants of my deep past."

"Need help?"

She studied him as if not believing the sincerity of his offer, then shook her head and walked into the bedroom.

He went outside and joined Prairie on the wooden bench. "Sam's getting me a photo of Lehrer," he said, speaking softly to avoid being heard by eavesdropping neighbors. "Dreyfus is gonna give it to the media, so more'n likely it'll be on TV tonight."

"That's smart," Prairie said. "Lehrer'd be a fool to come back here."

"That's not what you told me this morning."

"I know, but look what Carl Lowdy did. If that wasn't acting the fool, I don't know what is."

Devon kept quiet.

"Course I was a bigger fool, losing control of my gun. The

worst of it is, you're being called in front of a board of inquiry when it should be me for letting it happen."

"You'll get there."

"Yeah. My boss is flying in from Austin and all the facts'll come out. You think I'll lose my badge?"

He shrugged. "Dreyfus is threatening to take mine."

"For shooting Carl?"

He shook his head. "I punched out Lisa's uncle this morning 'cause I didn't like him."

She smiled with understanding. "What'll you do if Dreyfus does take it?"

"I don't know, Prairie. I'm beginning to wonder what wearing one's worth."

"It lets us make a difference in the world."

"Like stopping Lehrer? Or putting a crimp in the stride of Tierrasantas?"

"Maybe a little crimp."

He laughed and pulled her close for comfort, soaking in her warmth. When she looked up, tempting him to kiss her, he took his arm back and moved a scant distance away.

"This reminds me of your front porch," he said, trying to alleviate having put distance between them, "except here the railing's too far for me to put my feet up."

"I own that place free and clear," she said softly. "It'd make a good hideout for two lawmen on the run."

He chuckled. "Wouldn't Rufus hate it if I took up residence in his county?"

"That might make it worth doing right there."

They were laughing when Samantha opened the door.

"I found what you wanted," she said, biting off her words, "if you still remember asking."

Devon stood up. The photo she gave him was a wedding portrait of her and Jay smiling as they held hands in the sunshine of a California afternoon. Samantha had a wreath of flowers in her hair, and Jay wore a red rose in the lapel of his white jacket. Devon asked, "Do you care what happens to it?"

She shook her head.

He folded the photo down the middle and tore it along the crease. Giving back the half of her as a bride, he said, "So much for wedded bliss."

She tossed her head in anger and disappeared inside.

"You're pretty hard on her," Prairie murmured.

"That bother you?"

"No," she said. "I didn't marry Carl, and you've already made sure he ain't coming back."

Chapter Ten

At six o'clock that night, Prairie and Samantha were eating a veggie feast pizza while watching a western movie.

Prairie picked a black olive off her plate and said, "I've seen this already. Over all, it's pretty authentic."

"Everybody seems so dirty," Samantha murmured.

"That adds to the realism. But Janet Leigh blows it. Any woman who had short hair and wore pants on the frontier would've been tarred and feathered. I'm a student of westerns, and the heroines always conform to the fashions of when the movie was made rather than the time being depicted."

"How interesting," Samantha said dryly.

Prairie nodded. "I long ago gave up on ever seeing any true-to-life women in westerns. They're usually either saucy whores or wives reeking with virtue. That's 'cause they're written to play off the hero's violence, egging him on or reining him back depending on the need of the script."

Samantha reached for a second slice of pizza. "That doesn't sound so unrealistic."

"It is though." Prairie leaned back to sit cross-legged on the sofa. "One of my great-grandmothers gave birth while fighting Comanches. She suffered for near twenty-four hours, losing her husband to a heathen's arrow and killing two of the five braves later found in her yard. In the end, she delivered herself of a stillborn son, left him in the arms of her

142

dead husband, and walked fifteen miles to the closest neighbor. Two years later she had herself a new husband and a new baby, and I'd bet my boots she never once told her menfolk to leave home without a gun."

Samantha looked at Prairie's boots on the sofa.

Prairie put her feet down. "This is one of the finest westerns ever made. The best part is how the landscape reflects the hero's inner struggles. See, this part here: it's his darkest hour and they're in a cave. The climax comes in a river gone wild with spring thaw. That's what you call symbolism."

"Is it."

"Yeah, but I don't agree with Janet Leigh's thinking. After all the trouble they've gone through trying to get the killer to town so Jimmie Stewart can collect the bounty and buy back his ranch, she convinces him that buying it with blood money would be like walking on a grave. Shoot! I'd dance on a grave with glee if it meant keeping my ranch. It's the same one my grandmother fought the Comanches for, and land bought with blood is the best there is."

Samantha shivered. "How many acres do you own?"

"Hundred and eighty. Not enough to run more'n a coupla cows with the grama grass as sparse as it is, so it's not like I could make any kinda living off it. And being as I'm pushing thirty with no prospect of marriage, don't guess I'll have any heirs. That's partly why I joined the Rangers."

"To catch a husband?" Samantha asked, tongue-in-cheek.

Prairie shook her head. "Without heirs, my land'll be swallowed up by the Tierrasantas ranch, and the idea of that happening riles me. Soon as I got my badge, I wrote a will bequeathing my land to the Texas Rangers in perpetuity. They can use it for training or a retreat, but can't ever sell or give it away. My solution's a compromise, I know that, but least I got the satisfaction of knowing Sergio Tierrasantas won't ever put his boots on the railing of my porch."

"Do you know him well?"

"As well as I care to."

"What's he like?"

"He's a slimy sonofabitch who once told me he'd enjoy skinning a woman while he raped her."

Samantha looked away. "Do you mind if I change the channel?"

"Nah. I've seen this movie a dozen times and, like I said, I disagree with the ending."

Prairie carried her Diet Coke into the kitchen to look for something better. But the only drinks in the refrigerator were more Diet Coke, half a six-pack of Budweiser, an open bottle of white wine, and a quart of milk.

She noticed there wasn't a whole lot of food in there either, so she didn't think Samantha was much of a cook. The freezer, however, was stocked with Healthy Choice dinners. Prairie stared at the stack of cardboard, wondering if that's what Samantha served Devon for supper. Then she guessed maybe they ate out a lot, like cityfolk were prone to do. She wondered if he picked up the tab and opened doors for Samantha the way he had for her in Chinati, or if maybe their financial arrangement meant they always went dutch.

She closed the freezer and tapped the toe of her boot with impatience, thinking a stakeout must be the most boring job in creation. Abruptly she asked, "Mind if I use your bathroom?"

Samantha shook her head without looking up. She had changed the channel to MTV, a form of entertainment Prairie considered almost as depraved as Sergio's movies.

Crossing the bedroom, her gaze fell involuntarily on the bed, and she stopped a moment, unable to keep herself from wondering if Samantha was pleased with Devon's loving or if she had let her ex-husband back into her life because she was hungry for something she wasn't getting.

The nightstands held identical brass lamps but different telephones. One was blue like the bedspread, the other black with a built-in answering machine. Prairie figured it must be Devon's. The room otherwise was all Samantha. Over the bureau was a lithograph of a city in Europe, probably Venice because it had a canal in the foreground. Prairie could just see Devon in Venice, his cowboy boots on the cobblestones as out of place as Geronimo in the White House.

She hadn't really needed to use the bathroom, only to change the sights in front of her eyes. Now she looked in the mirror, thinking Devon used it to shave in the mornings, though there wasn't anything remotely masculine in view. The towels were pink, the shower curtain a motif of pink tulips with long wavering stems. On the vanity was a basket holding palettes of makeup. She wondered why Samantha hadn't made more of an effort to make Devon feel at home. Even the book on the back of the commode was *Modern British Poetry*.

Prairie had old issues of *Field and Stream* stacked on her commode, though before Devon's shower no man had been in her bathroom since she moved back from Austin. She kept up her grandfather's subscription not because she read *Field and Stream* but because she had seen it there all through her childhood. She couldn't understand why Samantha didn't want something of Devon's to prove he was more than a guest who slept over most nights.

Using Samantha's brush to straighten the pixie cut of her black hair, Prairie met her blue eyes in the mirror and wondered what Devon saw when he looked at her. Then she remembered how he had pulled her close on the bench outside Samantha's front door. He had taken his arm back right quick, but in the manner of a man putting out a spark whose flame was unwise in the peculiar situation they were caught in. Left alone, Prairie suspected she could kindle a fire he wouldn't want to put out. Before that happened, though, they had to get shut of Samantha's ex-husband, to say nothing of Samantha. Prairie turned off the light and walked back to the living room.

Samantha had put away what was left of the pizza and was making coffee in the new pot Devon had bought her. She looked up and asked, "Want some?"

"No, thanks. Coffee jitters my nerves."

"Would you like more tea?"

"About all I drink is Dr Pepper."

"I'm sorry. I should have asked when I ordered the pizza. They could've brought you some."

"No sweat," Prairie said.

"Devon has beer in the refrigerator."

"That's about all he's got in this house, ain't it."

Samantha met her eyes. "His clothes are in the closet. Would you like to look at them?"

Prairie shook her head. "How'd you two meet?"

Samantha smiled as she finished putting together the coffee and turned on the pot. "We had a flasher in the library one night. When we called the police, Devon was in the neighborhood so he answered the call."

"You're a librarian?" Prairie asked with surprise.

Samantha nodded.

"Doesn't seem a librarian and a cop would have much in common."

"Not as much as a cop and a Texas Ranger, I'm sure. But I think Devon felt drawn to me because I'm different from the people he works with. As dedicated as he is, he needs a change when he comes home."

"I can understand that," Prairie mumbled, wondering what it said of her chances while she and Devon were both wearing badges. She gave Samantha a smile of commiseration. "Too bad your ex-husband had to ruin everything."

Samantha sighed deeply. "I wish I'd told him to go away as soon as he showed up."

"Doesn't mean he would've done it. I kicked Carl Lowdy out lots of times, but he always came back."

"Who's Carl Lowdy?"

"We dated in high school, but when I came home from college I'd raised my standards. He refused to accept that and kept acting like he owned me."

"What did you do?"

"Not much. It was Devon who finally solved the problem."

"How?"

"We went to question Sergio at his ranch, and Carl showed up. I went out to talk to him, just trying to be kind, you know?" She snorted in self-denigration. "He got hold of my gun and kidnapped me." She nodded at Samantha's surprise. "Devon came after us. When Carl opened fire with a shotgun, Devon killed him."

"Yesterday? In Chinati?"

Prairie nodded. "I was locked in a closet but I could hear the guns going off. I felt like the biggest fool in creation for getting Devon into that. I still do. Now he's facing a court of inquiry for my mistake."

Samantha smiled sadly. "Seems like we have something in common after all, Prairie."

The balcony of Darryl Brent's condo afforded a view from the rugged Juárez Mountains south of downtown to the moonlit Rio Grande meandering north of Mount Cristo Rey.

All the other balconies were empty, their windows closed against the cool breeze, stiff so high in the air. It fluttered the drapes on either side of the open glass door behind Devon, lifting and letting them fall in a restless rhythm. He disliked being idle, but with an APB on Lehrer and Prairie with Samantha, he didn't have a lot of options other than waiting.

Brent came out and stood a few feet away. "We can eat anytime. The pasta only takes five minutes."

"Okay," Devon said.

At the sound of a siren, they turned their heads and watched the blue lights of a squad car hustle up Schuster to disappear beneath the trees of Kern Place. A minute later, a fire truck left the station on Stanton, then an ambulance was heard coming down Mesa. It turned on Cincinnati and followed the squad car and fire truck into the canopied neighborhood.

"Some old geezer had a heart attack most likely," Brent said.

Devon nodded.

"Prob'ly the dude on McKelligon. We've been there three times lately. One of these days we won't have to go again."

After a while, Devon asked, "You ever think about that?"

"What?"

"Not having to answer calls."

"Sometimes."

"What do you think when you do?"

"When I go, I'm generally hoping the civilians get out of my way so I don't end up in the ambulance."

Devon chuckled.

"When I think about not going, I wonder what I'd do with my life if I wasn't a cop."

"What do you come up with?"

"Nothing. I'm younger'n you, though. I imagine a man's

feelings about the job change with time."

Devon looked at the city spread over the hills like a rumpled blanket of lights. He had grown up in El Paso and knew it well, the land and its people; but what in his youth had been a friendly border town was becoming a sprawling metropolis out of control. Like the train he could see but barely hear snaking against the far mesa, he felt nudged with an inclination to move on.

"How you figure on handling it if Lehrer shows tonight?" Brent asked. "Go in with your gun drawn?"

Devon pulled his thoughts back. "I'm going in unarmed."

"You're kidding, right?"

He shook his head. "If we have to shoot, the fact that I was living with Sam will muddy the issue if I'm the trigger."

"Yeah, okay, but are you sure you want to be there without a weapon?"

"I'm hoping to talk him out. If not, you and Prairie'll be there."

After a moment, Brent said, "This thing with Sam will blow over, you know, after the guy's in jail and your life settles into a routine again."

"Maybe," Devon said.

The coffeepot sighed with a hiss of steam just as the doorbell rang, making Samantha jerk.

Prairie nodded, encouraging her to look through the peephole.

When she did, she whispered, "It's Jay."

As Prairie hurried to the black phone in the bedroom to punch in the number Devon had given her, Samantha felt herself tremble, waiting by the door. When Jay rang the bell again, she hugged herself for comfort.

"Sam, it's me," he called. "I'm on my way home and brought you a present."

She looked through the peephole and saw he was holding a flat box wrapped in pink-flowered paper. Behind her, Prairie whispered, "All set." Sam watched her step behind the bedroom door, leaving it barely ajar, then reached up with shaking hands and unhooked the chain.

"That's right, Sam," Jay responded with pleasure.

She turned the deadbolt and backed away.

"Don't be like that," he cajoled, setting a small duffel bag down as he came through the door. He was wearing a black T-shirt tucked into jeans over running shoes, the lines too smooth and snug to conceal a weapon. "I know it's not much," he said, offering the box, "but I want to try'n make up for what happened."

She accepted his gift, thinking he seemed boyishly excited. "Would you like some coffee?"

"Why not?"

She slid the box on the table as she walked into the kitchen.

He took a stool at the breakfast bar. "Where's Devon?"

"I don't know." She filled the cup she had set out for herself, then pushed it toward him.

"Aren't you having some?"

"I don't want any."

"Who'd you make it for then?"

"I thought I wanted some, but now I don't." Replacing the pot, she glanced at the open front door.

He stood up. "It's stuffy in here, but I'll close it if you want."

"Don't!" She tried to soften her voice. "It is stuffy."

"Maybe you better sit down, Sam." He walked around the counter. "You look like you're about to faint."

She backed away the length of the kitchen.

He stopped in front of the refrigerator and smiled. "You still got a mark down your belly?"

She nodded.

"What'd Devon say when he saw it?"

"He didn't see it."

"You mean you didn't make love after being apart for two whole nights?"

She shook her head. "When he found out what happened, he left me."

Jay leaned against the refrigerator. "Looks like I messed things up for you, Sam. That wasn't my intention, but now that it's happened, why don't you come back to L.A. with me?"

She doubted he would go back after having killed someone there. But then, he was still here. Did that mean he hadn't killed Lisa? But he *had* lied about Devon arresting her killer in Chinati. Confused, she asked, "What did you mean about taking only one of my shoes?"

"What would I want with your shoes? It's not like we wear the same size." He laughed, opening the refrigerator. "I like milk in my coffee, Sam. Guess you forgot that."

He poured in a generous amount and put the carton back. "If you don't want to go to L.A., we could go to Baja." He opened a drawer for a spoon to stir his coffee. "You ever been to Mexico, Sam? Besides Juárez, I mean."

Staring at the steak knives in the drawer he had left open, she murmured, "Devon took me to Acapulco last year."

"We could go there. Maybe get the same room in the same hotel." He followed her gaze to the knives, then gave her a smile. "You could open your present where you and Devon made love. Tell me, Sam: what's it like to fuck a cop? Does he want you to respond, or does he prefer his women submissive?"

In the bedroom, watching through the barely open door, Prairie thought: Yeah, tell us, Sam. What does Devon like?

They all heard the cadence of his footsteps approaching, but though both women pricked their ears to listen more closely, Jay apparently expected whoever it was to walk on by.

Devon had expected to surprise Jay, hopefully engrossed in giving Sam the pink dress probably wrapped in pretty paper to entice her. Instead he crossed the threshold to see the two of them standing close in the kitchen. She was obviously distressed, but in that moment he wasn't sure if she felt frightened or guilty. She looked the same as when he had first seen them together, and the suspicion that she might want to be with Jay after all threw him off balance.

Suddenly she cried out as Jay caught hold of her hair and pulled her head back to press the edge of a steak knife against her throat. "What's happening here, pal?" he snarled. "A little set-up?"

Whatever her previous inclination, Devon knew she didn't want what was happening now. "Let her go."

"How's it gonna look down at the precinct if you shoot a man just 'cause he fucked your girlfriend?"

"Assault with a knife's more'n a straight-ahead fuck."

"Some women like it rough. Guess you know all about that."

"I know you killed Lisa."

"Can you prove it?"

"The semen taken out of her matched what you left on Sam's pillow. That proves you were with Lisa just prior to when she was murdered."

" 'Cause I fucked her doesn't mean I killed her."

"It means you lied. After she called, you caught the

red-eye and got here at two, rented a car, and drove to the Camino Real. How'd you know she was there?"

Jay's smile was smug. "It's the most expensive hotel in town. Lisa wouldn't stay anywhere else."

"Why did she let you in?"

He jerked his head at the box on the kitchen table. "I came bearing gifts."

Samantha whimpered when he moved, but Devon stayed focused on Jay. "As for motive, once she left L.A., you couldn't trust her to back up your alibi for killing your neighbor."

Jay's eyes narrowed. "The L.A.P.D. couldn't pin that on me any more'n you can."

"They found her bloody shoes under your pillow. That's pretty strong evidence. Tie it in with Lisa's bare feet and it shapes up to a pattern. Course it would help if we found the weapon. Do you still have it?"

Jay glanced at the duffel bag he had left by the door.

Devon made a clucking sound of sympathy. "Keeping evidence isn't smart, Jay. But what I can't figure is why you took her shoes."

He smiled. "I like to line 'em up alongside my bed every morning so I can tell myself that bitch isn't going anywhere ever again."

Devon met Sam's eyes, searching for recognition that Jay had just confessed to murder. But she was beyond reason, her pupils glazed with terror, her face pale above the trickle of blood down her neck.

In a tone of gentle entreaty, Devon said, "Why don't you put the knife down, Jay. You got away with the others 'cause you didn't have a witness. That's not true this time."

"If I put this knife down, you'll kill me to tell Sam she can't have fun when you're not around."

Devon lifted his empty hands. "I'm unarmed."

"You're lying!" Jay shouted. Yanking Sam's head farther back, he dragged the knife so the flow of blood spread.

"Are you gonna let him kill me?" she sobbed.

Devon met her eyes. "You let him in."

His tactic worked. Jay laughed and raised the blade away from Sam's throat.

"We understand each other, don't we, Devon? There're certain bitches who ask for it and others who deserve it. Men're better off without women like that."

"Maybe you're right," he said. "Go on and leave if you want. I won't stop you."

"I'm taking Sam," Jay said.

Devon shrugged.

Jay took a step toward the door, dragging her with him. She whimpered, her eyes incredulous on Devon. He glanced toward the bedroom and saw light glint off Prairie's badge. Calculating she had gained a better angle, he nodded, hoping her boast of being a sharpshooter hadn't been idle.

The bullet caught Jay like a grappling hook snagging his forehead. Samantha screamed as blood sprayed out behind them, then the knife clattered onto the floor and his body slumped with a thud. She skittered away to stand awkwardly staring at Devon.

Still holding her pistol, Prairie came out and knelt by the body to check for a pulse. It was a redundant gesture, but Devon admired her for making sure the man was down.

Samantha ran for the bathroom, then Brent sidled around the corner, his gun in both hands. Scanning the room, he took it all in: Prairie kneeling by the corpse, the sounds of Sam retching in the bathroom, Devon empty-handed on the edge of it all. He gave Brent a small smile, then walked out to sit on the bench in the dark.

Closing his eyes, he surrendered to fatigue as he listened to Brent on the phone. Sam came back, and he heard her hysteria dissipate beneath Prairie's soothing control. He heard his name a few times, Sam accusing, Prairie explaining that his apparent callousness had been tactical, then he stopped listening to hone his ears to the distant rumble of a freight leaving town. The rattle of boxcars whispered off the mesas urging him to move. He was gathering his impetus to do that when Sam came out and sat down beside him.

The blood was gone from her neck, a long Band-Aid now covering the cut, and apparently Prairie's reassurances had done the job because she said without rancor, "I've decided to check into a motel tonight and find another apartment tomorrow. I think I'll even hire movers to get my stuff out. I don't ever want to see this place again."

He nodded, hearing the wail of sirens coming closer. When she made no move to leave, he asked, "Want a ride?"

"Please," she said. "I feel too shaky to drive."

He pulled himself to his feet.

She stood, too. "I'll just be a minute."

He listened to the sirens grow louder. Brent came out and asked, "You want to talk to Dreyfus?"

"Tell him he can reach me at my brother's in the morning."

Brent passed Prairie in the door. Devon knew she needed both praise and expiation for having made the kill, but right then all he could do was ask, "Can you get to Connie's on your own?"

She nodded, and they almost smiled at each other, but just then Sam came out and Prairie turned her back to watch the clusters of curious neighbors on the patio below.

Devon took Sam's suitcase and held her arm as they descended the stairs. On the street, he opened the passenger door of his confiscated Lexus and watched her slide in, closed the door and walked around, tossed the suitcase on the backseat, then took the wheel. "Where to?" he asked, turning the ignition.

"The Sunset Inn?"

He turned right off Santa Fe and north on Oregon before cutting across Mesa to the motel. He went into the lobby and paid cash for a room, gave her the key and drove to the door. After killing his engine, he faced her in the dark.

Finally she said, "Our rift is irrevocable, isn't it, Devon?"

He smiled, admiring her choice of words.

She reached across and touched his cheek, then got out and opened the back for her suitcase.

He waited until she had gone inside and closed the door before he drove away.

Chapter Eleven

In the dark upstairs bedroom of his brother's house, Devon unbuckled his belt and pulled it free of the holster in the small of his back. He put his gun on the nightstand, laid the wallet holding his badge next to his gun, then stripped himself naked and slid between sheets fragrant with the scent of wildflowers. In the extremity of his exhaustion, he fell quickly and deeply asleep, only to be awakened in what felt like minutes but must have been hours by someone sitting down beside him.

Barely visible in the shadowed light, Prairie asked, "You want me to sleep on the couch, Devon?"

"No."

She smelled like her scent left on the sheets, only fresher, more vital. Her body was limber, amazingly graceful. For a long time he merely allowed her tongue to play on his chest like sunlight dappling stones through the cold current of a river. But like the sun, she was undauntable, and finally he rose, breaking the surface of his inertia to cover her. Cut loose from the shackles of restraint, he discovered that as deep as he could fall, she could lift him higher, until the blue field of her eyes was filled with flowers born blossoming in the light of love.

In the morning, he awoke to a knock on the door. Arranging the sheet to protect Prairie's modesty, he called softly, "Yeah?"

Connie opened the door, grinned at the sight of them together, then whispered, "Dreyfus is on the phone."

"I'll be right there," Devon said.

Gently disentangling himself, he quietly dressed and went downstairs. In the dining room, his family sat around the table watching him with concern, having gleaned the gist of what had happened from the news on TV. He gave them all a smile as he walked through to the living room. He picked up the phone and said, "Morning, Dick."

His lieutenant's voice was heavy with regret. "I gotta put you on leave, Devon, but you'll get full pay 'til this mess is cleared up. Go fishing or something. I'm postponing the inquiry and anything else you gotta show up for 'til the middle of March."

"Good enough."

"Where'll you be in case I need to get in touch?"

"At Prairie's house in Chinati."

The line hummed between them before Dreyfus asked, "You gonna stay out of trouble over there?"

"Guess that depends on whether trouble stays out of my way."

"Any more incidents and I won't be able to save your badge."

"Maybe I don't care."

"You don't mean that. Don't make any decisions 'til you've had a chance to let the dust settle. You hear me, Devon?"

"I hear you."

He hung up and walked back into the dining room to sit facing his brother at the opposite end of the table.

Laura went into the kitchen to fix his breakfast. After a pointed look from her father, Misty went in to help.

The men sat in silence a moment, then Connie asked,

"What'll you do now?"

"Soon as Prairie gets her butt out of bed . . ." Devon smiled, watching Eric blush, "I'm gonna take her home."

Devon made a quick stop at a drugstore while Prairie waited in the Lexus. He tossed his purchase on the console between them, then drove downhill on Stanton toward I-10. With her usual impetuosity, she opened the bag and looked inside. As he accelerated onto the Sunday morning freeway, she said, "I ain't got any diseases, Devon. Do you?"

"There's another reason for using 'em."

"We didn't use one last night."

He met her bright blue eyes beneath the black jagged cut of her bangs. "Do you have any idea where you are in your cycle?"

"About the middle."

"Maybe we'll be lucky."

She smiled impishly. "You worried you're gonna knock me up?"

He watched the scant traffic in his rearview as he nudged the speedometer to eighty. "I'm Catholic. Did you know that?"

"No."

"One of the things that means is there's no easy out if it ends up there's three instead of two people on this trip."

"What makes you think I'd want out?"

He glanced at her slender hips in her snug jeans. "Your gunbelt wouldn't fit."

She laughed. "I'd love to have your child, Devon."

"Thanks, but don't you think motherhood might interfere with your job?"

"Nope. I'm a state employee with the same right to maternity leave as any other."

159

"It would interfere with mine."

"The one you're suspended from?"

"Suspended, not fired."

"Thing of it is," she argued softly, "I don't like the feel of condoms. Wasn't it nice having nothing between us?"

"You could put yourself on the pill."

"Yeah, but it'd be a full month 'fore it took effect. By then, you'll be back in El Paso and we'll only see each other catch as catch can. I ain't gonna mess up my hormones for an occasional roll in the hay. 'Sides, I want an heir."

"An heir?"

"Someone to keep my ranch in the family when I'm gone." After a moment, she said, "Anyway, ain't birth control as much a sin in the Catholic Church as sex outta wedlock?"

"I don't want to get married."

"Me, neither."

"Don't ever lie to me, Prairie."

She sighed. "Okay, maybe I wouldn't mind getting married. But I'm pushing thirty, and what I'd mind even more'n not having a husband is not ever having a child." When he didn't say anything, she asked, "What'd you and Samantha do?"

"She had her tubes tied."

"Well, shoot, I ain't getting myself spayed just 'cause you're shy of fatherhood."

"She had it done before I met her."

Prairie took the box out of the bag and read aloud, "Super lubricated for an easy slide." She sighed again. "Reckon that'll be okay. But you know something, Devon? I once bought a coffeemaker they called quick-drip, and damn! if it wasn't the slowest maker in creation."

"No pun intended," he muttered.

★ ★ ★ ★ ★

Watching a black Lexus turn off Highway 90 and drive into the back country of Jeff Davis County, Jack Greco decided that what he needed were wheels. If he pulled into Big Bend in a respectable car, with maybe a credit card or two heisted off its owner, he could clean himself up and make a good impression on the drug dealers he was hoping would take him into their organization.

After following the tire tracks on the dirt road for half an hour, he spied the Lexus parked all by itself in the middle of a field. Though it was locked, he peered through the windows, thinking it was definitely a classy car. When he backed off, he caught a reflection of himself in the window and nearly died of fright.

He hadn't shaved in a year and didn't own a comb, so his long hair was matted and hadn't been washed since the last time he shaved. He wore a perky blue mariner's cap, but between its bill and his beard, his dark eyes glittered with warning that he wasn't a man to be messed with. In the distance, he heard a woman laugh.

Skulking toward the sound, he crested a small hill to see a couple on a blanket under a tree. The woman was nude from the waist up, sitting astride a man who lay flat with all his clothes on. When she leaned closer to dangle her tits in front of his face, the man slid his hands up her bare back as he tasted what she was offering.

Jack saw a stick in the dirt by his feet. It was about two feet long, a couple inches around, and rock solid. Hefting it in his hand, he decided to wait until the couple got a little deeper into it, then hit the woman on the head and pop the man in the face before either one of them knew he was there. Slowly he approached, almost silent in the sand.

Looking up from Prairie's feast to see a filthy cretin

descending the hill with a stick in his hand, Devon whispered close to her ear, "We've got company."

She froze. "What'll I do?"

"You're a Texas Ranger," he teased, "why don't you get your gun?"

She slid her hand under her shirt on a corner of the blanket, flipped the keeper strap off her pistol, and began pulling the .45 out of its holster. "Where is he?"

"About twenty feet straight behind you."

She leapt up, twirling in the air to land facing the intruder.

Watching the man's eyes dart back and forth between her gun and her nipples proud as tin soldiers, Devon couldn't help but laugh. He slowly stood up, glancing at her breasts himself before taking her gun so she could get dressed.

Staring into the business end of the .45 now in the man's hand, Jack asked, "What the fuck?"

"We weren't quite there yet," Devon said. "Why don't you put that stick down before I shoot you for interrupting us?"

Jack tossed the stick and let his hand fall limp.

"What's your name?" Devon asked.

"Jack."

"Well, turn around, Jack. Put your hands on your head and start walking toward the car."

Jack did as he was told, struggling to climb the sandy hill. By the time they reached the Lexus, Prairie caught up, dressed and carrying the blanket wadded in front of her. Devon tossed her his keys. She opened the passenger door, then the glovebox for his handcuffs. When she turned around again, sunlight flashed on the silver-circled star of her badge.

"Shit," Jack complained. "Are you cops or something?"

"That's right," Devon said. "Put your hands behind you."

Prairie snapped the cuffs tight. "Jesus Christ," she said,

backing off. "Don't you ever take a bath?"

The breeze shifted, putting Devon downwind. "As bad as you smell, I ought to make you ride in the trunk."

Jack stared at it. "You wouldn't do that."

"Afraid of the dark?"

"I'll suffocate."

"If you do, it'll be on your own stink. Open it, Prairie."

"I don't know if this is a good idea."

"You want to ride with him?"

She hesitated only a moment longer, then opened the trunk.

Eric sat on the bed Devon and Prairie had slept in the night before, indulging himself in the masochistic game of imagining his uncle making it with her. The pleasure was like biting a sore tooth, feeling the agony shoot through his jaw, then jerking his teeth apart only to begin searching for that pain again. In exactly the same way, Eric's gaze would wander the room before returning to the rumpled sheets and two pillows nestled close.

They had gone to Prairie's house in Chinati to wait out Devon's suspension. That was supposed to last two weeks, then Devon would resume his duties in El Paso and Prairie would continue being the Ranger assigned to West Texas. Unless he brought her home as his bride. If that happened, she would be off-limits forever.

Eric had one week of college before spring break. Then he figured he would show up in Chinati and flaunt his stuff. Prairie was ten years older, so if she turned him down, he could handle that. But at eighteen a man was at the peak of his prowess while at thirty-five he was losing his stride. Prairie didn't strike Eric as a woman who wanted a man the least bit off his game. As near as he could tell, he'd had as many lovers as his uncle had, though Devon kept a closed mouth about such things. But even if he wasn't quite as seasoned, Eric figured Prairie might appreciate the freshness of his come-on.

On Friday morning, Sergio Tierrasantas called Prairie at home and asked that she come see him in her official capacity. She pinned on her badge and strapped on her gun under Devon's watchful eye, then drove out of her yard knowing he would spend the day drinking on her porch.

She told herself he was a man of action disabled by forced inactivity, that it was partly her fault he had been suspended, and when he went back to work he would again be the detective she had coveted from afar. But by then, they would be hundreds of miles apart and she would have lost her chance to find love with this man she so intensely admired. Half of their time together was already gone.

When she came home at sunset to see the bottle of Old Crow he had opened the night before nearly empty, she decided it was time for a change. Sitting cross-legged on the opposite end of the swing, she squared off in front of him.

"There's no answer in the bottom of a bottle, Devon."

"I know that." He smiled. "But the bottom feels better when you hit it drunk."

"You're a long ways from hitting bottom."

He shrugged.

"Remember when we first met and I told you you're cute?"

"If you're working up to saying I'm not cute anymore, the truth is I never was. You didn't know me. Maybe you still don't."

"That's the way you like it, ain't it?"

"What way?"

"For no one to know you."

He lowered his gaze, and she understood by his gesture of avoidance that she had hit home. "What are you afraid of? That if I get to know you, I won't like you anymore?"

He met her eyes. "Are we having this conversation because you like me more than you did a week ago?"

She was tempted to say yes, because in that week she had fallen in love, but she stuck to her guns: "A week ago you didn't get drunk every day, to say nothing of the nights."

"You don't like our nights?"

"I almost do."

"What's missing?"

"A hint that you care about what I want."

"Let me see," he mused, as if seriously considering how he might accommodate her. "What if I build an alcove off the bedroom? You could call it the nursery." He gave her a wry smile. "Would that satisfy you?"

She stood up. "It's hard to talk to you when you're drunk."

"Because I'm slurring my words? Or don't you think I'm sharp enough to catch your intent?"

"Because you act like I'm an enemy you're out to beat." She turned around to stare into the desert, at a loss for how to set things right between them.

He took hold of her hand and pulled her to sit beside him. "Didn't you expect," he asked gently, "that telling me you want to get pregnant would make me wary?"

She shook her head. "I make enough money to support a child. You wouldn't ever have to see us if you didn't want to."

"You think I'd let you do it alone?"

"It's my choice."

"No, if you include the child, it's one you're making for three people. You know how often a policeman's killed in the line of duty?"

"It happens every five days in this country," she said, remembering that statistic from her training.

He nodded. "Who'd take care of our child if you were killed? Or I was? Or both of us were? You don't have any family. I've got a brother barely able to take care of the kids he's got."

"Most policemen have children."

"Most police*men* have wives who don't wear a badge."

She sighed.

"What'd Sergio want?"

"He's got a transient camping on his land, wants me to roust him."

"Why'd he call you instead of the sheriff?"

"Rufus had a heart attack. He's in the hospital."

"What about his deputy?"

"Hank Gentry couldn't run a chigger off a dog."

"Why doesn't Sergio have his *vaqueros* run the guy off?"

"I didn't feel that was a question I could ask. I mean, it's the law's job."

"Didn't you wonder though?"

She nodded.

"Did you tell Sergio you'd do it?"

"Sure. I stopped on my way home and found the guy's camp, but he wasn't there. Figure I'll go back later tonight."

"Alone?"

"Texas Rangers nearly always work alone, Devon. If I can't roust a transient, I ain't worth much."

"You expect me to sit here and wait for you to come back?"

"I ain't taking you drunk."

"What if you go out there and his camp looks empty, but while you're poking around he jumps you from behind?"

"I'll have to make sure that doesn't happen."

"Are you willing to shoot him?"

"If I have to."

"You should've said yes, Prairie. By the time you decide you have to, it'll be too late." He grinned with victory. "I'll stay in the Jeep."

Feeling she had lost their argument all the way around, she picked up his bottle of whiskey. "Reckon I can put this away."

He shrugged. "We gonna have supper 'fore we go?"

"Sure. What'd you cook while I was at work?"

"We're eating out."

The camp was a firepit and a tattered sheet of black plastic draped over creosote bushes, its corners anchored with rocks. A low fire flickered in the pit and an empty can of Ranch Style beans lay nearby. Its lid had been cut open with a knife, leaving a jagged line. The interior of the tent was deeply shadowed, but Prairie thought she saw a rumpled form inside.

"Hey, buddy," she called. "Wake up."

The guy didn't move.

Inside the Jeep, Devon blasted the horn.

Prairie jumped at the noise, then mentally winced, scolding herself for not having thought of honking to wake the guy. He lurched to his feet and came staggering out to squint at Prairie standing between him and the headlights.

Recognizing the man who had tried to attack her and Devon in Jeff Davis County, Prairie wondered why the sheriff had cut Greco loose, or if maybe he hadn't walked. "You can't camp here," she said. "This is private property."

He glanced at the Jeep, but she didn't guess he could see past the headlights. "I got the owner's permission."

"What's his name?"

"Sergio Tierrasantas."

"Yeah, he's the owner," she agreed, wondering what Sergio was up to, "but he told me to roust you."

"I talked to him just today, and he said I could camp here long as I want."

"Don't move."

Without taking her eyes off him, she backed toward her Jeep, reached inside for her radio, and called Andy Packer, the nightshift clerk in the sheriff's office. "Ranger Drake here. I've got a Jack Greco camping in Rattlesnake Draw. He was arrested in Jeff Davis last week. Call the sheriff over there and find out if they let him go or he walked."

"Okay," Andy mumbled, then clicked off.

She waited, watching Greco.

After a few minutes, Andy came back through the static. "Prairie? Jeff Davis let him go."

"Did they say why?"

"I didn't ask. Should I call 'em back?"

"No, thanks, Andy."

"You want me to find Hank and ask him to give you a hand?"

"I got it covered."

She clicked off and dropped the mike on her seat, then approached Greco again. "You can't stay here."

"Where am I s'posed to go in the middle of the night?"

"Ain't you got any money?"

"If I did, you think I'd be living like this?"

"What're you traveling for, if you don't have money?"

"I didn't have any where I was either."

"Where's that?"

"Barstow."

"You running from the California cops?"

"No!"

"You ever been arrested before the other day?"

"Yeah."

"What for?"

"Burglary."

"Why would Mr. Tierrasantas want a thief camping on his land?"

Greco kicked at the sand at his feet.

"Don't move!" Prairie shouted.

He gave her a sleazy smile. "You're wearing more clothes than last time."

"Doesn't smell like you've had a bath." She decided if she rousted him he would just change locations so she wouldn't know where to look. "I'll let you stay 'til morning. But I'll be back early and you best be gone."

"I got the owner's permission."

"No, you don't. So unless you wanta be arrested again, you best be gone by sunrise. Understand?"

He nodded.

She backed into her Jeep and sat down on the radio mike. Embarrassed, she pulled it out and hung it up, then shifted into reverse. Her headlights swept across his camp as she left.

Driving along the sandy floor of the canyon, she felt tempted to ask Devon what he thought of her performance, but she kept quiet, not wanting him to think she needed his approval.

Finally he said, "Law enforcement's a bit loose out here."

She downshifted as she approached the highway.

"The sheriff of Jeff Davis should've held Greco for trial," Devon said.

"Prob'ly didn't want to feed him." She accelerated onto the pavement.

"You think Greco was lying about having permission?"

"Sure."

"How'd he know Sergio's name?"

"Could've heard it somewhere."

"It's not easy to remember, especially with a fried brain."

She watched the flashing white lines in the middle of the blacktop. "You think Sergio was hoping I'd fall on my face?"

"Only if Greco's a backdoor man."

She met his teasing eyes in the green glow of the dash.

"What's your next move?" he asked.

"Go out there tomorrow and make sure he's gone."

"If I were you, I'd call Sergio in the meantime and hear what he has to say."

"Yeah, I might do that too," she muttered, not admitting it was another good idea he'd thought of first. She reminded herself that everything he did was a trick he had learned along the way. Given time, she would know as much as he did.

Without the whiskey, his lovemaking was gently soothing, relaxing her into a languor that ebbed her toward arousal as easily as moonlight seeped through their open window. After caressing her to a moist readiness, he rolled over to open the nightstand for his box of condoms. She watched him discover it was empty, then meet her eyes with an unspoken accusation that she had thrown the last one away as a ploy to get what she wanted, but she figured if he hadn't been so drunk last night he would have known the truth. Sighing, he turned around and put his feet on the floor.

"Here," she said, sliding down to kneel between his knees, "let me bring you to a come."

"No."

She looked up at him. "Why not?"

"I don't like it."

She lowered her gaze to his erection, still strong between his thighs. Running a fingertip its length, she whispered,

"You wouldn't like to come inside my mouth?"

"No!"

Unable to believe him, she said, "Most men love it."

"I don't."

Puzzled, she asked, "Hasn't any woman ever gone down on you, Devon?"

"Only whores."

"You use whores?"

"Coupla times, years ago."

Knowing it was a traditional rite of passage for men who grew up on the border to first have sex with prostitutes in Mexico, she smiled. "Well, all women do the same things, you know. It's just that whores do it for money. I do it for love."

"How many men have you done it with?"

"A few," she answered, cautious now in the face of his anger. "Mostly in college. It's just mutual masturbation, a way to have sex without intercourse."

He stared at her with utter condemnation.

Confused, she sat back on her heels. "You're the one so intent on not getting me pregnant. This is a way to get off without risking that."

"I'm not gonna fuck your mouth."

"You make it sound obscene."

"How do you think it looks?"

"No different'n anything else." She laughed, trying to ease his anger.

"You think this is funny?"

"Kinda. I mean, no, I guess ironic is a better word, or maybe pathetic."

He slapped her.

She jumped to her feet and hit him with her fist.

He touched the corner of his mouth, then looked at the

blood on his fingertips.

"I want you out of here," she said. "Now!"

Too late she realized he had been about to smile and maybe the storm could have passed, leaving them a lull to find peace. But after ordering him out, to take it back without his apology would be crawling.

Sitting near the pillows, she watched him get dressed, reach under the bed for his suitcase, toss it on the rumpled sheets, and snap it open. He went into the bathroom to gather his stuff, then opened her chiffonnier for his clothes, carelessly throwing everything in. She sat stock still, willing him to apologize, if only with his eyes. But he walked out without looking back. Listening to the sound of his engine fade into silence, she could scarcely believe what had happened.

"Shit," she whispered, trying hard not to cry.

Devon was eating breakfast in Felipe's Cafe when he saw Eric's black Shadow park at the curb. He sipped his coffee as his nephew sauntered through the door and along the row of booths.

"Morning," Eric said, sitting down across from him as casually as if they were home.

Devon nodded, then went back to his *huevos rancheros.*

"How'd you split your lip?" Eric asked.

"Prairie hit me."

Eric laughed. "Why?"

"I slapped her."

"What for?" All humor gone.

"None of your business. What're you doing here?"

"It's spring break," he answered buoyantly. "I came for a visit."

Devon glanced at his watch. "You must've left before dawn."

"I got in last night and drove straight out to Prairie's. She told me I might find you here."

"You sleep at her place?"

"She made me a bed on the couch."

Devon went back to finishing his breakfast. The waitress came over, refilled his cup, and asked Eric what he wanted.

"I'll have the same." He watched Devon eat, then asked, "How come you slept in town last night?"

"What'd Prairie say about it?"

"To ask you."

"I've already given you my answer."

"It's none of my business, right?"

"You got it."

Eric laughed again. "Does that mean you don't have any claim on her?"

Devon set his empty plate aside. "It was a passing fancy."

Eric grinned. "Great, 'cause I think she's dynamite! You got any objection to my making a move on her?"

Devon shook his head. "She's looking for a stud."

"Then I'm her man."

"I meant that literally. If you don't want to be a father, I suggest you use protection."

The waitress brought Eric's breakfast. He waited until she was gone again, then whispered, "It'll be something to have shared a woman, huh, Uncle Devon?"

"Ask me after it's happened." He looked out the window and watched Sergio Tierrasantas park a yellow BMW on the other side of the street.

Chapter Twelve

Eric was shoveling runny eggs dripping with red chili into his mouth when Sergio pushed through the door. A hush descended on the cafe, making Devon suspect it was a rare event for the citizens of Chinati to see their lord and master mingling with his peons.

Sergio walked over and extended his hand. "Detective Gray. What a pleasure to see you again."

Devon accepted the handshake without standing up. "Is this a chance meeting?"

Sergio laughed. "I confess, it's not." He looked at Eric. Devon introduced them.

"Your son?" Sergio asked with apparent delight.

"Nephew," Devon said.

"Do you mind if I join you?"

Devon shook his head but otherwise didn't move. Eric slid closer to the window and continued to eat, throwing curious glances at the man who sat down beside him.

The waitress quickly appeared. "What can I get'cha, Mr. Tierrasantas?"

"Coffee, please." He gave her a regal smile.

She blushed and hurried away. Sergio and Devon watched each other until she returned and left again, taking Devon's empty plate with her.

Sergio added cream to his cup. "Did Boots have any trouble rousting that squatter off my land?"

"You'll have to ask her," Devon said, noting Eric was quick to catch on that they were talking about Prairie.

"I understand he told her I gave him permission."

"Did you?"

"My foreman had the same compassion she did and let Greco stay overnight. That was the extent of it. I came into town to ask Boots if he's still there, but she's neither at home nor her office."

"You could've called."

Sergio sipped his coffee. "Yes, but I was hoping to also see you."

"Why?"

He smiled. "You still don't like me, do you?"

Devon shook his head.

"Even though it has been proven I'm innocent of the murder of my ex-wife?"

"They call it not guilty in a court of law."

"But we're not in a courtroom. Shall I assume, if we were, you'd find me guilty?"

"I think you were morally complicit, but I know you're responsible for the death of Carl Lowdy."

"Carl," Sergio said in a dismissive tone. "Perhaps, being the shooter who accomplished the deed so adeptly, you feel what happened was unfortunate, but his death was a matter of indifference to me."

Eric had stopped eating and was watching back and forth between them.

"Would it have been a matter of indifference," Devon asked, "if I hadn't arrived in time to stop him?"

"I don't know his intention."

"The deed you traded for the use of your stud."

"That had nothing to do with you."

"Or Prairie?"

"I'm fond of Boots and have put out the word that anyone who harms her will answer to me."

"It strikes me odd that Lowdy hadn't heard."

"Carl wasn't operating from a full deck at the end. You did this county a favor by stopping him before he hurt someone."

Devon shrugged.

Sergio's smile was conniving. "Sheriff Bowlin is going home from the hospital today. I've asked him as a personal favor not to interfere with your presence in his jurisdiction."

"He has no legal right to interfere."

"I'm afraid he doesn't agree. Since the inquiry on Carl's death is yet to be held, he feels you've overstepped your bounds by coming back. But let's not discuss that. As I said, I've secured his promise to leave you alone."

"What do you want to discuss?"

"I admire your directness, Detective."

"Why don't you quit lauding me with compliments and get to the point?"

Sergio laughed. "I'm having a few friends for dinner tonight and I was hoping you'd join us." He paused to give Devon a playful smile. "I promise not to show any blue movies."

"Will Estefen Escobar be one of your guests?"

"He's no friend of mine." He chuckled. "I was pleased beyond measure when I heard you knocked him down. I sincerely wish I could have seen it happen."

"If you'd bothered to pay your respects to Lisa, you might have."

"I attended her funeral. Since you now know I wasn't responsible for her death, I wish you could forget your former suspicions."

"They weren't only concerned with her murder."

"What else?"

"Complicity in Lowdy's scheme, for one."

"I assure you I had nothing to do with that."

"Smuggling through Coyote Canyon, for another."

Sergio frowned. "Without proof, you're skirting slander, Detective."

Devon shrugged. "Smuggling's not my beat. Neither is Presidio County."

"Precisely," Sergio answered, beaming again. "Will you join me and my friends for dinner? I'm certain you'll find it interesting."

"Maybe. I wasn't doing anything anyway."

"Excellent." Sergio stood up. "Dinner's at eight. Shall I send a car for you?"

"I have my own."

Sergio nodded. "Bring your nephew. He may find it educational."

Devon watched him walk out and drive away, then looked at Eric. "Want to come?"

"Maybe I'll bring Prairie." Eric grinned. "How would you feel about that?"

"If Sergio wanted her there, he'd ask her himself."

Eric frowned. "Is he dating her?"

"No, she's the Ranger for the part of Texas he owns. Unless I miss my bet, he won't want a badge at his table tonight."

"He invited you."

"Uh-huh. A suspended cop from El Paso. I think he's gonna offer me a deal."

"You won't take it, will you?"

"I don't know," Devon said. "I'm getting damned bored."

Prairie drove west on Highway 90 toward Rattlesnake Draw, hoping Jack Greco had moved on. She had called

Sergio's ranch and spoken with his foreman, J. C. Cooper. J.C. had been friends with Prairie's grandfather, and she felt more comfortable talking to him than Sergio anyway. Having learned J.C. had also told Greco to move on but Greco hadn't done it, Prairie suspected she would have to roust him by force.

She had spent an hour before she left bolting the heavy-gauge screen between the front and back seats of her Jeep. On her way out of town, she drove by the courthouse on the off-chance she could get Deputy Gentry to accompany her, since the duty technically fell within the scope of the sheriff's office. But Gentry wasn't in yet, so Prairie drove toward Rattlesnake alone.

The air was cool under a blue sky speckled with bits of clouds like whitecaps on a rough sea. She drove with one hand on the wheel, the other fingering the brass knuckles in the pocket of her denim jacket. She didn't expect to fight Greco, but she sure wished she had some backup in what lay ahead. His eyes had a flat indifference that left no doubt he had long ago lost whatever semblance of a conscience he'd ever owned.

She found him standing over a paltry fire in the arroyo where he had made camp. After killing her engine, she flipped the keeper strap off her pistol as she stepped into the sand.

"What're you doing here, Jack?"

He looked at her a long moment, his hands clenched into fists. "I got the owner's permission."

"I talked to his foreman this morning and he told you the same thing I did, only he said it three days ago!"

"I ain't talking about no foreman. Mr. Tierrasantas himself asked me to stay."

"When?"

"Yesterday. He came by on his horse with a coupla other

men, but he told 'em to keep off and he came in and sat down while we talked matters over."

"What matters?"

"What your tits look like, for one thing!"

"You slimy excuse for a toad! You would've never seen 'em if you hadn't been sneaking up to commit a crime."

Greco grinned. "I told the sheriff of Jeff Davis how all that came down, and he thought it was real funny a Texas Ranger would take her shirt off for a bounced cop from El Paso. The story's prob'ly all over Texas by now."

"You best shut your mouth if you don't wanta go to jail 'stead of being sent on your way."

"You can't arrest me! I got the owner's permission to be here!"

"Then why would he tell me to roust you?"

"I don't know," Greco mumbled, kicking sand.

"Quit that!" Prairie shouted. "Put your hands on your head and turn around!"

He dropped to his knees and scooped up sand he threw in her face. Closing her eyes, she pulled and fired her gun high to keep him at a distance until the brittle grains slid off her cheeks. Then she aimed her weapon at the furrow between his flat dead eyes. "On the ground! Face down!"

He propelled himself off his knees to butt her belly with his head. Staggering backward, she smacked it hard with the barrel of her gun, but not before she felt his hands like pinchers on her breasts. She struck him again with the full force of her strength, and he crumpled, out cold.

For a moment, she trembled above him. Then she holstered her gun and yanked her handcuffs out of her belt, pried his arms behind his back and snapped the cuffs on tight. When she stood straight again, she kicked him in the ribs for good measure before she retreated to the open door of her

Jeep and sat down on the edge, breathing hard as she waited for him to wake up.

Remembering his hands like claws closing on her breasts, she shuddered with revulsion. Her anger jerked her to her feet and she yelled, "Goddamn sonofabitch!" As her voice echoed in the canyon, she walked over and kicked Greco onto his back, then kept kicking until he opened his eyes, squinting against the sun. She aimed her pistol at his face. "Get up or I'll leave you here to feed the buzzards."

He staggered to his feet.

She wagged her pistol toward the Jeep. "Over there."

She opened the tailgate and nodded for him to get in. He did, stumbling to land on his nose, so it was bleeding when he managed to sit up inside the cage. She slammed it shut, holstered her pistol and jabbed herself behind the wheel. Gunning the engine, she spun sand as she left Rattlesnake behind.

Devon sat on his bed in Borough's Motel and called the library in El Paso. He dialed Samantha's extension but the stranger who answered put him on hold. While he waited, he scooped a plastic glass into the ice bucket, broke the seal on a bottle of Old Crow, then filled the glass and watched the ice settle as it dissolved in the whiskey.

"Samantha Sawyer," she said, smoothly in control.

"How you doing, Sam?"

"Devon?" she whispered.

Picturing her behind her desk, he asked, "What are you wearing? Your red paisley with the full skirt?"

"Oh Devon." She laughed softly. "Where are you?"

"Chinati." He lifted the glass and shook the ice down.

"With Prairie?"

"Alone in a motel. Or I was alone 'til Eric showed up." He

emptied the glass and refilled it with whiskey. "Just thought I'd call and see how you're doing."

"I moved into a condo a couple of doors down from Darryl Brent."

Devon dropped in more ice. "You buying or renting?"

"Renting for now, though it's for sale. Maybe I'll buy it. I haven't decided."

He drained the glass.

"What are you drinking?"

"Whiskey."

"It's not yet noon, Devon."

"Which proves we're in the same time zone."

Eric came out of the bathroom in a black pair of swimming trunks. He routinely worked out with weights, and his body was lean and curved with muscles. Devon figured Prairie would appreciate it. Away from the phone, he said, "Enjoy your swim." Eric smiled and waved. Devon listened to the door close, then slowly refilled his glass and dropped in more of the fast-melting ice. "I'm having dinner with Sergio Tierrasantas tonight."

"I thought that case was closed."

"It is, but he invited me, so what the hell." He took another sip, beginning to feel more at ease.

"Why are you drinking so early?"

"I'm on suspension, as in dangling in nowhere?"

"Can't you consider it a vacation?" Her voice was carefully solicitous. "Just relax and enjoy yourself?"

"You know me."

"Yes," she murmured.

He emptied the glass. "I feel so damn angry, Sam."

"Maybe you should talk to a therapist."

He poured another drink and dropped in more ice.

"Or a priest," she suggested. "Have you thought about

finding someone you can talk to?"

"I called you."

She sighed. "Devon, I'm sorry for everything that happened. I wish I could go back and change it."

He took another sip and set his glass down.

"There's a nice view from my balcony, Devon. If you want to drink all day, you can do it here and be a lot safer than having dinner with the likes of Sergio Tierrasantas."

"What do you know about him?"

"It's common knowledge he has ties to the Mexican mafia."

"Can you prove that?"

"I could find documentation, but the references are oblique. Mentions of him riding in a car with Rafael Otero, things like that."

"Circumstantial."

"There's a meeting in Mexico City next week, known kingpins of the Colombian drug trade coming to supposedly discuss the archeological heritage shared by Colombia and Mexico, ways to preserve the sites and promote tourism, but the men coming to the meeting aren't archaeologists."

"How'd you hear about it?"

"Tom Hernandez told me. He was reading an article in a Juárez newspaper, and he pointed out that the men attending the meeting had all been connected to the drug cartels. Tierrasantas was one of them."

"Which cartel is he connected to?"

"Evidently he moves freely among them."

Devon shook the ice down in his glass.

"Don't go out there drunk, Devon. You need your wits to deal with men like that." She waited, then said, "You shouldn't go at all if you want your job back."

"My comfy little life working homicide?"

"Yes."

"You know something, Sam?" He emptied his glass. "Killers are easy compared to women."

"I never meant to hurt you, Devon."

"See what I mean? A killer would never say that. When he hurts someone, it's 'cause he wants to. That makes him easier to understand."

"Don't drink any more, Devon."

"I guess you really are okay. I mean, as long as a woman feels she can tell a man what to do, she hasn't lost her purpose in life. Course it doesn't count for much if he doesn't listen."

"And you won't, will you."

"I won't go to Sergio's drunk. But I've got a whole day in front of me with nothing to do, a privilege I owe to you and Prairie. Now you want me back and she wants to get pregnant. But what I'm gonna do is have dinner with Sergio. If there's any women there, they'll be whores trained to please. Maybe it's time I learned how that feels."

"Devon, listen to me."

But he hung up because he didn't want to hear it.

Eric came in, dripping water as he walked to the bathroom. On the tile, he peeled off his trunks and hung them on the shower curtain, then glanced at the whiskey bottle before giving Devon a smile. "Figured I'd drive out to Prairie's and see if she's back yet."

"From where?"

"She had to roust some transient. Said it shouldn't take more'n an hour."

Devon nodded, wondering how well she had handled Greco alone. "You coming to Sergio's tonight?"

"I'd rather go out with Prairie."

Devon studied his nephew standing there naked. With his

shoulder-length dark hair dripping wet and his muscles shining in the light, he could have been a generic ad for a stud. "Good luck," Devon said.

Eric laughed and turned on the shower.

Devon poured himself another drink. He sat sipping at the whiskey and staring at the pattern in the carpet—cabbage roses in varying shades of orange—until Eric came out again and put on clean jeans and a baggy black T-shirt. He sat on the other bed to pull on socks and sneakers.

Watching him tie the laces, Devon thought about Eric's running shoes costing a hundred dollars, but Eric hadn't paid for them. His father had. His father and his uncle had bought his car. And generous ol' Uncle Devon kept up the insurance, suspecting Eric would drive without it if he didn't.

The whole family was coddling the kid, but Devon wondered if what Eric really needed wasn't responsibility. Having a child with Prairie might give him that. Maybe they would be one of those New Age couples practicing role reversal. Devon could see it: Prairie coming home at night and hanging her gunbelt on a peg by the door, kissing the baby and asking Eric what he'd cooked for supper. Prairie with her feet on the porch railing while Eric set the table. Eric servicing her in bed every night with his eighteen-year-old hormones, she controlling his every move with her take-home pay. What would Eric turn out to be? Would he ever stand on his own like a man, or was Devon's concept of manhood as dead as the dinosaurs?

Finished lacing up the hundred-dollar sneakers he hadn't paid for, Eric asked, "What're you thinking about, Uncle Devon?"

"I want you to come with me tonight."

He looked like a kid who had just been told to mow the lawn, but he shrugged and said, "How late you figure we'll be?"

"You gonna make a date with Prairie for afterwards?"

"I was thinking about it, yeah."

"We should be back before the bars close."

Eric nodded and stood up. "See you later then."

"Don't make me come out to Prairie's to get you."

"I'll be here by five," he said, walking out.

Devon finished his drink, noting the bottle was well gone. He didn't feel a thing. Not drunk, but at least not angry. He felt almost inanimate, sitting in an anonymous motel room with the drapes drawn. Remembering he had called Samantha, he couldn't remember what he'd said. He had a vague recollection of her telling him to see a priest, and he smiled as he reached for the bottle again.

Maybe Chinati was purgatory and because basically he had been a good person—at least tried—he was given the anesthetic of alcohol while watching his nephew seduce the woman he loved. If he squinted he could almost see Samantha with her legs wrapped around Eric's butt. No, that wasn't Eric. It was Jay Lehrer, the man Prairie had killed in the second act leading to Devon's suspension. No, the third. He had killed Carl Lowdy and punched out Estefen Escobar as the opening two acts. Was this the epilogue then? Watching his nephew fuck Prairie?

There was only a puddle of cold water left in the ice bucket. He emptied the bottle into his glass, filling it almost to the brim. How much whiskey could a man accustomed to drinking only beer swallow before poisoning himself? A man in good physical shape, even though he was pushing middle age, who earned his living with his wits, taking pride in the sharpness of his mind. A man whose pride was too much maybe, it being the worst of the seven fatal sins. A man who had slapped a woman for calling him pathetic, now proving her right.

He looked at his watch. Between the two dials in his line of vision, he managed to make out that it was one o'clock. Seven hours before he had to show up at the Tierrasantas ranch wily enough to sidestep whatever dirty deal Sergio surely meant to offer, sidestep it long enough to keep Sergio talking, adding details as enticement, so he could figure out if he was still a cop or had gone over to the other side.

Someone knocked on the door. The maid, probably. "Go away," he shouted over his shoulder.

The door opened, flooding the room with light.

Squinting at the silhouette of a woman against the painfully bright sunshine, he said, "I don't need anything."

"The hell you don't," Prairie said, mercifully closing the door.

He let his gaze slide over her unfairly svelte hips, the rise of her breasts beneath a shirt the same blue as her eyes, as bright as the shine on the silver circled-star of her badge, then he said with a smile, "He went that-a-way."

"Who?"

"The stud you're looking for. He's on his way out to your place right now."

She glanced at the empty whiskey bottle. "You've been drinking."

"The power of women's intuition is amazing."

She walked over to stand in front of him as she dropped the full glass and empty bottle into the ice bucket.

"Tidying up?" he teased.

"Think you had enough," she said.

He unbuckled her gunbelt and tossed it onto the bed behind her, then clumsily unfastened the clasp of her badge and threw it to clink against her gun.

"What're you doing, Devon?"

He unbuttoned her blouse, let it fall on the floor,

unhooked her bra and tossed it to land on her gun, then unbuckled the beaded belt running through the loops of her jeans. When he started unzipping her jeans, she caught hold of his hands. "You're drunk."

He met her eyes, blue as a prairie sky at twilight. "I'm dead. That's what Sam said."

"You talked to Samantha?"

"She told me to see a priest."

He lay back on the bed, pulling Prairie to straddle his chest, her boots alongside holding him together, her breasts like moons shining above him. "Oh bury me not," he sang, "on the lone prair-ee."

"Devon," she whispered.

"Has anyone ever told you you're beautiful?"

She shook her head.

"Dynamite's what Eric said. He's got the hots for you, Prairie. You gonna let him burn your grass?"

She laughed.

He reached up and touched her cheek. "I'm sorry I slapped you. Do you care that I'm sorry?"

"Yes."

He smiled. "Want to kiss and make love?"

"I don't think it's a good idea."

"I do."

"I can see that. But when you sober up, you're gonna say I took advantage of you being drunk."

He rolled her over beneath him and finished unzipping her jeans. "If you hadn't wanted this, you wouldn't have locked the door."

"You're pretty sharp for noticing I did that, but we got a little problem: I don't have a condom. Do you?"

He leaned down to pull off one of her boots. "Think I've figured out a solution to that." He dropped the boot and took off her other one. "If you get pregnant, you can marry Eric and keep him as a house-spouse." He stood up to tug at her jeans. "He's good with kids."

"So're you."

"But I don't want to be kept." He pulled her jeans and panties all the way off, then smiled at her naked beneath him.

She sat up and unbuttoned his shirt. "I got a problem with your solution."

"What's that?" Watching her breasts.

"I don't wanta marry Eric."

He shrugged out of his shirt while she unbuttoned his fly, then she stood up, pushed him onto the bed, pulled off his jeans, and climbed on top of him. "Want me to get on the bottom?"

He shook his head, watching her image ripple against the ceiling. "If I was up there, I'd lose my balance."

"Yeah, it's pretty scary."

"It's scary down here, too."

"I know," she said.

He woke up thinking it had been a dream, but his clothes were folded neatly on the other bed and the ice bucket was gone, neither of which made sense if he had spent the afternoon alone. Wondering if he had really polished off a fifth of whiskey, he pulled himself out of bed and into the bathroom. The bottle was in the trash. He took a step back from what he saw in the mirror, then turned on the shower and stood under the hot water waiting for his memory to return.

He had called Samantha and she asked him to come home. Prairie had opened the door and he had pulled her into bed. He wondered if he'd managed to finish before passing out. Surely he hadn't quit in the middle. His body wouldn't betray him like that. No, he'd finished on cruise control, then passed out.

Brushing his teeth in front of the mirror, he heard someone knock. He spit out the toothpaste, tucked the towel around his waist, and padded barefoot across to open the door.

"Five o'clock," Eric said with a grin. "On the button."

Devon walked back to hang the towel in the bathroom. Eric was sitting on the unrumpled bed when he came out and opened his suitcase. He had thrown his shirts in willy-nilly and doubted any were wearable, as wrinkled as they were. He rummaged through the chaos to find a pair of underwear.

"I saw Prairie," Eric boasted.

Devon stepped into a clean pair of jeans, buttoning them as he crossed to the phone. When Tom Borough came on the line, Devon asked, "Is there someone could iron some shirts for me?"

"Why sure," the old man drawled. "When ya want it done?"

"Right now."

"I'll send my girl lickety-split."

"Thanks." He hung up and walked back to study the options in his suitcase.

"Neat packing job," Eric said.

Devon scooped all the shirts out and carried them toward the door just as someone knocked. He opened it to a blond teenager who eyed his naked chest as if it were ice cream. "I'd like the blue one right away," he said, handing her the wad of shirts. "Tomorrow'll be soon enough for the others."

"Dollar apiece?"

"Deal." He closed the door and looked at Eric. "What'd Prairie have to say?"

"She's gonna meet us in the Range Rider at midnight."

"Us?"

"Me, but I figured you'd come along. She said she'd bring someone named Cynthia."

Devon remembered that Cynthia kept Prairie's house and fed her horses while she was gone. He went back to the bathroom and shaved. When he was finished, he studied Eric still sitting on the bed. "You make any headway with her?"

Eric shrugged. "She was pretty busy, being a Texas Ranger and all. That's why I'm hoping to see her tonight when she's off duty."

Someone knocked on the door. Devon opened it to see the girl holding his shirt on a hanger. He had to look for his wallet. When he found it in the jeans Prairie had left on the bed Eric was sitting on, Devon felt a twinge of guilt. Giving the girl five dollars, he said, "On account."

"Thanks." She laughed, her eyes on his chest.

"You want to give me the shirt?" he asked, thinking teenagers were at the mercy of their hormones. Unlike him and Prairie, always in control.

The girl handed him the hanger.

"You did a good job."

She giggled, looking past him at Eric. But Eric had his sights set higher than a girl his own age.

Devon closed the door and put the shirt on, then took his .38 out of the suitcase. Without a badge, he didn't have a license to carry a concealed weapon, but he threaded his belt through his jeans, catching the holster in the small of his back, and faced Eric again as he buckled the belt. "I hope you don't get your heart broke if Prairie turns you down."

"You think she will?"

"You're ten years younger than she is."

"I'm mature for my age."

Devon laughed. "What makes you think so?"

" 'Cause of what happened last summer."

He shrugged into his jacket. "You think killing someone makes you mature?"

Eric nodded. "I went to church last week and confessed it. Took me this long to get the guts to go. I kept arguing that I didn't really think shooting Truxal was wrong, but I couldn't go to confession and not mention it, so I guess at some level I knew it's always wrong to kill someone, even if you do it for a good reason. But it was knowing I was coming here to see Prairie that made me clear my conscience, as if taking communion and making love with a woman have something in common. You think that makes sense, Uncle Devon?"

He nodded, wondering if his own anger might stem less from what had happened with Sam than from having killed Carl Lowdy, and if maybe the weight of that hadn't contributed to his decision to conceive a new life with Prairie, assuming he could call what he'd done a decision. He found his car keys in the jeans she had folded so neatly just a few hours before, then met Eric's eyes with more than a twinge of guilt. "Long as we're talking about women, do I have to tell you to keep your hands off anything you see at Sergio's tonight?"

Eric's eyes lit up. "There's gonna be women there?"

Chapter Thirteen

The front patio of the Tierrasantas hacienda was illuminated with rose-colored lanterns. A quartet of flamenco guitarists played in a corner, their strings evoking the subtle mysteries of gypsy melodies, while a dozen men in the open-shirt style of casual attire seen on the pages of *GQ* lounged in the shadows sipping drinks and smoking cigars. Serving the drinks were several lushly beautiful young women dressed only in fur g-strings and stiletto high heels. Devon scanned the scene for Sergio, then saw him leave a trio of men near the fountain and approach with a smile.

"Detective Gray. I'm glad you came. And Eric," he said, also shaking his hand. "Good to have you with us." He turned back to Devon. "Do you mind if I call you Devon? Among my friends, your title might be intimidating."

Devon shrugged.

Sergio chuckled. "Please, allow me to introduce you." He gestured toward the men he had left by the fountain.

Their names were Emilio Calderon, Zalo Terrazas, and Jorge del Soltana, and they all spoke English with a bare trace of the softly rolling Spanish of South America rather than the abruptly dancing enunciation of northern Mexico. They also all wore a lot of gold—Rolex watches, jeweled rings, thick mesh necklaces—flaunting their wealth in the manner of men who had grown up poor. Dismissing Eric with flickered glances, their dark eyes settled in unison on Devon as if

192

assessing whether he would live up to whatever Sergio had told them about him.

Their conversation meandered through NAFTA, the Zapatista uprising in Chiapas, and the recent assassination of Luis Colosio, PRI's presidential candidate. Devon kept quiet, not feeling qualified to critique Mexican politics, though he had heard Colosio was killed by the drug cartel controlling Tijuana. Despite the fact that they spoke in English, Eric watched the men with the bland expression of someone politely listening to a discussion in a foreign language. Only when one of the fur-clad young women approached with a tray of drinks did he perk up.

Devon accepted a bottle of beer, but seeing Eric about to lift one off the tray, he told the waitress, "*Mi sabrino desea una Coca-Cola.*"

She smiled, dimpling her cheeks with charm. "*Un momento, señor, por favor.*" She looked at Eric and added, "*Señorito, por favor.*"

The men chuckled at the diminutive, traditionally used only for the very young son of a nobleman, and watched her walk away. From behind, her body was nearly naked, cut only by the thong of her g-string, all the fur being in front.

As she returned across the patio with a tall glass of ice and bottle of Coke on a tray, Devon wondered if he had been right to bring Eric. When she leaned over to set the tray on a low table, all the men in their circle watched her butt. She stood up pouring the Coke, then handed the glass to Eric.

It slipped through his fingers and shattered on the flagstones. The men quickly stepped back, then drifted away while Devon watched Eric trying to help gather the shards of glass when he couldn't seem to get his eyes off the woman's breasts.

A man more to Devon's liking approached. He was American, close to sixty, his wiry body dressed in boots and jeans, a wide leather belt and a white shirt with snap buttons. Extending his hand, he said, "I'm J. C. Cooper, Sergio's foreman."

"Devon Gray," he said, shaking hands.

He looked back at Eric in time to see the woman leading him toward the house as she insisted on drying the soaked leg of his jeans. Though Eric didn't understand Spanish, he was following her with no hint of hesitation. Devon called his name. Eric stopped and waited, his hand still grasped in the woman's. Devon came close, laid his arm across Eric's shoulders, and said softly, "Don't fuck her."

Startled with more than surprise, Eric met Devon's eyes. Devon smiled. Eric nodded. Devon turned back to J.C.

"Care to sit down?" Cooper drawled.

Devon accompanied him to a corner table where they both sat with their backs to the adobe wall, watching the lantern light flutter in the breeze, the music and murmured conversations punctuated by the patter of water falling in the fountain.

Cooper had pale blue eyes in a narrow, weathered face. He studied Devon a moment before saying, "I ain't sure why Sergio asked me here tonight, but I'm glad to have the chance to tell you something I think maybe you need to hear."

Devon waited.

"It's about Carl Lowdy," Cooper said, his eyes as direct as his voice was soft. "Ain't nobody in the county holds it agin you for what happened."

Devon felt the muscles in his face relax, as if they had been hardened into a rigid mask he only became aware of in the moment he lost it. "I appreciate your saying so."

Cooper nodded. "Carl wasn't right in the head for a long time. I don't know if it was Prairie giving him the cold shoulder when she come back from Austin or if his hatred for

Sergio finally drove him over the edge, but we all knew he was losing control." Cooper sighed. "Was a time folks looked after each other. Nowadays we just get outta the way."

"Why'd he hate Sergio?"

"Carl never had much. Sergio always had more'n maybe anyone should." Cooper shrugged. "It was jealousy, pure and simple. I don't guess there's anything more destructive when it takes ahold of a person." He let his gaze scan the patio. "All these men got more'n what a lotta folks would call a fair share. If you combined their individual worths, you could bankroll a small country."

"What're they doing here?"

"They're on their way to a shindig in Mexico City."

"Out of their way to come this far north, isn't it?"

Cooper smiled. "You're thinking they're South Americans, and most of 'em are, but that don't mean they spend much time at home."

"Any idea why I was invited?"

"Sergio likes you." He sipped his beer, taking time to savor it before letting himself swallow. "There ain't hardly nobody he trusts. Me, I guess 'cause I worked for his daddy, but he ain't got any brothers or sisters nor aunts or uncles. He's the last of his line, and I imagine it's lonely up there with all he's got. I s'pect he's wanting to put you in his saddle. But I'll tell you something, Devon . . . You mind if I call you Devon?"

He shook his head.

"I've been riding a Tierrasantas saddle all my life, and for the most part it's right comfy. But hidden inside is a sharp blade that can be used for or agin you, and it strikes without warning. So all the time you're riding along feeling you got it made, when you remember a knife can come outta nowhere to whack your balls off, well, it takes some of the

195

pleasure outta the ride."

Devon looked away, wondering why J.C. was telling him this.

"I know what you're thinking," Cooper said softly, "and the answer is I was friends with Prairie's granddaddy."

Devon watched the old man smile.

"I was with him when he died," Cooper said. "We was sitting on his porch with our feet up, sipping at a coupla beers and thinking about something he'd said, when his ticker quit. Just like that." Cooper snapped his fingers. "Wanta know what the last thing he said was?"

Devon nodded.

"He said, 'I hope to shout Prairie finds herself a man with balls and puts some blood back in the gene pool of Texas.' " Cooper smiled. "Josiah din't have much schooling, but he was smart and picked up concepts from Prairie when she'd come home summers. Gene pool was one of 'em. Reckon concepts is too, so guess I picked up some of the schooling Josiah gave Prairie." He sipped his beer. "The reason I'm telling you all this is I've heard you're seeing her, and I felt I owed it to Josiah to tell you in no uncertain terms you can't be Prairie's man while riding in Sergio's saddle. It'd be like putting a rattlesnake in a nest of baby songbirds. I ain't got nothing agin rattlers. Living as long as I have, I've come to respect 'em, but the world would be a sorry place without songbirds. Some mornin's, they're what makes me get up."

Devon smiled. "Me, too."

"Is that right? You still got birds in El Paso?"

"A lot of 'em."

Cooper looked at the men clustered about the patio. "I hear tell the birds in Mexico City are dropping from the sky 'cause of the smog."

"I've heard that," Devon said.

196

Sergio appeared under the shadowed portal. "Gentlemen? Dinner?"

Cooper gathered himself to his feet. "Reckon I'll skip that part. I never can figure which fork to use."

Devon stood up to shake hands. "Glad we met."

Cooper nodded. "Kiss Prairie's cheek for me, will you? And be sure'n tell her who it's coming from."

Devon watched the foreman walk out the front gate, then he turned around and looked for Eric.

Two hours later, Devon was alone with Sergio in a small office at the back of the house. Unlike the other rooms he had seen, this one looked utilitarian. The books on the shelf were texts on bovine parasites, regulations governing the transport of livestock across the Mexican-American border, botanical analyses of indigenous and imported grasses in the American Southwest, and ancestral pedigrees of Arabian horses. Several portraits of stallions hung on the walls, and there was a glass-enclosed display of ribbons and trophies.

Sergio sat in one of the leather horseshoe chairs, facing Devon across a low table of polished redwood burl. On the table were a crystal snifter of after-dinner cognac and a sweating bottle of Dos Equis beer.

"Your nephew is charming," Sergio said. "On the very cusp of manhood. He's heterosexual, I presume."

"To the hilt," Devon said.

"One of my guests inquired," Sergio explained with an apologetic smile. "I told him the boy was off-limits regardless of the answer, but the question piqued my curiosity. I hope you aren't offended." He stressed the last word as a tease.

Devon shrugged.

Sergio lifted the snifter and swirled his cognac. "I've done some investigations, I must confess, and everything I've learned has served to heighten my opinion of you."

"What have you learned?"

"Prior to this recent debacle, you had an exemplary record with the El Paso Police, having been honored three times for quick results in solving your cases. You're admired by your colleagues, but not especially liked because you don't attend their social functions. You're a loner, preferring to work without a partner, a privilege your lieutenant allows given your value to the department. You've never been married and have no dependents, have no mortgage on the house you inherited from your father and drive a city-issued car, so are free of debt. Your brother lives in the house with his family, which includes his pregnant wife, your charming nephew, and a fourteen-year-old niece who's quite pretty." He paused to smile. "I've seen her picture."

Devon felt a flash of anger he camouflaged by sipping his beer.

"Your brother served time in Huntsville for armed robbery," Sergio continued, not having missed what Devon tried to hide, "but has since kept himself clean, no doubt due to your influence. Until recently you were living with a woman named Samantha Sawyer who's head of reference at the public library. She was raped by her ex-husband. The denouement of that affair caused your suspension from the police force. Despite having achieved the man's death, you rejected Miss Sawyer as damaged goods, an attitude I find especially indicative of your high standards, for which you accept no excuse of failure."

Devon resisted an impulse to explain himself, not liking Sergio's spin on what had happened.

Sergio smiled. "You're Catholic and attend Mass almost every Sunday at Our Lady of the Angels, the small parish church you grew up in. You don't patronize prostitutes and have no bad habits. You're an excellent marksman but usually manage to solve your cases without using a gun, though you have been known to exhibit violence when faced with people whose lack of cooperation crosses your threshold of patience, which nevertheless is extraordinary given the cretins you confront. Your attire is nondescript in the extreme, consisting of, as now, scuffed boots, jeans, a tailored shirt and a conservative jacket. You never wear a tie, have a preference for Mexican restaurants, speak a passable Spanish, and keep a closed mouth about nearly everything." He leaned back, smugly proud of his sources.

"I wear a tie to weddings and funerals," Devon said.

Sergio chuckled. "The car you're driving cost more than your annual salary. Do you ever think about that?"

"I think the crook who bought it got cheated."

"Your salary is forty-two thousand a year. Your car costs forty-seven plus tax. I spend many times that on annual fees to golf courses around the world."

"I don't play golf."

"What do you play?"

"Mind games with killers."

"Would you play them on my behalf for a salary of five thousand a week? Off the books, if you like."

"That's a lot of money to sweep under the rug."

"I have an excellent accountant."

"Would he be there when I went to confession?"

"Perhaps you could use my parish priest. He's notoriously broad-minded."

"I'm surprised he's not defrocked."

Sergio laughed. "Every man at my table tonight is Catholic."

"Not my kind of Catholic."

"Your kind is sainthood. I'm asking you to use your

worldly talents to protect a man who admires you immensely."

"I'm listening."

"There's a conference in Mexico City next week. I'd like you to accompany me for the purpose of ensuring I come home alive. For that duty, I'll pay you the amount we discussed. If you find the work amenable, we can continue the arrangement."

"What's the subject of the conference?"

"Protecting archeological treasures."

"Not pharmaceutical?"

"I don't deal in drugs."

"Your friends do."

"As do many of the men you associate with."

"My purpose isn't to assist them."

"Neither is mine. I'm pursuing goals that are independent of theirs but require the umbrella of their organizations. Much like a rider on an insurance policy. An innocuous addendum which seemingly would take effect only in disaster, though in reality it's the advent of that disaster I'm banking on."

"You're gonna have to be more specific."

"Come, come, Detective. I'm offering you a lucrative moonlighting job while you're on suspension. If at the end of the week you're convinced you can abide my employ, I'll apprise you fully of my endeavors. Surely that's fair."

"Your endeavors must be illegal or you'd apprise me now."

Sergio tched. "Many instances of skirting the law are more moral than following it to the letter. I know of one young man who escaped the consequences of murder because his uncle decided justice lay with the boy rather than the law." He swirled his cognac. "Elise Truxal is a true beauty, don't you think?"

Devon managed to say, "She's underage."

"Not in Mexico. Which is where she is. In my apartment in the Zona Rosa, pining for me right now." He smiled ruefully. "Unless she's out spending my money."

"Does her mother know where she is?"

"Oh yes. She's of the old school."

"You're a sonofabitch," Devon muttered.

"On the contrary, I'm considering marrying Elise. You see, I have no heir, and she obviously carries exceptional genes."

"Does she know about your proclivity for razorblades?"

"Not yet. Would you like to tell her?"

Devon stood up. "When are you leaving?"

"Monday afternoon."

"I'll let you know." He started for the door.

"Prairie has my number."

Devon turned back, nudged with dread.

Sergio smiled. "She's someone else hoping for an heir. It's a pity, don't you think, that God made us so we need a partner to procreate?" He finished his cognac and left the snifter behind. "Shall we see what's become of your nephew?"

At one-thirty, Devon and Eric were walking across the gravel parking lot of the Range Rider Saloon, the raucous country music from inside discordant under the stars.

Eric said eagerly, "There's Prairie's Jeep!" Then in a more subdued tone, "You won't tell her I dropped my Coke on Sergio's patio, will you?"

Devon shook his head as he opened the door to be hit with a blast of deafening music. Unlike the last time he had been there, the barn-like structure was packed. Couples swayed on the floor, single men lined the bar, and the booths were filled with mostly women who had come with girlfriends. As soon as he had paid the cover charge and had his hand stamped with a purple bucking bronco, he looked up and met Prairie's eyes through the congestion of smoke.

Winding his way through the crowd toward her booth, he noted the woman with her was pretty, with long blond hair and brown eyes. Like Prairie, she was watching him and Eric approach.

Eric quickened his pace and beat Devon there. Prairie slid over to let Eric sit down, so Devon sat beside the other woman just as the music stopped. Prairie introduced them. Cynthia's eyes were frankly curious about Devon and gently amused with Eric. Both women were drinking Lone Star.

When the band started another song, Eric asked Prairie to dance. Devon watched them walk onto the floor. Cynthia leaned close and asked if he would dance with her. He stood up and held her hand to lead her through the crowd, then slid his arm around her waist as they began the Cotton Joe Shuffle.

Cynthia had the moves down smooth, though at first she seemed surprised he knew the Cotton Joe. They fell into a reciprocal rhythm of parting and coming together, shifting hands when she twirled under his arm, matching strides as they shuffled around the circle, taking two steps back and starting all over again.

Devon guessed her age to be right around thirty, her height five-six, and her weight a hundred and twenty-five. He also suspected she was divorced with children, and that she often spent her Saturday nights picking up men she rarely saw again. He garnered all that from the ease with which she followed his lead, the nonchalance of her flirtatiously close dancing, and the seasoned wisdom behind her eyes. When the band began a slow tune, Cynthia stepped as easily into

Devon's arms as she would any other man's, the opening maneuvers of stylized courtship obviously old hat.

Snuggled close, she smelled of jasmine, one of his favorite scents, and he found himself sliding both arms around her waist as he forgot his present situation and even lost the weight of knowledge accumulated over his years of working homicide. For as long as the music lasted, he was a kid as fresh and clean as the perfume of the woman he held with an intimacy transcending who they were in the light of day. When the song ended, they met each other's eyes knowing they had shared something special in the hungry heat of a crowded saloon. Feeling more than a tinge of regret, they returned to the couple who made what had happened complicated when otherwise their next step would have been so simple he could have led her out the door and driven her to his motel without either of them saying a word.

The band began packing their instruments and last call was announced as he and Cynthia sat down. Prairie's eyes were sharp, looking back and forth between them.

Eric asked, "Where'll we go now?"

"Why not my place for a beer?" Prairie suggested, looking at Devon.

"All right," he answered.

Eric piped up, "Can I drive your Jeep, Prairie?"

She watched Devon, obviously waiting for an invitation to go with him.

"I'll bring Cynthia," he said.

Prairie's head jerked in one abrupt nod.

Cynthia had the grace to ask, "Is that all right with you, Prairie?"

She shrugged with apparent indifference. "Let's go, Eric."

When they were gone, Devon asked Cynthia, "How do you feel?"

"Like I'm walking on eggs."

He smiled. "You're light on your feet."

Her laughter was a purr from deep in her throat that made him want to taste the sound coming out of her mouth. She licked her lips, watching him, and it was his turn to laugh.

Chapter Fourteen

Prairie's house was brightly lit when Devon drove in. She and Eric were sitting on the porch sipping beers. Walking across the yard with Cynthia, Devon frowned at seeing there wasn't any space on the swing between Eric and Prairie. Eric misinterpreted the frown.

"Aw, come on, Uncle Devon, I can handle one beer. 'Sides, I'm not driving again tonight."

The implication created such a strained silence that Eric laughed with embarrassment. "I mean I don't have my car, so I'll be going back with you, won't I?"

"I'm leaving pretty quick."

"You're not staying for a beer?" Prairie asked.

"No, but I want to talk to you." He held out his hand. "Let's take a walk."

Her Appaloosa and pinto watched them approach the corral. Devon put his elbow on the top rail and faced Prairie, who leaned with her back to the fence. He kissed her cheek.

"That's from J.C."

"I'm always glad to have a kiss from him, but I was hoping for a different kind of one from you, Devon."

"Things have changed."

She looked back toward the house. "Boy, that Cynthia."

"It has nothing to do with her."

"I saw the way you were dancing. You do that with every gal you meet?"

"Why is it a woman always picks a fight when a man's trying to tell her something important?"

"Well, damn, Devon! After this afternoon, I thought . . ."

"This afternoon I was drunk."

She stood up straight and confronted him head-on. "I knew you were gonna say that! I would've bet my boots on it."

"Prairie, calm down and listen to me."

She flopped back against the fence. "I'm listening."

"Sergio offered me a job. I've decided to take it."

She stared in disbelief.

"I'm doing it 'cause there's a girl involved I feel partly responsible for."

"How old is she?"

"Sixteen."

"Is she pretty?"

He nodded. "J.C. said something tonight that hit home."

"What he'd say?"

"That to be with you while working for Sergio would be like putting a rattlesnake in a nest of songbirds. But I don't think it's just Sergio."

She stomped her foot in the dust. "I ain't no baby bird! And I'd shoot any snake poking its nose into my nest."

"That's what I mean. You've already killed one man 'cause I dragged you into a case that without me you wouldn't have been anywhere near."

"I'm proud of killing Jay Lehrer! That was a damn fine shot, and he deserved it sure as hell."

"You're right," Devon said, deciding not to mention killing Carl on her behalf. "Lehrer did deserve it. And it was the best shot I've ever seen."

A tremor ran down her body as she blinked back tears.

"But if it happens again anytime soon," he said gently,

"you're apt to lose your badge for being a little too quick on the trigger. What would you do then?"

"Maybe I'd find me a man to bring home the bacon 'stead of one who's always dumping a can of worms on my head!"

"Prairie, stop it. Can't you see I'm trying to protect you?"

"I don't need protection from Sergio! I grew up with him! Reckon I know my range better'n you!"

"It's my range I'm talking about."

She sniffed. "Oh, go on and save your little nymph from his razorblades. But if you fuck Cynthia, Devon, I swear to God I'll forget I ever loved you."

He smiled and pulled her close. "You never said you loved me. I thought all you wanted was my sperm."

"Well, shoot," she mumbled against his shirt, "you think I'd want it if I didn't like the whole package?"

He kissed her the way she wanted to be kissed, then disentangled himself and walked away.

"Let's go, Eric," he shouted across the yard. "Good night, Cynthia."

"Good night," she called, a question in her voice.

He was turning the ignition when Eric jumped in and slammed the door.

"Holy shit! I thought you didn't care if I made a move on Prairie."

"I changed my mind." Nosing the Lexus out of her yard, he glanced at Eric. "That okay with you?"

"Yeah, sure." He shrugged unhappily. "I mean, she's a helluva woman and I like her a lot, but . . ."

Devon accelerated onto the highway. "But what?"

"I've always felt proud of how the men in our family play it as a team, and I don't want to be the one who drops the ball."

Devon gave him a smile. "How do you feel about spending

207

spring break in Mexico City?"

"Sounds great!"

"There's a catch."

"Figures. What is it?"

"Elise Truxal."

Eric looked away, his face suddenly hollow with hurt.

"We're gonna try'n get her out of there without putting her back in your bed. Think we can do that?"

"Whose bed are we gonna get her out of?"

"Sergio's."

Eric met his eyes. "I'm good, but I don't know if I'm that good, Uncle Devon."

"Sure you are." He laughed with a wink.

Watching the swarthy face of Sergio Tierrasantas through the bars of the cell, Jack Greco wanted to believe his luck was finally taking a turn for the better, but it was hard to grasp in jail. Sergio's voice droned on, throwing out a sales pitch.

The cop had called him, he said, so it was all set. In two days, the woman would be alone for a week. Sergio didn't want her hurt badly, just scared out of her wits so she would turn in her badge, maybe run to El Paso and hide out under the cop's protection for the rest of her life. By the time the cop got back, Jack would be in Miami. Sergio had the plane ticket all ready. He showed it to Jack. The ticket and a thousand dollars to kick start his new life. Sergio even had connections in Miami who might throw a little work Jack's way, if he proved himself able.

In the meantime, Sergio droned on, jail was the best place for him. If the sheriff let him out now and the woman got word of it, she might call the cop back. After all, Jack had assaulted a Texas Ranger. That was a felony. This way, after the cop couldn't be called back, the sheriff would confuse the paperwork so it looked like his deputy screwed up and let Jack loose by mistake. In three days, Sergio would ditch the cop in Mexico City, come home and check on Jack's progress, pay him if the job was done, then fly back to Mexico without the cop knowing he had been gone. Until then, Jack had a bunk and three hot meals a day, a shower he might consider using, unless he meant to traumatize the woman with how bad he smelled. Sergio laughed. Jack smiled. The deal was set.

"Plenty of cops work private security," Devon said.

"I don't like it," Dreyfus growled. They were sitting in his office in El Paso, heavy sunlight slanting through the blinds. "I told you to go fishing. You come back with this."

"I caught something."

"Tierrasantas isn't a fish, he's a whale. Even if you manage to reel him in, Presidio County's not your beat."

"It's Prairie's."

"So what're you doing? Using her as a beard to expand your jurisdiction?"

"If we stumble across a crime coming down in Austin, we let them make the arrest. What's the difference?"

"You sleeping with any cops in Austin?"

"I'm not sleeping with her, either. That part's over."

They stared at each other across the dust dancing in the sunbeams.

"Okay," Dreyfus grumbled. "But watch your step, Devon. I sure as shit don't want to go to your funeral."

Devon caught the freeway west to the North Mesa exit, turned left on Osborne, right on Teramar, and left again on Ripley. Pulling up to the loading dock of Great River, Inc., a small company manufacturing couplings, he saw his brother talking to a man in a suit. Devon got out and stood leaning against the front fender of his Lexus, its black finish now obscured beneath dust and its hood pocked with the pellets from Carl Lowdy's shotgun.

Connie finished with his boss and sauntered over with a wry grin, embarrassed to have been caught working. "When'd you get home?"

"Coupla hours ago, but I'm leaving again."

"Going back to the sweetness 'tween Prairie's boots?"

Devon laughed. "I came out here to talk about Eric."

Connie's face fell. "He fuck up again?"

"Just the opposite. I've got a short job working private security in Mexico City and I'd like to take him along, but I wanted to clear it with you first."

"What's Eric say?"

"He wants to come."

"Then there's no problem, bro."

"Yeah, there is. The man I'll be working for had me investigated before offering the job. One of the things he came up with is that I let Eric skate last year."

Connie frowned. "How'd he find out?"

"Elise Truxal's his mistress."

"Shit. Maybe you oughta stay clear of this, Devon."

"No, what we gotta do is make sure she quits talking."

"How you gonna do that?"

"I'm not. Eric is."

Connie nodded. "I'm catching on."

"I told him I wanted to pull this off without putting her back in his bed, but I'm not sure that's possible."

"Meaning?"

"Right now she's being kept by Sergio Tierrasantas, a millionaire several times over. If we buy her with anything short of true love, we're condemning ourselves to blackmail by a bitch for the rest of our lives."

"I knew it was too easy last year."

"You with me on this?"

"Damn straight."

From the cabin of Sergio's private plane, Mexico was a vast wilderness of uninhabited mountains beneath a dark sky. Devon marveled at how empty the country was. From Texas, it seemed crammed with a horde of refugees pushing against the border. And the border cities were crowded, but the country itself was wild and empty.

Mexico City was different. Ten million people lived in the valley nestled within mountains reaching to the clouds. Some of the inhabitants camped in caves on the outskirts, others occupied buildings originally constructed by the Conquistadores and barely improved in the intervening centuries. Yet it was one of the cosmopolitan cities of the world, its resplendent avenues and gracious parks overlaying the brutality of Toltec magnificence.

Riding the subway from the airport to downtown, Devon saw pre-Columbian relics embedded in the tunnels. Antiquities discovered during excavation and left entombed, they intermittently emerged from the dark: brightly-lit mosaics of broad-faced men wearing earrings and intricately executed ritual sacrifices flashed between long stretches of black void as the underground train hurtled through a graveyard of art.

At the Zocalo station, Devon and Eric followed Sergio up an escalator to the immense empty plaza between the governmental palace and the national cathedral, then into a taxi to Sergio's apartment in the Zona Rosa. The streets were alive with vehicles and pedestrians, the ancient buildings crowding close to the sidewalks, a plethora of multi-colored lights softly aglow beneath the night sky. After ascending in an elevator to the twentieth floor of a modern high-rise that Devon doubted was earthquake proof, Sergio led them down a long, austere corridor, unlocked a door, and walked in first.

The apartment was furnished with the understated splendor of a fine hotel, everything obviously expensive but lacking personality. Devon and Eric waited in the living room as Sergio went into the bedroom. They heard the murmur of voices, then Sergio returned and nodded at a door behind them.

"The guestroom is there," he said. "Please, make yourselves comfortable. I have a phone call to get out of the way, then we'll all go to dinner." He turned around and left them alone.

The guestroom was furnished with two single beds covered with yellow satin spreads on either side of a night table holding a yellow ceramic lamp with a white fringed shade, a corner mahogany table flanked by delicate Italian provincial chairs, and a matching bureau. Adjoining the room was a commodious bath with black and gold fixtures. Eric closed the door and murmured uneasily, "Pretty posh, isn't it, Uncle Devon?"

He nodded. "I think you should drop the uncle. No sense advertising we're any more'n partners on this job."

Eric smiled. "Hope I don't let you down."

"You won't. Are you ready to see Elise?"

"Guess I won't know 'til I see her."

"Let's do it, then."

They returned to the living room. Furnished with more mahogany and satin, it was a formal parlor. Devon peeked into a minuscule kitchen, then walked the length of the room to lift the drapes and look out the window. Except for a sliver of city visible past the corner of the next building, the view was of a brick wall. He figured that made sense for someone who didn't care to be seen, but wondered how Elise liked being so completely shut in. Hopefully she hated it.

He heard the slither of silk a second before she came in from the bedroom. She stopped dead still, staring at Eric. Her dress was a china blue sheath on her familiar statuesque figure, and her hair falling to her waist was still the platinum blond Devon remembered, but her blue eyes contained no trace of the innocence he had seen there before. Surrounded by adept smudges of blue and gray shadow, they simmered with the savvy of an experienced whore. Yet her lips trembled, as if she wanted to say things she couldn't let herself as she met Eric's eyes.

He was standing with apparent nonchalance, his hands in the pockets of his trousers, his best jacket sloping casually behind his wrists, his face set in a facade of cool indifference Devon knew he was working hard to achieve. She looked at Devon, her eyes puzzled now, her mouth closed in a pout he found charming despite knowing she had the heart of a steel trap.

Sergio came in and said with a supercilious chuckle, "I think you all know each other."

"You should've told me," she whispered.

"And spoil your surprise?" He cast an amused gaze around their faces. "Are we hungry?"

They rode the elevator down in silence. On the sidewalk, a dark mist floated in the air as a uniformed chauffeur opened the door to a black Cadillac limousine waiting at the curb. Devon and Eric sat on the jump seats in front of Sergio and Elise. She kept her face turned away, watching the streets shimmering with oily rainbows. Eric stared out the opposite side, though Devon hoped their thoughts were on each other. Sergio looked straight ahead, either deep in contemplation or hoping to give that impression.

The restaurant in Chapultepec Park was called Del Lago,

its dining room a series of descending mezzanines over-looking the lake. As soon as everyone had ordered drinks, Sergio excused himself to make more phone calls. Devon followed him up the tiers and into a corridor with a dozen telephone booths encased in glass. Halfway through the door of one, Sergio turned back. "Your presence isn't necessary, Devon."

"Damn hard to guard a body I can't see."

"I'll let you know when you're needed."

"No dice. Either I call the shots or I'm on my way home."

Sergio slowly blinked, then went in and shut the door.

Devon leaned against the opposite wall watching everyone who approached, all men en route to the lavatory at the end of the hall. The only other person using a phone, a man who had left an empty booth between himself and Sergio, seemed unhappy with his conversation while Sergio chatted and laughed as if flirting with a woman. Devon looked back toward the dining room, hoping Eric was taking advantage of his time alone with Elise.

Eric was trying to do that, though he felt tongue-tied. Elise kept her gaze on the room at large as she drank her *cuba libre* through a straw. Her pursed lips made Eric remember how well she kissed, and the chiseled planes of her face brought back memories of the hours he had spent admiring her in bed.

When he finally managed to force words out of his mouth, they didn't sound as nonchalant as he had hoped. "What're you doing here, Elise?"

She met his eyes. "What're *you* doing here, Eric?"

"I'm working for Devon."

"Who's he working for?"

"Sergio."

"So am I," she answered with a shrug.

"That makes you a whore."

"By working for Sergio, Devon's selling his integrity as much as I am. Maybe more, 'cause I like Sergio and it's obvious Devon doesn't."

"What's integrity mean?" Eric asked, baiting her.

"Conducting yourself in an honorable manner," she said.

"So by being with Sergio you're not being honorable?"

"You're twisting my words."

"You said you're selling your integrity."

"I said I'm doing it less than your uncle is."

"Maybe he has his own reasons for being here."

"Maybe I do, too."

"What are they?"

She stared at him in silence.

He smiled. "I'm taking an ethics course in college. It's taught me how to ask questions."

"You're going to college?"

He nodded. "I thought that was something you wanted to do."

"I gave up a lot of dreams," she said sharply, "after you ditched me."

"I never ditched you!"

"You never called."

"I called lots of times. Your mom always said you weren't home, but I figured you just didn't want to talk to me."

She hid her eyes as she sipped rum and coke through her straw.

"Seemed to me," Eric said, "that since I'd done your dirty work, you didn't want me around anymore."

She met his eyes. "Mom sent me to stay with my aunt and uncle in Missouri. She never told me you called."

"Why didn't you call me?"

She looked out the window at the lake shimmering under

spot lights. "I promised not to."

"Promised who?"

"Devon."

"What're you talking about?"

"He said if I wanted him to get you out of that mess last year, I had to promise not to see you again."

He stared at her.

She shrugged, looking away.

"You should've told me," he said.

"I thought it was what you wanted, too."

"It wasn't."

She shrugged again.

"How'd you hook up with Sergio?"

"I met him in a mall in St. Louis. I was admiring a dress in a window, and he came up and asked if I'd like to have it."

"So you let him buy it for you?"

"No." She smiled at Sergio coming back. "Not right then."

Eric winced, then cast his puzzled gaze at Devon.

Since she hadn't heard a car, Prairie assumed the person knocking on her front door was probably a wetback looking for work. Fresh from the river, illegal aliens often stopped by on their way north. They were humble, harmless people who had never given her any trouble.

Seeing Jack Greco on her porch, she wondered why he wasn't in jail, but only for a second. Then his fist slammed against her face, snapping her head back so she heard bones crack in her neck. His other fist drove into her stomach, staggering her away from him. He followed to hit her three more times as she stumbled backward across the floor.

He kicked her feet out from under her and dropped his weight on top, his knees nailing her to the floor as he unbuckled her gunbelt, yanked it off, and threw it against the wall. She heard it hit, then felt his fists on her face again, bouncing her head on the floor until she passed out.

Devon was lying, still dressed, on one of the beds in Sergio's guestroom, his hands clasped behind his head as he waited for his turn in the bath. When Eric came out and sat down at the foot of the other bed, Devon knew from the kid's expression that he had a bone to pick. "What's up?"

Eric's eyes glimmered with anger but he kept his voice low as he said, "Last year when all that came down, don't you think it was kinda high and mighty of you to tell Elise not to see me again?"

Having known this was apt to come up, Devon said, "I was running a risk by letting the two of you skate, so I figured that gave me some rights."

"She didn't kill her father. What'd you let *her* skate from?"

"I think her complicity went a little deeper'n you're willing to admit."

Eric shook his head. "It was an accident. A chain of events that got out of hand."

"She's the only one who benefited from it." Devon sat up, put his feet on the floor and leaned closer with his elbows on his knees. "I'm trained to look at motives, Eric, and you didn't have one."

"I was protecting her."

"No, you came out of that closet blind and fired in an instinctive act of self-defense. But Truxal wasn't threatening you. And even though he may have been heavy-handed, he had a legal right to punish his daughter. Of the three people in that room, she was the only one with criminal intent."

Eric's frown deepened. "If that's how you feel, what're we doing here?"

"She told Sergio that I jimmied the case to keep you out of it."

It took a minute for Eric to put it together. "Could you go to jail?"

"Yeah. So could you and your father."

The confusion in Eric's eyes was painful. "What do you want me to do?"

"Marry her."

Eric snorted. "I don't have much to offer compared to Sergio's money."

"Money's one thing. Abuse is another."

"What do you mean?"

"He's a sexual sadist."

"You mean he's hurting her right now?"

"Maybe."

Eric looked at the door. "Why don't we go over there and stop it?"

"All we'll accomplish is getting ourselves kicked out. Odds are tomorrow you'll have more time alone with her."

Eric looked at him.

"Our success demands you keep a cool head. Think you can do it?"

Eric sighed, then nodded.

Prairie came to naked and dazed. She tried to stand up, then gagged as pain swept through her body, stabbing her spine as if with a knife. Her hands were numb, her knees and elbows raw, her head aching with agony. She was on the floor, handcuffed to something heavy.

For a moment, she thought she was blind, then saw a gleam off the steel shackles attached to the bed. A flicker of light, that was all. So she was in her bedroom, and it was night. Exploring her mouth with her tongue, she found where her left canine was broken off jagged, and she remembered the face behind the fists: Jack Greco.

She pulled against the shackles, making them clink, metal on metal, the chain through the brass filigree. The footboard was one piece, so even if she managed to get the bed apart, she would be dragging the footboard and two posts. At the other end was her phone on a table. She could see the red light of her answering machine. Not the light itself but its dim glow in the dark. She moved.

Pain ricocheted down her spine. She sucked air, let it out slowly, took another deep breath, and slid onto her side parallel to the bed, stretching her feet toward the phone. When her toes touched a table leg, she angled one foot behind it and tugged the table closer. The leg scraped on the bare wood beneath it. She stopped to listen, then heard him snore.

Asleep. In the living room. Probably on the couch. She tugged the table closer, reached her toes up and pushed against its bottom. The lamp fell first, breaking the bulb, then the phone slid off to crash on the floor, its bell jangling.

She heard his footsteps and the door bang open before the overhead light came on, blinding her. When her vision returned, he was standing above her, his dark eyes cruel. He picked up the phone and held the receiver to her ear. The line was dead. Satisfied, he dropped the phone on top of her, turned off the light, and slammed the door on his way out.

She shook the phone off her belly, its bell again ringing as it hit the floor. She waited for him to come back. When he didn't, she again stretched her legs under the table, tipping it all the way over this time. She tried to roll out of its way, but the answering machine fell on her knees. Ignoring the pain, she dumped the machine on the floor.

The table lay on its side. She reached with her toes to grasp the knob and slide the drawer toward her. Her foot cramped and she had to stop and put weight on it, then try again. As she slid the drawer open, its contents spilled to the floor, but by the flutter of their falling she knew he had taken her gun.

She fell back in frustration, her mind momentarily mired in despair. Summoning her gumption, she used her feet to fumble through the things spilled from the drawer until she found a pen and a flyer advertising a Cajun band that had played at the Range Rider the month before. Picking up the pen with her toes, she clumsily printed a message on the back of the flyer:

Jack Greco here 3-8 raped/ beat me, think he'll kill me. Get the SOB!

P. Drake TX Rgr

With her toes, she slid the flyer under the small rug beside the bed, then flopped the rug back smooth. For a moment she took comfort from knowing she would be avenged. It wasn't much, but something. In the end, though, not enough.

She remembered her gun case against the far wall. Inside were five rifles. The key was on top. The case was too heavy to tip over, would probably kill her if it fell on her head. She could throw something, maybe the answering machine, and break the glass door. But even if she managed to touch a rifle with her toes, she couldn't get it into position, not with her feet, before he heard the glass breaking and came back.

The digital clock on her answering machine read 12:42 a.m. But the date was March 10! She had lost a whole day! It was Wednesday. On Monday morning, Devon had called her from El Paso to say he was leaving for Mexico City and would try to call again on Wednesday night. Would her phone sound as if it were ringing? Or would he know the line had been cut? Probably he would think she had accidentally left it off the hook. He'd wait and try again.

Why was Greco out of jail? If he escaped, she would have been notified. When the sheriff couldn't reach her by phone, he would try the radio in her Jeep. When that didn't raise an answer, someone would come looking. How long had Greco been free? It was dusk when she opened the door Monday night. So he hadn't escaped. The jailer would have missed him at supper and an APB would have been issued. He had been released. Why? It didn't matter. All that did was that she couldn't assume anyone would help her. Devon couldn't get here in time, even if he knew. But he wouldn't call for hours yet. Wouldn't suspect anything when he did call. Would simply try again later, if he wasn't too busy.

She yanked her hands against the cuffs, deepening the bruises on her wrists. What was Greco waiting for? He had both her handguns, the keys to her Jeep, her money and credit cards. Why wasn't he gone? How had he known where she lived? Could it have been a coincidence that the house he chose to rob was hers? Not likely. Someone told him. Maybe even sent him. That's what he was waiting for: his payoff. Did that mean he wouldn't kill her? Again, not likely. He had been booked into two county jails, maybe not photographed and fingerprinted in Jeff Davis but definitely in Presidio. After this, his apprehension would be top priority. Cops took care of their own. She was one of them. Even dead.

Devon shadowed Sergio to a morning meeting at the anthropological museum. Although admitting his Spanish was limited, he couldn't catch any hint that the discussion strayed off the stated subject of archeological treasures. The men he had met at the ranch—Calderon, Terrazas, and del Soltana—were there, each with his own bodyguard, and several other participants had backup too, so the perimeter of the room was lined with men wearing concealed weapons and assessing each other with amused forbearance. Devon felt like a hypocrite, flaunting his willingness to protect a man he despised. He also knew a bodyguard who hated his boss wasn't worth much, and wondered why Sergio trusted him. Growing in his mind was a nudging suspicion that he had been lured to Mexico merely as a ploy to get him out of Chinati. But whatever Sergio was hoping to achieve in Presidio, Devon's first priority was getting Elise back to El Paso.

Strolling with her through the Olmec Room, watching the smooth heads carved of massive boulders stare back at him with blind eyes, Eric whispered, "Don't you think they're creepy?"

"They can't hear you," Elise answered in a normal voice.

"I'm not so sure. Doesn't seem they're real happy being stuck in a museum with people staring at 'em all day."

"They come from the jungle, you know."

"I bet they miss the birds."

She looked at him curiously. "I do. There aren't many here, you know."

"Why not?"

"The smog kills them."

They walked into another room displaying a model of the pyramid at Chichen Itza.

"I miss the doves most of all," she said. "I used to wake up in the mornings and hear them calling to each other from the trees outside my bedroom window."

"I remember that window."

She met his eyes, then looked away again. "Why did Devon take this job? Isn't he a detective anymore?"

"He's on suspension."

She laughed. "Like in school?"

He nodded.

"What'd he do?"

"It was just a series of events that got out of hand." He watched her closely. "Like what happened with you and me."

They walked into a room whose walls were covered with friezes from Tenochitlán. When she stopped before a stone carving of a man wearing an elaborate feather headdress, Eric asked, "Do you ever think about how we used to be?"

She moved away to stand in front of a mural of farmers throwing seeds on ground irrigated with blood flowing from a sacrificial table. Eric thought the mural was morbid. Taking hold of her elbow, he guided her into a corridor streaming with light through a glass-brick wall. He met her eyes when he said, "Devon told me Sergio's a sadist. It drives me crazy to think of him hurting you."

She lowered her lashes.

"Why do you want that, Elise?"

She turned to look out the wall of glass bricks, though she couldn't see anything through them but light.

Behind her, he said, "Come home with me."

She laughed sadly. "Devon would never let that happen."

"It was his idea. That's why we're here."

She faced him, her beauty taking his breath. "You came all this way to save me from Sergio?"

He nodded.

"Why?"

" 'Cause I still love you."

"Do you?" She seemed pleased.

"Devon took a big risk, getting me out of what happened last year. Now Sergio's using it against us. Are you gonna let him?"

She bit her lip. "I'm the one who told him."

Eric nodded. "Let's put all that behind us for good."

"How?" she scoffed.

"Get married."

"Was that Devon's idea, too?"

"I'm the one who's in love with you. I'll be good to you, Elise. Devon will, too. So will my parents and sister. We're a tight family. We take care of each other in ways you probably can't imagine, coming from the family you did. I don't like talking against 'em, but I don't think they taught you what it really means to love someone. Me and my family can teach you that, and I'll do everything I can to see you're happy."

She watched him, her beauty making him dizzy.

He slid his arms around her waist. "Say yes," he whispered.

"Can I take the jewelry Sergio gave me?"

"Why not?"

She laughed. "Then I say yes."

Riding a rush of adrenalin, he led her toward the nearest exit. "We'll go to the apartment to get your stuff," he said, flagging down a taxi, "then I'll take you to the airport and put you on a plane." He looked at her in the bright sun. "Will you do that, Elise? Go home and wait for me?"

"Where's home?" she asked, frowning.

"My father's place, though it was really my grandfather's. He left it to Devon, but we all live there now."

"I'm not keen on walking in someplace I've never been and telling people I've never met that I belong there."

"I'll call and tell 'em you're coming. It'll be okay."

A taxi stopped. After hesitating, she got in. Eric followed her and gave the driver Sergio's address. Elise looked scared. As the taxi accelerated into traffic, Eric put his arm around her shoulders and pulled her close. "It'll be okay," he said again. "As my wife, you'll be part of the family."

"I'm not your wife yet."

He took a deep breath. "You want to get married here?"

"Right now?"

"I've got three hundred dollars in my pocket. Any priest'll perform a marriage for that. All we gotta do is find a church."

"How'll you pay for my plane ticket?"

"Devon gave me his Visa card."

She sat up and studied him a moment. "He must trust you."

"I told you we're a tight family. Trusting each other is part of that."

"Will you trust me? Even knowing all I've done, with Sergio and all?"

"None of that'll matter anymore."

She sighed, settling against him again. "It sounds too good to be true, Eric."

He leaned toward the driver and said, "Take us to the closest church."

Laura answered the phone. She hadn't been happy to learn Devon was taking Eric to Mexico City, and her first thought at hearing her son's voice was that they were in trouble. She didn't feel any better as she listened to what he was saying, but she agreed to pick up Elise at the airport. Other than that, Laura kept quiet, not wanting him to suspect she doubted his wisdom in marrying the girl. If it was already done, the family would make the best of it.

She had never met Elise, but she knew Eric had accidentally killed the girl's father and Devon had shuffled the deck to keep him out of jail. Connie told her the whole story, including that Devon made the girl promise not to see Eric again. Although it hurt Laura to watch Eric struggling to cope with what he thought was Elise's rejection, she agreed that no good was likely to come from their seeing each other.

Wondering what had changed, she called and told Connie what was happening. He spoke to her from the phone on the loading dock, so she knew his words were guarded for fear of being overheard. What he did say was that she should treat the girl with kid gloves because it was vital to the family that they made Elise happy. Reading between the lines, she decided she suddenly had a daughter-in-law because the men wanted Elise under their control. Their shenanigans may have achieved that, but Laura knew the work of maintaining it would fall largely on her.

So she drove to the airport and waited for the flight from Mexico City. When she saw the blond beauty come off the plane looking lost, Laura hurried over to give the girl a hug, then kissed her on the cheek and said, "Welcome to the family, Elise."

Elise looked at Laura's belly, ponderous in the eighth month of pregnancy, and Laura could see that the girl was contemplating her future with less than joy. Laura laughed and said, "I figured if I was gonna stay home all the time, I may as well have another baby."

"How many kids do you have?"

"This will be our third."

Elise sighed with relief. "I thought maybe you had ten or twelve, being Catholic."

"We're not that Catholic."

"I'm not Catholic at all," she replied. "And I sure don't want a passel of kids hanging on me."

"Yes, well," Laura said, forcing a smile, "you and Eric have plenty of time to think about that." She bit her tongue against saying that, at sixteen and eighteen, they were still kids themselves.

Walking to the baggage terminal, Laura couldn't help

thinking Elise's dress had probably cost more than Connie earned in a week, confirming her suspicion that they were in trouble. When she saw the expensive luggage Elise took off the ramp, suitcases easily worth the price of a good used car, Laura knew the trouble was deep.

Chapter Fifteen

Devon and Sergio returned to the apartment to find Eric alone. Sergio glanced toward the bedroom, then asked Eric, "Did Elise get another one of her headaches?"

He shook his head. "She went home."

Sergio walked to the bedroom and opened the door.

Devon gave Eric a small smile of congratulation. Though he wished the kid had left with her, he admired his nephew for sticking around to face Sergio's wrath.

Sergio came back. "Where is she?"

"In El Paso by now," Eric answered, standing up.

Sergio studied him, then looked at Devon. "What have you done with her?"

"He didn't do anything," Eric said. "I married Elise in Tlatelolco, then sent her home."

With his usual aplomb, Sergio laughed, though his eyes were dark with anger as he turned back to Devon. "So you've tucked the little bird under your wing to keep her from singing."

Devon smiled. "I'm not one to stand in the way of love."

"Especially when it keeps you out of prison."

"That's a goal any intelligent man would try to achieve."

"Do you realize," Sergio asked Eric, "that what you think is love in actuality is your uncle's Machiavellian plot?"

"I wouldn't want to see him with only one ear."

Sergio paled beneath his swarthy skin. He crossed the

room and took down a painting of a Brahman bull, revealing a wall safe. As he quickly twisted the dial and opened the safe, Devon frowned at Eric, hoping the kid hadn't overplayed their hand. Eric smiled with cocky confidence, which didn't reassure Devon. Sergio slammed the safe shut and glared at them both.

"What's missing?" Devon asked.

"A jewel box containing family heirlooms."

"Elise said you gave 'em to her," Eric said.

"I'm afraid you've taken on a woman who far outranks you in duplicity," Sergio drawled. "I sincerely wish you luck in keeping her happy, but whether you succeed or not, I want the jewelry back."

Eric stood his ground. "You can't take back what you gave away."

"Mexico is under Napoleonic law," Sergio said, "which means a man is guilty until proven otherwise. Since you've admitted taking the jewels, your innocence is nonexistent, so unless you relish picking maggots out of your flesh while waiting for a trial that won't happen, I suggest you leave now."

Devon said softly, "Go pack our bags, Eric."

"They're already packed."

"Then get 'em and wait outside."

Looking only slightly chastened, Eric walked into the bedroom. Devon and Sergio watched each other until the kid had come out with the luggage and left them alone.

As soon as the door closed, Sergio said, "I congratulate you, Detective, on recognizing that I do not make idle threats. Shall I assume this was your intention from the start?"

"I intended to take Elise home, no more'n that. You'll get your jewelry back."

"At which point, your family will be safe. If, however, the jewelry is not returned to my ranch before I arrive, I'll play a few games with your niece the mere contemplation of which will turn your stomach."

Devon stared into the cruel dark of Sergio's eyes. "If you touch her, I'll kill you."

"I'm sure you'll try. But if she's as feisty as your nephew, even if you succeed, I'll die happy."

"I guarantee you won't."

Sergio laughed. "Give my regards to your family, Detective."

It took all of Devon's discipline not to smash Sergio's laughter back down his throat.

Eric was waiting in front of the elevator. Devon punched the button with more force than was necessary, then asked, "What was that about an ear?"

"There was one in the safe," Eric answered, trying to maintain his bravado. "Looked like a man's, though it had a gold cross on a stud."

"How'd you get the safe open?"

Eric grinned. "Dad taught me how to listen for the tumblers."

Devon nodded, and Eric turned away from the anger in his eyes.

Prairie could hear her horses whinnying to be fed. She wondered if they had enough water, and if Bandit, her pregnant pinto, needed any special attention. In the front room, Greco was snuffling himself awake, clomping this way and that. She hoped to hear him leave, but he opened her bedroom door and stood looking down at her shackled naked to the bed.

When he came close, she kicked at him, but he caught her ankles and flopped her onto her stomach, then sat on the backs of her knees. She was afraid he would do it again, what she knew he had done before, though mercifully she had no memory of it. Instead, he ran his hand along the curves of her butt, his palm hot and sweaty.

"Jack?" she whispered.

His hand stopped.

"How'd you get out of jail?"

He snorted laughter. "They let me out."

"Who?"

"Dude with the keys."

"Why?"

"Said he was told to."

"Who told him?"

"I didn't ask."

"How'd you know to come here?"

"What is this, twenty questions?"

She squeezed her eyes shut as he caressed her again. Striving to keep her voice calm, she said, "You're in a lot of trouble, you know that, don't you? What you've done is a felony."

"You're the one in trouble! I can do anything I want. Nothing you can do."

"I can help you, Jack."

"You already have. With the money I get, I'll be set up."

"Someone's paying you to do this?"

"Yeah, you! Hundred bucks in your wallet and a coupla credit cards."

"If you let me loose, I'll testify that you could have hurt me again but had second thoughts and decided to make amends."

"None of that's gonna happen. Especially the part about me not hurting you again." He stood up. "Want me to feed your horses?"

She opened her eyes. "Would you?"

"What do I feed 'em?"

"There's hay in the stable. Just take an arm full and drop it over the fence."

He walked toward the door.

"Jack?" She looked over her shoulder and forced a smile. "Thanks."

He shrugged. "No sense making animals suffer just 'cause people are ugly."

She listened to him leave the house, then went to work on the gun case. Once he heard the glass break, she figured she had no more than a minute to get a rifle into position using her feet. It would be a miracle if she did it, but the only chance she had.

She pulled the comforter off the bed, wrapped it around her feet, then stretched her legs toward the case. Wrenching the sore muscles in her back, she kicked her padded feet through the glass. It shattered and fell. She kept kicking at the jagged edges so she wouldn't cut herself when she maneuvered without the blanket. After she had what she hoped was a clear path, she tried for a rifle. The Remington was the only one she kept loaded. Pushing against the stock with her bare toes, she freed the barrel from its cradle and was watching the gun fall toward her when she heard his running footsteps on the porch.

Devon slept in Eric's room that night, caustically amused by the posters of rock bands on the walls. One was of Guns and Roses with red flowers growing from the eye sockets of a skull, the other for a band called Rage Against the Machine. Their poster showed the four musicians running along the white line of a blacktop road, the last young man throwing something back at the camera. Probably a grenade, Devon thought, sipping a beer before going to bed. He wondered what Eric's mindset was to want pictures of death and destruction on his walls. But then life now was different than when Devon came of age, though some things hadn't changed. Despite all the advances in birth control, condoms were still the preferred method.

He hoped Eric was using them with Elise. They were sleeping in the bedroom upstairs, and Devon knew a box of Trojans was in the nightstand because he had kept them there when the room was his. The morning after his first night with Prairie, he had opened the drawer to see the condoms were still there, though he hadn't looked when he could have used one with her. So even before the motel in Chinati, he might have gotten her pregnant.

He finished his beer and turned off the light, then lay flat on his back, rigid with tension. His life lately felt like a runaway train, catapulting from killing Carl Lowdy to breaking-up with Sam, becoming embroiled with Prairie after using her to kill Jay Lehrer, then extricating Elise from Tierrasantas and manipulating Eric into an early marriage. Now he had to take something away from Elise in a confrontation he knew wouldn't be easy when what she needed was to feel she had gained, not lost, by joining the family. Unable to understand how everything had gotten so out of control, he couldn't help wondering if he hadn't set the course himself when he bent the law for Eric's sake.

Early in his career Devon had formulated a theory that murder always snowballs, creating an avalanche of destruction that sweeps everyone involved over a fatal precipice. He wondered if he hadn't dragged his family to the brink of that precipice by not turning in his badge after choosing to protect them instead of upholding the law. If he had turned in his badge, he wouldn't have left Sam alone with her ex-husband, would neither have met Prairie nor tangled with Tierrasantas, and wouldn't have killed Carl Lowdy. Prairie wouldn't have killed Lehrer, and Elise would still be only a memory to Eric. Now they were all in jeopardy, most especially Misty, the one person least capable of defending herself.

In the bare light of dawn, he awoke with the sound of the door clicking shut. Knowing he hadn't missed her knock, he watched Misty come in wearing a brown velvet robe that matched her eyes.

She gave him a tentative smile, testing her welcome. "The TV predicted it might snow last night, but it didn't."

"Late in the year for snow," he said.

"It's still cold, though. Can I get under the covers?"

"I don't think you should."

She lifted them anyway and slid in beside him. He got up on the other side, keeping his back to her as he found his shorts and pulled them on. It *was* cold in the room, and he quickly dove under the covers, tucking them tight for warmth.

"Do you think I haven't seen a naked man, Uncle Devon?"

"Guess I never really thought about it."

"One night the neighbor's dog was barking," she said, snuggling close, "and Daddy came into my room to look out the window. He didn't have anything on but a T-shirt. I pretended to be asleep, but I wasn't."

"You still dating Stone Curtis?" he asked, propping his head on his hand so he could watch her face.

"Yes."

"Have you had sex with him?"

"No," she whispered.

"Good girl." He kissed her forehead, then decided maybe his reward was premature. "Have you had sex with anyone?"

"No. Do I get another kiss?"

He gave her one on the tip of her nose.

"When I'm eighteen and legal, will you have sex with me?"

He met her eyes, such a deep, soft brown, her urchin face so sweet and loveable. "Ask me again when you're eighteen."

"You think I'll forget about it, don't you? But I won't 'cause I'm saving myself for you."

"That's the nicest compliment anyone's ever given me, Misty. But you and me together's not only against the law, it's a mortal sin and always will be, no matter how old you are."

"If two people love each other, what right does the law or the church either one have to keep 'em apart?"

"We can love each other without having sex."

"But I want to do it with you, Uncle Devon. Don't you want to do it with me?"

He figured the simplest answer would be to say no and send her skedaddling. He might have done it, except he needed her to listen to something more important, and he knew she wouldn't if he made her angry. She might even defy him to get even, which could lead her straight into Sergio's hands. So he said, "Sure I do, Misty, but it wouldn't be right."

She laughed. "Just my luck to love a cop. There're plenty of men who would sleep with their niece and not feel bad about it. You know that?"

"Probably better than you."

"I don't know how you stand it, working with those awful people all the time. Do you ever think about not being a cop?"

"All the time."

"Why do you keep doing it then?"

" 'Cause people like you need protection from those awful people. And anyway, you just admitted our having sex would be wrong 'cause it's something awful people do."

"Did I?"

"Think about it."

She sighed. "Life is sure complicated. I wish we could just do what we like and not have to think so much."

"There's something else I want you to think about, Misty."

"What?" she asked, pleased he wanted something from her.

"Sometimes the people I work with get mad at me. They think I've hurt 'em when the truth is they've hurt themselves and I'm just their own meanness catching up. But they don't see it that way, and when they get mad, sometimes they want to hurt me back."

"But you don't let 'em. You're too good at protecting yourself."

"Yeah, that's true, as far as it goes. But once in a while someone figures they can get at me by hurting someone I love."

"Like what happened to Samantha?"

He frowned. "What do you mean?"

"Didn't the killer hurt her to get at you?"

"Who told you that?"

"Nobody."

"Then what makes you think it's what happened?"

"I don't know," she said, wary of his anger.

"You must know, Misty."

"I saw a movie about it once. The killer went after the detective's wife, knowing he'd try'n save her. Isn't that what happened with Sam?"

"The killer was Sam's ex-husband. He would've gone after her regardless of me."

"Oh."

"You don't believe that?"

"I guess, if you say so, but you gotta admit he was pretty nervy going after your girlfriend, even if she was his ex-wife. I mean, most killers would stay away from her just 'cause she was living with a cop, seems to me."

"Okay, he was pretty nervy. But that's not what we're talking about."

"What're we talking about?" she asked, sounding relieved to change the subject.

"You," he said.

"Me?"

"I'm only telling you," he said gently, " 'cause I don't want you going anywhere with someone you don't know."

"I'm not dumb, Uncle Devon. I've been hearing all my life not to go anywhere with strange men."

"It could be a woman, or a kid. They could be a tool working for this man to get you in a helpless position."

"What man?" she whispered, her eyes filling with fear.

"His name doesn't matter, but he takes pleasure in hurting girls your age."

"And he's mad at you?" The fear sharp in her eyes.

He nodded.

She faced him and held on tight. "Let me stay with you, Uncle Devon. That way he couldn't hurt me."

He stroked her hair. "We can't be together every minute, Misty. You have to go to school, and I have to go to work." Feeling her tremble, he said, "I don't want to scare you, just make sure you're careful. This man wants something. I'm gonna give it to him, and that'll be the end of it. But it could happen anytime, with this man or another. If anybody ever hurt you, I'd kill him, but that wouldn't take your hurt away, so it's best to keep it from happening. You're the only one who can do that by staying alert and not letting anybody trick you. Do you understand?"

"Yes," she whispered.

"You gonna be brave?"

She nodded, her face against his chest.

"That's my girl." He kissed her ear. "Isn't it time you got ready for school?"

"Let me stay another minute," she pleaded, hanging on hard.

He held her, too, knowing her world would never be the same.

The door opened and her father stopped on the threshold. For a long moment no one said anything, then Connie asked, "Ain't you going to school today, Misty?"

"Yes," she said in a tiny voice as she slid out of the bed.

Connie stepped aside to let her pass, then closed the door and looked at his brother.

"I didn't touch her," Devon said.

"Jesus, Devon, you think I don't know you better'n that?"

He shrugged. "It's been known to happen in the best of families."

"Not ours."

Devon sat up to lean against the headboard. "I had to tell her something I didn't want to, though."

Connie chuckled. "I've known for a while she's got the hots for you. I didn't say nothing 'cause I figured you could handle it. From the looks of things, you did all right."

"It wasn't that. Sergio Tierrasantas threatened her."

"Threatened Misty?"

Devon nodded. "Elise took some jewelry he wants back. He said if he didn't get it, he'd hurt my niece."

"Where is it?"

"Upstairs, I hope."

Connie reached for the doorknob. "Let's go get it."

"Wait a minute," Devon said, not moving. "I thought you could ask Eric to drive Misty to school this morning so we can talk to Elise while he's gone."

Connie nodded thoughtfully. "With no one on her side, the two of us oughta be able to convince her easy enough."

"Eric wouldn't take her side over his sister's."

"Elise'll put him in the middle, though. This way it'll be over 'fore she can do that."

"And hopefully she won't hold it against him, 'cause the next thing we have to do is get Elise's mother to agree to the marriage. She won't if Elise balks. I figure the four of you can go see her this morning and get her approval."

"Weren't they married in Mexico?"

"A civil ceremony in this country will make sure it's legal. I thought I'd ask Judge Kelton to do it, if that's all right."

Connie nodded. "It'll feel more real if we see it happen. The way it is now, it just seems like Eric brought his girlfriend home."

"In the meantime," Devon said, "tell Laura about Sergio's threat and send her to the school with Eric so she can warn the principal that Misty needs watching. If Elise kicks up a fuss, we'll have to calm her down before they get back."

Connie sighed. "How many times we gonna have to do that, Devon?"

"As often as necessary. The trick is to win her loyalty so she stays 'cause she wants to."

"And we gotta start by taking her jewelry."

Devon nodded.

Before leaving, Laura had told Elise she was wanted downstairs but it still took the girl a long time. When she finally entered the dining room wearing a pink peignoir that Connie figured might have cost as much as the diamond on his wife's wedding ring, he glowered from his end of the table while Devon stood up and offered her coffee.

She shook her head, suspiciously looking back and forth between them.

"Sit down," Devon said, holding a chair for her.

When she was settled, he sat back down, glanced at Connie, then gave her a smile. "How'd you sleep?"

She laughed. "Where's Eric?"

"He took his sister to school," Connie growled.

She studied him a moment. "Is something wrong?"

Devon nodded. "Sergio wants his jewelry back."

"It's mine. He gave it to me."

Devon shrugged. "Said if he doesn't get it, he'll take his disappointment out on Misty."

"Misty's just a kid," she argued. "He wouldn't hurt her."

"Did you see any of those movies he's fond of?"

"Yeah," she answered softly.

"Those girls are just kids."

"He wouldn't do that to her."

"What's to stop him?"

"You!"

"The easiest way is to give the jewelry back."

"Where's Eric?" she demanded.

"I told you," Connie said, his voice heavy with threat. "He took his sister to school 'cause all of a sudden we're worried about her safety. Him as much as the rest of us."

"It isn't fair you do this when he isn't here!"

Devon kept his voice soft. "We didn't want to make him choose between his wife and his sister, which is how we figured you'd set it up. But if you take time to think it through, you'll see the choice isn't between you and Misty, but between us and a box of trinkets."

"Trinkets! That jewelry's worth a fortune! None of you'd

willingly give it up if it were yours."

"None of us," Connie said, "ever associated with the kind of scum who'd threaten a fourteen-year-old girl to get what he wants."

Elise jerked to her feet. "I'm not gonna listen to that for the rest of my life!"

Gently, Devon said, "Sit down, Elise."

"Not until he apologizes."

"The fuck I will!" Connie shouted. "I'm not the one who's wrong!"

To his brother, Devon said, "Tell her you won't mention her past again."

Connie glared at her, then at Devon, then sighed. "Okay, maybe I *was* wrong. We're not dealing with the past here."

She slowly sat back down, looking at Devon. "This isn't fair."

"Sergio's the one set it up. If you'd rather be with him, I suggest you go now before Eric gets home."

She flinched. "You've always tried to keep us apart. I bet you gave him a hard time for marrying me, didn't you?"

"No, I was hoping he would."

"Then why did you say that about me going back to Sergio?"

"We don't want anyone in this family who doesn't want to be here."

"Damn straight," Connie muttered.

She pouted, looking back and forth between them.

"Right now Connie's pissed off," Devon said, " 'cause Misty's been threatened. You don't blame him for that, do you?"

She shook her head.

"As your father-in-law, he'll come around to feeling protective of you. I know you didn't have a good father, Elise, so maybe you can't understand what it's like. In time you'll learn a father isn't an enemy but a friend in your corner. You do this one thing for us and we'll never let you down." He looked at his brother. "Will we, Connie?"

Connie took so long to answer, Elise looked at him too. Finally he said, "Not if you prove you really love Eric."

"I do love Eric, but I don't think he wants me to give up my jewelry. He's the one picked the lock on the safe!"

Connie grinned. "Eric picked the lock?"

Elise looked at him sharply. "He said you taught him how."

Connie glanced sheepishly at Devon. "I just did it in front of him once. Guess he's a quick study."

"As you well know," Devon muttered.

Elise laughed. "You two are a pair." She smiled at her father-in-law. "You should've played it the other way, though. Devon's the tough guy. You're a softie."

"I've been in prison, little lady. Don't call me soft."

"Okay. But if you're tough, Devon's steel."

Devon watched her, wondering what her frivolity meant.

"It's gonna be fun watching you two get old," she said. "You'll probably end up bickering on the porch over a bottle of whiskey while Eric takes care of business."

Prairie raged against the chain holding her in place. Then she tried to take the bed apart, suspecting she was so mad she could smash the whole footboard over Greco's head the next time he came through the door. But the bed was old, the joints welded with time. As she fell limp in defeat, she saw the broken glass littering the floor around the now empty gun case.

Searching for a shard that was long and narrow with a lethal point, she spied one close to the wall. Carefully she extended her feet into the field of sharp slivers, caught the shard she wanted under her toe, and slowly drew the weapon toward her. To figure out how to lift it to her hands without cutting herself was a challenge. If she tried to wedge it between two toes, she might cut them both. He would see the blood, maybe guess what she had done, and keep his distance. She needed to lure him close enough to cut his jugular. Any other wound would only provoke him. Slowly, with excruciating finesse, she worked the shard toward her hands. Her body was jack-knifed around the footpost when he came back. She flopped her legs out from under the bed and twisted around to stare at him standing in the door.

He was smiling. "We got comp'ny."

She looked toward the window, not having heard a car. Maybe whoever it was had arrived on foot, one of his transient friends, someone else who preferred jailhouse sex.

Greco picked her up and threw her on the bed. Her shoulders wrenched at the odd angle of her arms over the top of the footboard, her wrists burning as the manacles pinched against the stretch of the chain. He left her there, but in a moment returned with several pillowcases. He pulled one over her face, then another, then a third. She couldn't see now, but she could hear him opening drawers, searching through her clothes. He came back and tied a sash around her neck, not tight but enough so she couldn't work the pillowcases up her face, off her eyes. She could hear him breathing hard as he surveyed his work, then he called toward the other room, "Okay, she's ready."

Footsteps approached. Leather-soled shoes on the wooden floor. She shivered when a cold hand caressed her breasts, its smooth palm telling her it belonged to someone who did little physical labor. Though he didn't make a sound, she sensed he was pleased with Jack's work. The hand slid down her belly to nudge her legs apart. She didn't fight him, knowing it was useless. When he imposed his hand between her legs, she felt the chill of his fingers penetrating deep inside. Then the hand was gone and the footsteps retreated, Jack's heavy workboots following the leather-soled shoes out the front door.

Fighting tears, she dragged herself closer to the footboard, fumbled blindly at the sash, found the knot and untied it, recognizing from the feel that it was a scarf Cynthia had given her. She pulled the pillowcases off her head and looked out the window. She couldn't see a car, couldn't hear the men. Wishing she could escape through the ceiling, she leaned back to look behind herself. As if in answer to her silent prayer, she saw the key on the lintel above the bathroom door.

The bathroom was a late addition to the house, and the door had once led outside. It was solid oak set in a sturdy frame. The room itself was a cubicle of cinderblocks. With no window, no skylight, only a tiny fan to clear the air, the bathroom was a cell, as secure as a jail.

Though she couldn't remember Jack having used it, he must have been in there because he had known where the pillowcases were. He might go again. If she had the key, she could lock the door. Then she wouldn't have to risk luring him close enough to use the shard of glass when her reach was limited to a few inches of chain. He wasn't interested in her mouth, not even her breasts. He had only one point of interest in her body, and that didn't bring him close enough to cut his throat. The bathroom was a better plan.

With her feet, she tugged a pillow from the head of the bed into her hands. She twisted onto her belly, lifted the pillow as far as she could behind herself, and threw it at the lintel.

The pillow thumped against the wall and slid to the floor,

but the key didn't fall.

Rehearsing in her mind how the pillow must catch the key, she pulled the other one close and held it a moment, telling herself to concentrate the whole of her being into achieving success. She threw the pillow and watched the brass key spin, flashing end over end until it bounced with a ping on the floor.

She eased herself off the bed and crawled near to where the key lay, slid it closer with a toe, grasped it between two, lifted her foot to her mouth, took the key on her tongue, turned it around and carefully positioned it between her toes again. Flat on her back, she stretched full length, reaching her foot toward the door. She could do it. Touch the keyhole, anyway. Whether she could insert the key and turn the lock before he caught on remained to be seen. But it was possible. She had a chance. From outside, she heard her horses whinny, then his heavy footsteps on the porch.

Chapter Sixteen

At eleven-thirty, Devon walked into the library to ask Samantha to lunch. She was wearing her red paisley dress. With her auburn hair and the full skirt that blew against her body in the slightest breeze, he had always thought she looked on fire wearing that dress. Now, walking south with her toward the plaza, she wore a smile as fragile as the flame of a single match.

He put his hand on the small of her back when they crossed Franklin Street, and they shared a smile that said without words that they had missed each other. But the next block was a long one. As they were crossing the bridge over the railroad tracks, a freight train came in from the west and rumbled beneath them, vibrating the concrete under their feet.

Devon stopped to watch the tops of the boxcars flash by in a hypnotic rhythm. When the caboose disappeared in the tunnel, he felt drawn to its darkness, knowing the train wouldn't emerge into sunlight until the tunnel came up on the east side of town. From there the tracks stretched across the vast plains of west Texas all the way to Chinati and beyond.

He looked at Samantha. "Maybe this wasn't a good idea."

She closed her lips in the firm line he knew meant she was trying not to cry.

Below him, the empty tracks were littered with trash, the

dirt between them dark with oil from thousands of trains. Keeping his eyes on the grime, he said, "I have to go to Chinati tomorrow."

"To see Prairie?"

He shook his head. "To deliver something to someone else." He took hold of her elbow and guided her back toward the library. "How do you like your new place?"

She sighed. "I feel safe being in a high-rise with a guard in the lobby."

"See much of Darryl Brent?"

"We've had a few drinks, talking mostly of you."

He nodded, not wanting to know what they said. "Eric's about to get married."

"Eric? To who?"

He met her eyes. "Elise Truxal."

"How did that happen?"

"It's a long story." He looked up the facade of the library with its owl logo carved in stone. "Maybe I'll tell you sometime."

She smiled sadly, accepting that she was shut out of his family. "It was nice seeing you, Devon."

"Sorry about lunch."

She shrugged. "I brought one with me."

"You never used to."

"The condo costs more than my apartment did. And then, I guess I got spoiled, sharing expenses all that time."

"You need money? I could give you some."

"No, thanks, I'll make it."

He nodded. "I don't know what I'm doing, Sam. No sense dragging you through my problems."

She blinked back tears. "You're not dragging me."

"Yeah, okay. Maybe I'll call you when I get home."

She didn't answer, and when he turned around at his car

to give her a parting smile, she was gone.

He drove aimlessly for hours. North to Transmountain and across Hondo Pass, south on Gateway to Alameda, east into the Lower Valley, then west to downtown on the Border Highway, cruising the city he knew by heart. At one point he found himself well on his way to Chinati. He turned around and headed back toward El Paso. Sergio wasn't due home for another three days, so tomorrow would be soon enough to make the trip. And Devon would have the excuse of Eric's wedding to extricate himself from Prairie, if he needed an excuse.

At dusk he was on Interstate 10 just above the New Mexico line. He took the tourist stop exit, parked in the lot, and used the payphone to call her. When she didn't answer at home, he left a message on the machine in her office. Getting back in his car, he caught the on-ramp heading south.

Prairie had the pillowcases over her head and the scarf tied around her neck when Greco came back. She had hidden the key in the sheets, praying he wouldn't find it.

"We're alone again," he said, sitting down beside her. His hand was hot and moist, caressing her breasts. There was a gentleness about the way he did it, as if some vestige of decency survived behind his vicious veneer.

She remembered she had once felt sorry for Carl Lowdy and what her sympathy had gotten her. But the two men were different. Carl had grown up in a good home and had a chance. She suspected Greco hadn't. "Jack," she asked, "what turned you around?"

His hand stopped on her breast. "What d'ya mean?"

"I can tell by the way you touch me that you could've been a good man. What got in your way?"

He laughed harshly. "I know what you're doing. I've done

it myself in prison. When some big prick was fucking me hard, I tried to tell him what a good dude he was, but all the time I was hating his guts and he knew it."

"I don't hate you."

He pinched her. "You like that, do you?"

She winced. "No, but I can tell it's not what you want."

"What do you think I want?"

"Love. Just like the rest of us."

His hand resumed moving in circles on her breasts. "You get much of it?"

"Not enough," she answered with a sigh.

"What about that cop you were with? Doesn't he love you?"

"Some."

"Bet he makes a lotta money, driving such a fancy car."

"He didn't buy that car. It belongs to the department. What kind of car does your friend drive?"

"I don't have any friends."

"The man who was just here. Isn't he your friend?"

"Nah, it was just business."

"Oh," she said, as if surprised. "What kind of car does he drive?"

"I dunno. I've only seen him on a horse."

"What kind of horse?"

"Brown."

She laughed despite herself.

"You like talking to me?" he asked.

"Yes," she said.

"Huh. I bet you're hungry, since you ain't had nothing but water since I got here."

"Yeah, I am."

"Maybe I'll fix you something."

"That'd be nice."

He stood up. "I gotta go to the bathroom first."

She listened to him cross the room and close the door before she yanked the sash loose and the pillowcases off. Holding the key in her mouth, she worked herself into position as quietly as she could. She raised a foot and placed the key carefully between her toes. Then she extended her leg, eased the key into the lock, and swiveled her ankle, hearing the tumblers fall into place. She watched the knob turn back and forth as he tried to get out.

"You goddamned bitch! I was nice, was gonna feed you and all, look what you do!"

She smiled, falling limp on the floor.

He pounded with his fists, then shoved against the door, thudding his body without effect. "You fucking bitch!"

She lay savoring her shallow victory. Still shackled and with no way to call for help, she hoped they both didn't starve to death before someone found them.

It was full dark when Devon took the downtown exit and cruised the plaza. Vice had never been his beat, so normally he didn't look at hookers. This one had long legs under a short skirt, a blouse more like a bra, curly brown hair brushing her shoulders, a generous heart-shaped mouth. When he stopped at the light on her corner, she licked her lips in invitation. The light turned green but he didn't take his foot off the brake.

She ran the few steps to lean in his window, her breasts nearly spilling out of her blouse. "It'll cost you twenty."

Surprising himself, something astonishing in its own right, he reached across and opened the door. She brought in the smoky scent of a sultry perfume.

He drove around the plaza, turning left on San Antonio, then again into an alley to park in the shadow behind a loading dock. After killing his engine and lights, he gave her a twenty and turned on the seat to face her. She slid the bill into her shoe, opened her tiny white purse for a condom, then ducked down in the dark, out of sight. He could barely see glimmers reflecting off her hair from the distant streetlamp as he felt her tongue through the thin skin of latex, the blunted edges of her teeth. The pleasure was like a hot bath on a cold day, or the hands of a masseuse easing a knot in a sore muscle; a remedy, a fix, but nothing to write home about. He gave her his handkerchief and let her do the cleanup, figuring twenty bucks should include maid service. She threw the white cloth out the window as he started his engine.

"You happy?" she asked.

"Sure," he said.

Driving back, he glanced at her face beneath the intermittent streetlights. Her amber eyes were watching him. She was maybe twenty, not yet old enough to drink in a bar. When he stopped at her corner, she gave him a smile and got out. That was it. Fifteen minutes later Devon was walking into the home of Judge Kelton to ask him as a personal favor to marry two kids who probably enjoyed oral sex every night.

After visiting with the judge, he downed a few beers in the Tampico Bar at the border end of Santa Fe Street, then drove home to find his brother's house dark, everyone apparently asleep. He took a Budweiser out of the refrigerator and carried it into Eric's room to sit on the edge of the bed and share a nightcap with Rage Against the Machine. Someone knocked on the door.

"Yeah?"

Connie came in. "Hey, bro. How you doing?"

"Can't complain. You?"

Connie shrugged. "Mind if I sit down?"

Devon shook his head. Watching his brother pull the chair

out from under the desk, he wondered if Eric would return to school after spring break.

Straddling the chair, Connie said, "Something I need to talk to you about."

Devon offered the can of Budweiser, the room small enough that he could do it without getting up.

Connie took a sip and gave the can back. "You know Misty's been seeing a shrink?"

Devon shook his head.

"No big deal," Connie said. "Just her counselor at school thought she was having some adjustment problems, whatever the hell that means."

Devon smiled.

"Her teachers said she was kinda drifting off in class, as if what they're saying oughta hold her attention." He sighed. "Anyway, they recommended this lady over at Jewish Family Services. Rene Szold. Misty goes once a week and tells this shrink her problems. Whatever they are. She seems okay to me."

"Me, too," Devon said.

Connie nodded. "Well, this Dr. Szold called Laura today and asked if maybe you might stop in and see her."

"Me?"

"Yeah. Seems like you're a big part of what Misty talks about. If you don't wanta do it, I can understand. I mean, a shrink and all."

"You think I'm a big part of Misty's problems?"

Connie looked at the poster for Guns and Roses, then met Devon's eyes. "I don't know, bro. I just know this doctor asked to see you. Will you do it?"

"Sure."

Connie nodded. "Appreciate it."

"There's nothing wrong with Misty."

Connie nodded again. "Guess if she's gonna crawl into a man's bed, I'd just as soon it be yours, but I mean, Jesus Christ, she's only fourteen. Not that I think it's your fault. I'm not saying that. But, hell, something ain't right."

"I think she's scared. I'm a cop. We're supposed to protect people."

"So are fathers."

"If she was crawling into your bed, it'd be more of a problem."

Connie laughed. "Maybe so." He stood up, reached into the pocket of his T-shirt and handed Devon a slip of paper. "The shrink said she's free then, if you can make it."

Devon read Laura's handwriting: *Friday, 8:30 p.m.* "I'll be there."

"Appreciate it," Connie said again, putting the chair back under the desk. "When you going to Chinati?"

"Tomorrow."

"You gonna be back for the wedding?"

"Wouldn't miss it."

"The tumble never stops, huh?"

"Time keeps on slipping," Devon said.

"Into the future," Connie finished with a laugh.

Devon sat alone and drank his beer. When it was gone, he walked out to the phone in the living room and called Prairie at home to tell her he was coming tomorrow. She didn't answer, so he left another message on the machine in her office.

This time when Devon made the trip to Chinati, the only thing on the seat beside him was a black velvet box about the size of a ream of paper. He had glanced at its contents, seeing sapphires, opals, emeralds and rubies, some of the pieces old enough to actually be family heirlooms.

It was noon when he turned off Highway 90 onto 2810. He

didn't expect Sergio to be home, but he figured the house-keeper could relay the message that the delivery had been made. When the shadows were lengthening toward mid-afternoon, he parked in front of the hacienda and knocked on the door. Estrella opened it. He tried to give her the box and instruct her to make the call, but she beckoned him in and led him to the library, then left him alone.

Devon looked at the ceiling. No hint was visible of the mirror concealed behind a sliding panel. He studied the wall between the library and parlor. Even knowing he was looking at an illusion, he couldn't discern the subterfuge. Curious as to how the effect was achieved, he was about to move a chair for a closer look when the door opened and Sergio walked in.

Devon handed him the box.

Sergio slid it on top of a row of books.

"Aren't you going to check to make sure it's all there?"

"I trust you, Detective. And it's given me immense pleasure to have you do my bidding."

Devon wanted was to smash Sergio's grin against his teeth. "Are you satisfied then?"

"That's something I don't expect to achieve in this life-time."

"But we're even. You've got no grudge against me or my family?"

"As long as you stay out of my affairs, neither you nor your family are of any significance to me."

"Including Elise?"

Sergio laughed. "Despite my anger in Mexico City, I concede she and Eric were probably destined for each other. What could be more lasting than a marriage built on murder?"

"You can't prove anything."

"Come, come, Detective, did you really think that was my

intent?" He shook his head. "I want your talents at my disposal. Having you in prison won't achieve that."

"Nothing will."

Sergio smiled. "Shall I call Estrella to show you out?"

"I can find my way."

Prairie woke up to the sound of footsteps in the living room. She could tell by the slant of sunlight that it was afternoon, and she felt a flash of surprise that she had either passed out or slept half of the day.

The bathroom door was still closed, the key still in the lock, so whoever was crossing the front room wasn't Jack Greco. She watched the bedroom door swing open to reveal Hank Gentry in his brown deputy sheriff's uniform.

"Holy Christ," he whispered.

She moaned, shaking her shackles. "Get me outta these."

He hurried across to kneel beside her. "Jesus, Prairie. Who did this?"

"Jack Greco! Why'd you let him loose?"

"I had orders." He gently brushed her hair off her face. "God, you're beat to hell. You saying Greco did this?"

She jerked away from his hand. "He's locked in the bathroom."

Hank studied the door. "You sure?"

"The key's still in the lock, ain't it?"

He nodded, then looked back at her. "We got a call from the El Paso Police saying they couldn't reach you. That's the only reason I'm here. When I saw your front door standing open, I knew something was wrong, but Jesus Christ, I never expected this."

"You wanta try doing something more helpful than calling on the Lord?"

He stood up. "You got a robe or something?"

"Fuck that!" She shook the chain between her wrists. "Let me loose."

He took his handcuff key from a pouch on his gunbelt and unlocked her. "I better call for an ambulance."

She jerked the cuffs off and threw them against the wall. "I don't need no ambulance."

But when she stumbled to her feet, her knees buckled and she would have fallen if he hadn't caught her. He pulled a sheet off the bed and wrapped it around her, then carried her out to the porch and set her in the swing.

She pushed him away. "I wanta know who told you to cut Greco loose."

Hank frowned as he backed down the step to the dust of her yard. "I got written orders, is all."

"Who signed 'em?"

"Don't be asking questions that'll get me fired, Prairie."

"Somebody's gonna answer 'em."

"He'll say it was a mistake. You know it well as I do. Long as a certain party wants him in office, he'll stay there."

"I ain't beholding to no certain party. The gov'nor's the only one can kick me outta office, so I reckon I got rank even on Rufus. You can bet your boots he's gonna eat shit for letting this happen."

Hank shrugged unhappily before turning away. She watched him cross the yard and get in his squad car to call for help, though she couldn't hear what he said.

The clouds were crimson above the Chinati Mountains, the eastern horizon darkening to the slate of dusk. Her horses watched from the corral, their ears pricked with concern, while from the cottonwood a dove cooed its melancholy song and a meadowlark's silver sweetness pealed from the chaparral. A faint scent of creosote rode the breeze, strengthening her with each breath. She was alive. And because she had won by outwitting rather than killing her opponent, she felt she had finally earned her badge.

Sirens broke the quiet, thin wails escalating into a howl that silenced the birds and frightened her horses until a sheriff's car and Presidio County's only EMS van stopped amid a settling churn of dust.

Andy Packer had been roused from bed to assist Hank in the arrest. Prairie had never seen the night dispatcher with a weapon, but she thought he looked effective with his big belly behind a shotgun. She made the EMS crew wait until the deputies brought Greco out.

With his hands cuffed behind him, he looked churlish as he faced her on the porch. "You gonna tell how I fed your horses and all?"

She squelched an almost irresistible impulse to spit in his face. "I'm gonna tell 'em the truth, Jack."

He didn't seem glad to hear it, but she felt happy, watching him being driven away in the squad car. Only when she was certain he was well off her land did she allow the EMS crew to load her into the ambulance.

Forlornly watching her horses as she left them behind, she remembered Hank saying the El Paso Police had reported her missing. So Devon had called but hadn't come back. Knowing his suspension was just about over, she wondered if she would see him again before the pending court of inquiry.

Fresh from Sergio's unpleasant company, Devon recalled his earlier suspicion that he had been lured to Mexico as a ploy to get him out of Presidio. Certainly his services as a bodyguard hadn't been Sergio's motive, and though the man was obviously a sadist, it was far-fetched to think Eric had been included merely for the piquancy of causing Elise emotional distress. Kicking these thoughts around, Devon drove into Prairie's yard nudged with a mushrooming dread.

Her Jeep was parked near her barn, as usual. Though her front door was open, the afternoon breeze was cooling on the sun-baked plains of a warm winter day, so that in itself was no cause for alarm. But something felt wrong. Devon cut his engine and let the Lexus coast to a stop in almost near silence as he studied her home through his dusty windshield.

In the corral, the nervous pinto and Appaloosa ran in short tight circles before facing him with their ears pricked. He could see now that the pinto was pregnant, her belly such a ponderous barrel between her four legs he could almost envision the foal folded within. The Appy stood with its legs sprawled aggressively, eyeing him as if sensing trouble.

He unsnapped his holster, pulled out his .38, and turned the cylinder to a live shell before quietly easing his door open and stepping into the dust. Except for the drumbeat of hooves as the horses again circled the corral, the homestead was quiet.

He approached the house from the side and leaned across the railing to peer through the living room window before announcing his presence by stepping onto the planked porch. A rumpled blanket and pillow lay on the sofa. He didn't think they were left from Eric's overnight stay, but if Prairie had been gone in the meantime, they might be. The kitchen, however, suggested otherwise.

Cupboard doors were open, the counter cluttered with torn boxes and empty cans, dirty dishes crowding the sink. Even if Prairie weren't home, Cynthia wouldn't leave the house such a mess. He tried to look into the bedroom but could see only the edge of the open bathroom door.

Carefully he eased his weight onto the porch. As he had expected, the boards creaked under his weight. He stopped and waited, but discerned no response. Holding his gun in both hands, he crossed the living room and sidled around the bedroom door.

The mattress was stripped of all but one sheet. The gun case had been broken into and emptied. The nightstand lay on its side, its lamp, phone and answering machine scattered by its fall. In a far corner, a pair of handcuffs gleamed in the soft light of dusk.

He glanced into the bathroom, saw it was empty, turned around and surveyed the front rooms again, then walked back onto the porch and holstered his gun. As he pulled the door closed, the most reassurance he could take from the scene was its absence of blood.

Prairie was drifting close to sleep when she heard someone come into her hospital room, but it took her a moment to focus. She smiled. "Hey, Devon. When'd you get back?"

"Just now," he said, his voice so comforting she wanted to snuggle between his words.

She tried to touch him but was restrained by the I.V. in her hand. Realizing she was as high as that bottle from the drugs they had given her, she laughed.

Devon sat down in the chair and curled his fingers under hers. "How you feeling?"

"I'd feel better if you were in this bed with me."

He smiled.

She touched her broken tooth with her tongue. "It was Jack Greco, but I think somebody hired him."

He nodded. "It's why Sergio took me out of town."

Squeezing her eyes shut as she tried to think through the drug-induced cobwebs, she remembered the cold hand on her body when she had been chained to the bed. Greco had said the man came on a horse, which was something Sergio might do. And if Sergio wanted Greco released, Rufus would make damn sure it happened. She looked at Devon. "Wasn't he in Mexico with you?"

"We'll figure it out later. Try to think of something good, so you sleep well and heal fast."

She sorted through her mind, then smiled. "Our baby's okay. Only two weeks old and it came through everything. It's gonna be a scrapper, ain't it?" She waited, hoping against hope for some hint of happiness from him.

After a moment, he said, "Couldn't be anything else."

She thought he smiled but his face was fading, then she was lost in oblivion.

Moments later, a nurse came in and kicked Devon out. He left with regret, feeling belatedly protective of Prairie. Cynthia stood up from one of the white plastic chairs against the wall in the bright corridor.

"I saw you go in," she explained.

They fell in step, walking to the elevator, then rode down in silence. In the parking lot, she unlocked the door of a blue Chevette before asking, "You staying over?"

"I have to get back for my nephew's wedding."

"Do you know all of what happened to Prairie?"

He shook his head.

"Besides a bad concussion, she was sodomized."

Devon turned away, tasting hatred for Tierrasantas.

From behind him, Cynthia said, "If she didn't tell you, reckon she doesn't want you to know." She took hold of his arm, turning him to face her. "I won't take that away from her. Don't you do it either, Devon."

He shook his head.

"Do you know she's pregnant?"

He nodded.

"She needs your approval, Devon. You don't have to marry her, you don't even have to take responsibility for fathering her child, but you gotta tell her she's a good peace officer. She needs to hear that from you."

"What if she isn't?"

Cynthia studied him. "Do you believe that?"

"You think she'd be in the hospital now if she were a man?"

"She'd be dead."

"None of this would've happened to a man."

"So what you're saying is she can't earn your approval no matter how good a job she does."

He searched for an answer that wouldn't condemn him.

In a conciliatory tone, she asked, "Can't you give her a shoulder to lean on?"

"If that's what she needs, she's got no business wearing a badge."

"How many women you got ready to buck you up when you're off your oats?"

He realized he could count four without stopping to think.

"Oh, go on back to El Paso, Devon. Stand up at your nephew's wedding and celebrate the enslavement of another woman to the patriarchy. Maybe I'll send her a set of handcuffs as a wedding present."

She got in and cranked her engine, then rolled down her window. "Do me a favor, will you?"

He waited.

"Don't come back 'less you got something good to give Prairie." She put her car in gear and sped away.

He watched her taillights disappear, then ambled over to his confiscated Lexus and started his long drive home, feeling lonelier than he could ever remember.

When he passed the turnoff to the Tierrasantas ranch, he toyed briefly with going in and blowing the fucker's head off. But he figured a man like Sergio would post a night guard,

261

and not being familiar with the layout diminished any reasonable chance of success. He didn't even know where Sergio's bedroom was, let alone the best way to enter the house unnoticed. As with a lot of police work, he had to bide his time and wait for his prey to walk into a noose.

He was so tired when he reached El Paso, he missed the Mesa exit so caught the next one, which took him downtown, then missed Mesa again and drove along the north edge of the plaza as if he were heading toward Sam's apartment in Sunset Heights. Correcting his mistake, he turned south on Santa Fe to circle back. Beneath a light on the dark street leading to the border, he saw the same hooker working another corner. He coasted to a stop at the curb, and she opened his door and got in.

"Recognized your car," she said.

He checked the rearview before pulling into traffic. "You got a room?"

"Yeah. Concordia Hotel."

He dropped a ten spot at the front desk, and they rode the elevator to the fifth floor, then walked down a dank corridor smelling of disinfectant. The room faced a parking lot, empty now in the dead of night.

She locked the door and tossed her purse on the bureau. "Same thing?"

He nodded, handing her a twenty before he sat down in the only chair. She didn't turn on a lamp, but he could see by the light through the window. Her body looked soft, her full breasts overflowing her scant blouse, her face bland beneath the flourishes of makeup. He watched her this time, how she handled him, her expertise with the condom, the way her jaw muscles rippled as she worked. She took a little longer, but the pleasure was the same.

Certainly nothing to risk his badge for, which was what he

was doing. Of course most cops would let him skate as soon as they saw who he was, and anyway, it was departmental policy not to waste personnel on hookers. He was breaking the law, though. Violating the ethics code and committing a sin. All of that mattered more than the pleasure gained by ejaculating into a condom inside her mouth.

She peeled the condom off, carried it into the bathroom and flushed it down the toilet. Admitting she could be one of the women Cynthia had been talking about, he watched her return with a warm washcloth. She cleaned him and put him back together, then sat on the floor and smiled up at him.

"Happy?"

"Ecstatic."

"Anything else?"

He shook his head.

She walked to the bureau and took her lipstick out of her purse. Meeting his eyes in the mirror, she asked, "Give me a ride back to my corner?"

When he dropped her off, she walked into the shadows and disappeared. He wondered about her life, where she lived and with whom, if she had kids or was supporting a man, maybe a pimp. He went to the Tampico and drank several beers, working at thinking about nothing before he drove home.

The wedding was a simple affair, only the families and Judge Kelton. Devon had spent the day secretly brooding while the house bustled around him. By mid-afternoon he had taken enough nips to be gently coasting on whiskey. Even Mrs. Truxal's arrival didn't rough his ride, though he had anticipated that seeing her again would be awkward. He spoke softly, knowing she had every right to hate him. But the words they exchanged could have passed between any two people at a wedding: a hope for the couple's happiness, an unspoken agreement not to interfere for reasons predating the marriage.

Elise wore blue; Eric a white shirt and his only suit, which was brown. The ceremony was brief, concluding with the cutting of the cake and a champagne toast.

His voice husky with emotion, Connie raised his glass and said, "I was the same age as you, Eric, when I married your mother. If not for your Uncle Devon, you might've walked the same hard road I did. But Devon came through for you. If I'd been smarter, he would've done it for me when I was your age. It took me another ten years to appreciate his wisdom. Now I know that, if not for Devon," he met his brother's eyes, "this family wouldn't be celebrating a new beginning." Connie beamed at Eric and Elise. "The blessings of God and Devon on both of you."

Devon felt small beneath the weight of his brother's praise. Judge Kelton slapped him on the back with a laugh, then left the families alone. Connie had made a tape of love songs, and he started everyone dancing.

Devon danced first with Anne, Elise's older sister and now a teacher in an elementary school in the barrio of Chihua-huita. Although the rest of her family were long-legged and blond, Anne was short and dark. She kept her distance, and the only time she spoke was when she said, "It was Eric who was secretly dating Elise when my father was killed, wasn't it." Devon nodded, and Anne looked away.

He danced next with Sunny, Elise's younger sister. At ten, she was fat and clumsy, obviously nervous and missing the beat as often as not. "Sorry," she kept whispering until he finally said, "It's gonna be okay, Sunny."

She met his eyes in a flash of embarrassment, then smiled. "Guess it doesn't make much sense, but I like you."

He smiled back. "I like you, too."

When the song was over, he invited Mrs. Truxal to dance. At first he thought she would refuse, but finally she rose and let him take her in his arms. Meeting his eyes from so near, she asked, "Now that you've got us all tucked under your wing, Detective Gray, what're you gonna do for us?"

"The best I can."

"Including my son?"

"He won't be home for a while yet. We'll deal with it then."

"Do you think his being in prison is just?"

"Yeah, I do. Someday we'll sit down and talk it out. But this is a wedding, and we should at least pretend to be happy."

She nodded. "Elise loves Eric. I'll give him that."

"It'll be enough."

She put her head on his shoulder, surrendering control, as she always had, to the strongest man in the family.

After that he danced with Laura. Because of her pregnancy, he turned her back to his chest and slid his arms between her belly and breasts, inhaling the flowery scent from her hair. Close to her ear, he whispered, "What do you think?"

Laura laughed, conveying both her recognition of the situation's complexity and her willingness to tackle it. He kissed her cheek with gratitude.

Next he danced with the bride, the music this time a salsa tune. As she melded her body to his in the intricate rhythms, she teased, "I would've never guessed you're such a good dancer, Devon."

He smiled. "Controlling your feet and your mouth aren't too different."

"There's a message in that, isn't there?"

"If the shoe fits."

She looked wistfully at Eric dancing with his sister. "You know something? I feel like it's a glass slipper I was damn lucky to get into."

Devon hugged her close, hoping she would never change her mind. When the song was over, he saw Misty looking at him with expectation shining from her eyes. They laughed, falling in step to the Cotton Joe.

"I almost invited Stone today," she said, "but I wanted to be alone with you."

"You call this alone?"

"As close as I can get."

He twirled her under his arm, then held her waist as they took two steps back and started over. When he escorted her to her chair, he winked at his brother, then glanced at the clock. The evening seemed interminable and he felt a strong urge to get out.

After slipping away unnoticed, he was turning the key in his ignition when Eric appeared in the driveway, his cheeks flushed with too much champagne. Devon unlocked the passenger door and Eric got in. They sat for a moment listening to the engine before he said, "Timing's off. You oughta get it tuned."

Devon nodded.

Finally Eric asked, "Did you see Prairie when you were in Chinati?"

"Yeah."

Eric shrugged. "I was just wondering how she is and all."

"She's okay. How're you?"

"I can't believe I'm married!" He looked at his uncle. "Do you think I did the right thing?"

"How would you feel if you knew you'd never see Elise again?"

"I'd feel pretty bad, but I feel that way about Prairie, too."

"You'll be seeing her," Devon said. "She's carrying my child."

Eric stared at him, then smiled, though it was a little crooked. "You gonna marry her?"

"I don't know."

"If you don't, she's just gonna be around, with the kid and all?"

"Maybe."

Eric stared straight ahead. "Where you going now?"

"To pick up a hooker."

Eric laughed at what he thought was a joke. "Can I come?"

"On your wedding night?"

He sighed and got out, then waved with a slightly sick smile as Devon backed down the driveway.

When he pulled up to the curb at her corner, her smile made him think maybe she was glad to see him. This time he took her to the parking lot of the Hacienda restaurant, which was closed for remodeling. Coasting into a shadow under one of the ancient cottonwoods, he killed his engine, then they sat in a silence broken only by the river running through Oñate's Crossing hidden in the cavern of darkness under the trees.

Softly she asked, "Same thing?"

He gave her the money and suggested they move to the back, then locked the doors before she began. When she ducked down out of sight, he touched her for the first time, running the silky strands of her hair through his fingers. Thinking of Samantha and Prairie and Misty, even of Lisa Escobar, who had been murdered nearby, he gave his seed to a stranger who threw it away.

She left the window down, and the breeze whispered in the trees above the sound of the river slithering through its banks. When he made no move to leave, she leaned back and gave him a smile. "You're nice."

"Thanks," he said, though he guessed she could only think that because he hadn't done anything cruel. Maybe that was being nice among the company she kept.

"What's your first name?"

"Devon."

"That's a nice name."

"What's yours?"

"Alma."

He smiled. "That means soul in Spanish."

She nodded. "Don't know how I got a Spanish name. My parents were from Czechoslovakia."

He didn't say anything, curious about her but figuring the parameters of their relationship limited what he could ask.

She broke the silence. "You married?"

He shook his head.

"Got a girlfriend?"

"Not anymore."

She clucked with sympathy.

"We had a fight 'cause I wouldn't let her do what you've been doing."

"Why not?"

"That's what I'm trying to figure out."

The light from the restaurant drew a silver line along her silhouette. "Do you like it with me?"

"Not much."

She met his eyes and laughed. "What're you paying twenty bucks a shot for then?"

"I don't know," he admitted, giving her a smile.

"You have a nice smile," she said.

He laughed, wondering if nice was the only adjective she knew. "You hungry?"

Her eyes widened with surprise.

"We could get something to eat if you want."

She shook her head. "I gotta go back to work. Thanks, though."

"Let's do it," he said, opening his door.

When he dropped her at the corner, she leaned back in the window. "I would've, but my old man'd beat me blue if he caught me out with another man."

"When you're not working."

"Yeah." She gave him a smile and walked away.

He drove to the Kern Place Tavern and nursed a beer, waiting out the time until his appointment with Misty's shrink.

Chapter Seventeen

Jewish Family Services was in a tan stucco building with a Star of David over the doors. Outside the lighted entry was a list of doctors. After Rene Szold, Ph.D., it said: Adolescent Psychology, Hypnotherapy. Devon wondered if her treatment of Misty included hypnosis, an idea he found unsettling.

Behind the desk in the predominantly beige lobby sat a smiling, silver-haired lady in pink. When he said, "Devon Gray to see Dr. Szold," she nodded, reaching for the phone as she said, "Down the hall, fifth door on your right."

The corridor was carpeted with more beige, the paintings along both walls seascapes. Before he reached the fifth door, a woman stepped out and watched him approach.

She was younger than he had expected, maybe twenty-five. Her lanky dark hair fell straight to gently cup her chin, her eyes were brown, her makeup discreet, her slender figure encased in a navy blue suit with a snug skirt and a triangle of yellow silk showing between the lapels of her jacket. "Detective Gray?"

He nodded and shook her hand.

"Thank you for coming," she said, her voice soft.

Professionally comforting, he thought, following her into her office. The carpet was the same beige as in the hall. A bare desk was tucked into the corner behind the door, and a white leather sofa faced a glass wall overlooking a subtly lit Zen garden: dry pools of glossy black pebbles surrounded by white sand raked in concentric circles, the design protected from the wind by a red stone wall.

"Please sit down," she said, taking one of the matching chairs at either end of the sofa.

He chose the chair facing her, leaving the length of white leather between them. On the wall behind her was a portrait of Georgia O'Keeffe contemplating a bald bust of herself.

Dr. Szold smiled warmly. "I'm glad to have this opportunity to get acquainted. But first, I want to reassure you that you've done nothing wrong. In cases of adolescent maladjustment, it's helpful to know the family, and though I've met Misty's parents, she speaks of you so often, I wanted to meet you, too. That's the only reason I asked you to come."

"What makes you think she's maladjusted?"

"She's been experiencing difficulties at school. Her counselor there suggested she see someone on a regular basis."

"What difficulties?"

"The most obvious is that her grades have dropped drastically. Her I.Q. tested at a hundred and forty, did you know that?"

He shook his head. "That's good, isn't it?"

"Very." They sat in silence, appraising each other, then she said, "Last year an event transpired within your family that has frightened Misty. When I asked her parents, I felt they knew what it was but wouldn't tell me. Misty herself knows only that knowledge is being withheld from her. Do you know what that event was?"

He nodded.

"Will you tell me?"

He shook his head.

"I see," she said. Then after a moment, "You're a homicide detective."

"That's right."

"Does the event have something to do with your work?"

"Why do you ask that?"

"I think Misty's problems arise out of being prevented from sharing knowledge of something terribly threatening. She's told me her father was in prison before she was born. That could account for a fundamental lack of faith in his presence: the fear that he might abandon them, even unwillingly. Then, too, her mother is pregnant, and a new child in the family is often threatening to those already there. But I don't think that's the problem with Misty. She seems sincerely happy about the baby and denies anxiety about her father being incarcerated again. She seems most concerned about losing you."

He waited.

"I have no wish to pry into your personal life, Detective Gray. My only purpose is helping Misty. But since her sense of well-being is so deeply involved with you, your actions in areas of your life that you may think are unconnected to her are, in fact, directly connected to how she perceives the world."

"Such as?"

"I understand you terminated a long-standing relationship with a woman because she was raped." She gave him an apologetic smile. "I'm not judging you, merely suggesting your having done that may have contributed to Misty's insecurity."

"I'm sorry if it did," he managed to say.

Her smile was forgiving. "Misty's told me that on several occasions she's tried to seduce you. From what she's said about those occurrences, I'd like to commend you for the gentleness of your rejections, and the rejections themselves."

"I have no intention of fucking my niece."

"Your actions prove that. Why are you angry?"

"It's got nothing to do with Misty."

"What does it have to do with?"

"You started out by saying I hadn't done anything wrong; now it sounds like you're accusing me of something I didn't do."

"I've commended you."

"Okay," he said, catching hold of himself. "Maybe I feel guilty because of what happened last year. We didn't tell Misty because we decided she'd be better off not knowing. Maybe that was a mistake. Mistakes snowball, I know that. What happened last year isn't over. We thought we'd put it behind us but suddenly it came up again, and Eric got married because of it. He's only eighteen and that'll probably ricochet for years, me and Connie trying to hold things together every time they start falling apart. I expected trouble with Eric, not Misty. But when this thing that happened came up again, a man who wasn't even involved then, but is now, threatened her life. I told her about it, so yeah, she's scared." Feeling Dr. Szold's almost palpable sympathy, he shrugged. "I'd do anything to protect Misty, but I can't make her feel safe when she isn't."

Dr. Szold nodded. "You were right to tell her she's in danger. I think you should level with her about everything. She can handle knowledge better than being kept in the dark."

"Okay, we'll tell her."

"That'll help."

They watched each other in the silence of the room. Then he looked out the window at the perfectly symmetrical circles of sand. "I killed a man a few weeks ago. Did you know that?"

"As I understand it, you acted in the line of duty."

His eyes on the Zen garden, he mumbled, "I feel like I've been derailed."

"How so?"

He shook his head. "Maybe it doesn't matter. I'll be back at work next week. Probably everything'll fall in place again." He cast his gaze down her legs, long and smooth beneath the hem of her skirt. "There's something I'd like you to understand: I didn't leave Samantha because she was raped."

"Why did you?"

"It was a mutual decision. The way she put it, our rift was irrevocable."

"What caused the rift?"

"Okay. But the guy was her ex-husband. Don't you think I had good reason to suspect she wanted him there?"

"No woman wants to be raped. If she does, it isn't rape."

"Maybe she was only figuratively raped."

"What does that mean?"

"She wanted the sex. After it happened, she felt he'd betrayed her. That was the rape."

"His betrayal."

He nodded.

"Please don't get angry. I'd just like you to consider this: do you think it might be possible that at some level you want to have sex with Misty and are subliminally communicating that message, so by denying her, you are in essence 'fucking your niece' in the same way you did by excluding her from knowing what happened last year?"

His mind slammed shut.

She smiled. "Will you think about it?"

He nodded.

"Thank you," she said, rising to indicate the interview was over.

"You can't shove me out the door after saying something like that."

She sat back down.

"I left Samantha 'cause she's too needy. I can't have a woman hanging on me all the time. It interferes with my work. I love Misty a lot. But there's no shortage of fuckable women in the world. If you think I'm not good for her, just say the word and I'll be out of that house in two seconds."

Gently she said, "I think that might be best."

He stood up and left, seething at the woman's audacity to think she could meddle so deeply in his family's affairs. But once on the road, he didn't go home. He drove to headquarters and walked into the detectives' bullpen as if he had never been gone.

Alma was arrested at one-thirty on Saturday morning. By two-thirty, when the case was dropped in Devon's lap, the crime scene had been trampled by so many cops and curious neighbors its integrity was far from intact. He didn't get there until four, by which time there wasn't much to see except a disheveled apartment with a mostly-dried blood stain on the living room carpet.

The case seemed as obvious as if Alma had killed her husband in public with a dozen witnesses. But she hadn't. To the arresting officer, Detective Gray was the obvious investigator since his desk was clear after his two-week suspension. But Devon wasn't officially due to start work until Monday. After bringing himself up to speed on the cases being worked by his colleagues, he had glanced through the window of the interrogation room and recognized the hooker he had been seeing in a manner he would loosely call social but anyone else would say was professional, the expertise being hers. The only aspect Devon found obvious was that he had no business accepting the case.

Yet he felt antsy with pent-up energy, and when he looked through the window and saw Alma shaking her head at Sergeant Bartlett, who stood leaning over the table as if to catch her words between sobs, Devon knew she hadn't been arrested for plying her trade.

Seeing Devon through the window, Bartlett shut off the tape recorder, came out, and closed the door. "Will you talk to her?"

"What about?"

"She killed her husband, but I can't get her to stop crying long enough to make sense of anything she says."

"What makes you think she killed him?"

"Neighbors called in a domestic dispute. When we were knocking on the door, we heard a gunshot. Broke in and found her husband shot through the head, her in the kitchen washing her hands. Nobody else in the apartment. Found the gun in the alley outside an open window. She claims another man was the shooter, climbed out the window and ran away, but whenever I ask why she was washing her hands, she starts bawling."

Devon watched her shoulders shake as she cried, her face hidden in her arms folded on the table. "Have you booked her?"

"Detective Ochoa's s'posed to handle it, but he's out on another case and asked me to get a confession. With five arrests for solicitation, she's no babe in the woods."

Devon nodded. "I'll take over."

Bartlett sighed with relief. "Name's Alma Rose."

She looked up when they walked in.

"Mrs. Rose," Bartlett said, "this is Detective Gray. He'll be handling the investigation from here on out."

She stared at Devon, tears running down her cheeks.

"You want me to stick around?" Bartlett asked him.

He shook his head, not taking his eyes off Alma, silently commanding her to keep quiet until they were alone.

"Let me know when she's ready for booking," Bartlett said. "I'll be downstairs."

Devon waited until Bartlett was gone, then pulled a chair out from under the table and sat down across from her, leaning back to increase the distance. "Did you kill him?"

She shook her head.

"I'll do what I can to help," he said. "But if you breathe one word about seeing me before tonight, they'll assign your case to another detective who won't give shit what happens to you. Do you understand?"

She nodded.

He took his handkerchief out of his pocket and handed it to her, remembering the other times he had done that, though what she wiped up then hadn't been tears. This time when she was done, instead of throwing it out the window, she tried to give the handkerchief back.

"Keep it." He switched the tape recorder on. "Have you been read your rights?"

She nodded.

"I need an audible answer."

"Yes," she whispered.

"Do you understand anything you say will be used against you in a court of law?"

"Yes."

"Do you understand you're being charged with murder?"

She nodded again, then remembered and said, "Yes."

"Do you want an attorney present during questioning?"

"No."

"Okay. Tell me what happened."

She watched the tape wind around its reel. "Bobby killed him."

"Bobby who?"

She met his eyes. "I don't know his last name."

"Why'd he kill him?"

"I don't know."

"Were they arguing?"

She shook her head. "No."

"Your neighbors reported a domestic dispute."

"That was me and Steve."

"Steve's your husband?"

"Yes."

"What were you arguing about?"

"My money. He thought I was holding out on him."

"Where do you work?"

"On the streets."

"Doing what?"

"You know."

"How would I?"

"The other officer," she said, recovering herself, "had my arrest record."

"I haven't seen it. And what you told him doesn't count. I need to hear it from you."

"I'm a prostitute."

"When you were arguing, did Steve hit you?"

"No."

"If he did, and you shot him, you could plead self-defense."

"He didn't."

"Okay. What was Bobby doing while you were arguing?"

"Just sitting there."

"Did you know he had a gun?"

She shook her head. "It was Steve's."

"Where was it?"

"On the coffee table."

"While you were arguing, the gun was on the table?"

"Yes."

"So what happened?"

"I went to the kitchen to fix them something to eat. I was washing my hands when I heard the gun. The next thing I knew, cops kicked the door down."

"Didn't you hear them knock?"

"Yeah, but I thought I'd let Steve handle it. He'd been the one doing all the yelling."

"What'd you do between when you heard the gun and when the cops came in?"

"Finished washing my hands."

"Didn't you react to hearing the gun?"

"It took a minute to register. I mean, gunfire's not all that unusual in my neighborhood."

He nodded. "Then what happened?"

"A cop dragged me into the living room shouting I'd been washing my hands, like it was a crazy thing to do." Her voice broke. "I saw Steve on the floor. Nobody tried to save him. We all knew he was dead."

"Where was Bobby?"

"He jumped out the window."

"Did you see him jump?"

"No, but there wasn't anywhere else he could go."

"Did you hear him and Bobby talking before the cops came?"

She nodded, then glanced at the tape. "Yes."

"What were they talking about?"

"I wasn't paying attention. I was mad, you know, about Steve thinking I'd hold out on him."

"So you and Steve were arguing, you left the room, the cops knocked, Bobby shot Steve, jumped out the window and ran away. Is that what you're saying?"

"That's what happened."

He studied her amber eyes red from crying, light brown hair limp on her shoulders, the generous heart-shaped mouth he had found so attractive when she first smiled at him. She wasn't smiling now. "What's Bobby look like?"

"Tall. Six feet. Kinda thin. Brown hair and eyes." She shrugged. "Just an ordinary guy."

"What was he wearing?"

"I don't remember."

"Blue jeans?"

"Yeah."

"Sneakers, boots?"

"Sneakers."

"What color shirt?"

"I don't remember."

"Any jewelry? Scars? Tattoos?"

"I didn't notice any."

"Had you ever seen him before?"

"Coupla times."

"At home?"

"Yes."

"Was he your friend or Steve's?"

"Steve's."

"What was their connection?"

She shrugged. "They met in a bar."

"Which bar?"

"The Tampico, I think."

"What'd they have in common?"

"I don't know."

"Think, Alma! Did they talk sports, business, what?"

She stared at him with fresh tears. "Sports," she finally said. "Bobby was a Cowboys fan. Steve hates the Cowboys." She sniffled. "Hated."

"You want me to find a man named Bobby, six feet, kinda thin, brown hair and eyes, who wears jeans and sneakers and is a Cowboys fan. Do you realize how many men fit that description?"

"A lot."

He nodded. "Did Steve have a job?"

"No."

"Any family in town?"

She shook her head.

"Other friends?"

"None he ever brought home. I think he was seeing another woman, though."

"What makes you think that?"

"Sometimes I'd smell perfume in the bed, a different kind than what I wear."

"Always the same kind?"

She nodded.

"I didn't hear you."

"Yes!"

"Do you know what it's called?"

She shook her head. "No."

"What's it smell like?"

"Strong, real sweet."

"Did you love your husband?"

Her eyes filled with tears. "Yes."

He watched her.

"Devon?" she whispered.

He switched off the tape.

"Help me," she pleaded.

"You haven't given me much to go on."

281

"I didn't do it!"

Gently he said, "I believe you. But without Bobby, I don't think anyone else will."

"Why do you?"

"Maybe 'cause your story's too flimsy to be a lie." He smiled. "Or maybe just 'cause we're friends."

She smiled, too.

"You ready for booking?"

"Who's ever ready for that?"

He called downstairs, then walked her to the elevator. When she got in with Bartlett, he returned to the interrogation room and briefly rewound the tape, played it back to hear her say she loved her husband, then pushed the record button to erase her whispering his name.

It was five a.m. when he walked into his brother's house and found Misty asleep in his bed. He lay down on the living room sofa and crooked an elbow over his eyes. When he woke up, he was under a blue blanket and Laura was sitting across the room crocheting a yellow baby bonnet.

"I kicked everyone out so you could sleep," she said.

He looked at his watch and saw it was nearly noon. "Thanks."

"Why didn't you sleep in Misty's bed?"

He sat up and ran a hand through his hair. "Guess I thought it'd make me look guilty."

She smiled. "We know you're not."

He walked across and kissed the top of her head, then continued into the bathroom. When he came out, showered and shaved and dressed in clean clothes, she had the table set for his breakfast, a steaming cup of coffee already in place alongside the paper.

A small headline on the bottom of the front page read:

WESTSIDE MAN KILLED AT HOME. He sipped his coffee as he read the article on the murder of Steven Rose, learning only that Alma, at eighteen, was two years younger than he had guessed.

Laura brought him fried ham, eggs over easy, and a stack of buttered toast. Glancing at the headline as she set the plate in front of him, she asked, "You working again?"

"Walked into headquarters last night and had the case dropped in my lap."

She sat down and read the article while he ate. "Sounds like the wife did it." When he kept quiet, she asked, "Have you seen Samantha since you got back?"

He sipped his coffee. "I asked her to lunch the other day, then chickened out and walked her back to the library."

Laura smiled sadly. "And Prairie?"

He set his cup down. "She's pregnant." He nodded at her surprise. "I feel like she picked me out of the field, then maneuvered herself into position like a mare in season."

Laura laughed. "How do you feel about being a father?"

"That's a question she never bothered to ask."

"I guess she makes a good salary, with benefits and all."

"Money isn't everything a kid needs."

"No," she agreed.

He stood up and kissed her cheek. "Thanks for breakfast."

"Will you be home for supper?"

"Probably not," he called back.

He drove down Mesa to the plaza, jagged around it to catch Santa Fe, then parked at the curb across from the Tampico Bar, the last known haunt of Steve Rose.

Chapter Eighteen

Devon liked the Tampico and often went there for a beer in the middle of the day, when the place was usually empty. The bartender's name was Jorge Obregón.

Setting a can of Tecate in front of him without being asked, Jorge said, "Good to see you, *amigo*. You get clear of those killings?"

"Sure," Devon said, though the inquiries were yet to be held. "Nobody'll miss a coupla extra cockroaches in Texas."

Jorge laughed.

Devon sipped his beer. "I'm looking for a man named Bobby."

"You asking 'cause of Steve Rose?"

He nodded.

"They was always arguing about them Cowboys. Who gives a shit, I wanta know. Cowboys, Injuns, Lakers, Jazz. I see a lotta money change hands on those names. I don't pay no attention. They don't mean nothing to me."

An old woman came in and sat at the far end of the bar. She wore a spangled white sweatshirt and too much makeup under a cheap blond wig. Again without being asked, Jorge gave her a bourbon and water neat, then came back.

Softly Devon asked, "What was Bobby's last name?"

"Sonofabitch, maybe. That's what I'm saying, *hombre*. I don't pay no attention to names."

"You knew Steve's."

"I read it in the paper. That's the only reason."

"How'd you know it was the same Steve?"

"I met his wife. You ever meet her?"

Devon nodded. "I'm trying to help her."

"You don't think she did it?"

He shook his head.

"Women're crazy. Who can tell what they'll do?"

"Maybe Bobby did it."

"I could believe that."

"Why?"

Jorge shrugged. "Like I said, they was always arguing. Get drunk, hang on each other like *amigos,* yak-yak-yak." He held his hand up and bounced his thumb off his fingers. "Pretty soon, they're mad, ready to fight."

"Cokeheads?"

He shrugged again, then leaned close, his elbows on the bar. "Steve put his woman on the street. She should've killed him a long time ago."

"She'll be locked up a long time if I don't find Bobby."

Jorge walked to the end of the bar and gave the old lady another drink, though she hadn't said a word. He came back and whispered, "She'll drink five or six, go home'n sleep 'em off, come back for more."

Devon sipped his Tecate.

"Steve told me him and Bobby did time together."

"Here in Texas?"

"I don't ask questions. One time when Steve was ripped, he said him and Bobby were brothers in death."

"What'd he mean?"

"Most people in here quit making sense years ago, *hombre.*" He turned his back to the woman and scratched his crotch. "I got something maybe could help you, but I got expenses too, you know? This job don't pay so much."

Devon took out his wallet and laid a twenty on the bar.

"Beer's a buck-fifty," Jorge said.

He laid another two on top.

Jorge curled the bills into his fist. "Bobby lives with Sabrina. You know who she is?"

Devon shook his head.

"Ask Vice. They call her the Angel of Death 'cause she's got AIDS, gives it along with her rides, a free kiss you can't wash off."

"Sabrina what?"

Jorge shrugged. "Is good to see you back on the job, *amigo*. When you're gone, the cockroaches take over everything." He leaned close again. "Like this business with Steve. I think a big cockroach come down and step on him."

"Does this big roach have a name?"

"He should be a saint, he has such a name."

Devon felt his pulse quicken. " 'Cause he comes from the Holy Land?"

"I heard you know him."

Devon nodded.

"You're not the only cop who does. Now get outta here. I've given you a lot more'n twenty dollars' worth."

"Appreciate it," Devon said.

As he walked into the sun, he felt a rush of anticipation, knowing the cockroach from the Holy Land had to be Tierrasantas.

Devon drove north on Mesa and pulled into the Seven-Eleven at Brentwood because it had a payphone he could use from his car. After punching in the home number of a detective in Vice, he listened to the phone ring a long time, wondering if he wasn't calling one of the cops on Sergio's payroll. When Ernie Minos finally answered, Devon asked if he could stop by to talk shop.

"Thought you didn't start 'til Monday," Ernie grumbled.

"You know me."

"Let yourself in the side gate. I'm out by the pool."

He lived in a big house off Shadow Mountain. The view from the street was a panorama of the Upper Valley, pale pinks and tans cut by the green ribbon of the river. The back yard was private, enclosed by an eight-foot stone wall. Sitting in a chaise longue with his ankles crossed, Ernie was drinking ice tea and reading the *Racing Gazette*. He had a fringe of dark hair around a bald pate, a thick stubble of salt-and-pepper whiskers, a bulbous nose, and eyes sharp as the crack of a whip.

Reaching up to shake Devon's hand, he smiled through his bristles. "Good to see you. Have a seat. Want some tea?"

"You, too. Thanks. No, I'll pass." Devon sat in the middle of a matching chaise longue.

The yard had been professionally landscaped with palm trees and a rock waterfall feeding the pool, suggesting Ernie was on the take. But nobody stayed in Vice long unless they were running a lucrative sideline. It was the nature of the beat to corrupt anyone within range, and a cop with checkers on the board was often able to ply effective leverage when the game tilted toward the rough side. Devon could accommodate that into his overall opinion of Minos as a good cop, seeing the graft as only a bruise that hadn't yet spoiled the apple.

"You nervous about the inquiry?" Ernie asked.

Devon smiled. "I had due cause, except for punching Escobar, but they won't take my badge for flooring a cockroach."

Ernie laughed. "So which roach on my beat interests you?"

"Sabrina. The hooker they call the Angel of Death. You know her last name?"

"Cuervo. Someone oughta tattoo a black A on her forehead."

"We should get her off the street. Set her up on welfare so she doesn't have to work."

"Then she'll give it away. You can't change whores, and you can't force 'em into a nunnery. That's the problem with this goddamned disease: everybody's got the legal right to spread it around."

Devon watched the aqua water rippling in the sparkling pool. "I really came over here to talk about the man she's living with."

"Which one?"

"His name's Bobby. Alma Rose fingered him as the killer of her husband."

"Alma Rose. The first time I busted her, she was seventeen and so scared I let her slide. Didn't do any good. The next time I had her booked, but that didn't do any good either. Every cop in Vice has booked her by now."

"Have any of 'em had her?"

Ernie shrugged. "Did she give Bobby a motive for knocking off her old man?"

"Said she didn't know."

"Bobby's a pimp. Maybe he wanted her in his stable and Steve wouldn't go for it, wanted her money all to himself."

"You know Bobby's last name?"

"Tutts. You got any evidence other than her?"

Devon shook his head.

"Prints on the gun?"

"Haven't talked to the lab yet."

"Witnesses at the scene?"

"Haven't talked to them either. Got the case at two-thirty last night."

"Dreyfus know you're on it?"

"If he checks the roster, he will."

Ernie scratched the stubble on his cheek. "Bobby hangs out at the Tampico a lot."

"Jorge's the one told me he's living with Sabrina."

"What you'd pay him?"

"Twenty."

Ernie chuckled. "He'll prob'ly get another from Bobby for telling him you asked."

"Let's pull Bobby in before he finds out."

"You got no evidence."

"Maybe we'll find some, or shake him up enough that he makes a mistake."

"He don't shake up."

"You've tried?"

Ernie shook his head. "I make sure our paths don't cross."

"When'd you start running scared of pimps?"

Ernie's eyes flared with anger.

Devon smiled.

"Ah hell." Ernie hefted himself to his feet. "Let me get my gun."

The Angel of Death lived in the projects on Paisano near the Coliseum. Which meant she *was* on welfare, and that probably meant she had kids. Some of the two-story tenements were clean, with wet laundry dripping onto potted flowers on the porches, but Sabrina Cuervo didn't live in one of those. She lived at the back, next to the railroad tracks, and her neighbors didn't care any more for the aesthetics of their homes than she cared for the health of her customers.

Or the well-being of her children, Devon thought, as he

and Ernie stood in the open door of her apartment.

Two toddlers wearing only diapers were sitting on the floor watching cartoons on a big-screen TV while eating Rice Krispies out of the box. The TV was so loud that they hadn't noticed the men standing in their door. Dirty clothes were scattered around the dingy room, and piles of dog shit added to the stink of soiled diapers and rotting garbage.

Devon looked beyond the kids to the kitchen, littered with festering food crawling with flies that buzzed through the air like bombers dropping disease. Next to the kitchen was a hall leading deeper into the darkness.

He met Ernie's eyes. They both drew their guns, then Devon walked behind the kids, stepping around the dog shit and laundry, while Ernie waited at the door. The kids still hadn't noticed they were there.

The hall was dim, its wood floor stained with soaked-in pools of piss. Devon glanced into the empty bathroom, shielding himself from seeing the source of the foul stench wafting from the commode. Ahead of him were two closed doors.

He listened at one, heard nothing, so gingerly turned the knob and opened the door enough to see into the kids' room. A mattress on the floor fitted with a Star Wars sheet, cardboard boxes for furniture, the closet door gone, a board across the space to keep a litter of puppies inside. Dobermans, still young enough to be nursing, the bitch nowhere in sight. Probably in the last room, protecting whoever else was there.

Approaching the door, he heard a threatening growl about the height of his knees. He figured he would have to kill the dog, then see who was left. He turned the knob and warily swung the door open. A snarling blur of fur and fangs flew straight at him. He fired between the teeth and she stopped in mid-flight, her snarl diminishing into an abrupt whimper ending with the thud of her body hitting the floor.

Past the dead dog, a naked woman sprawled on the bed, staring blind at the ceiling. Her long black hair was soaked in blood still oozing from a gap in her neck, the wound less than a few minutes old. Beside the bed was an open window, its tattered curtain shivered by the breeze.

He walked to the window, avoiding more dog shit, thicker here, as if the dog had spent most of its time confined in this room, and looked out at an alley overflowing with Dumpsters but empty of people. Behind him the kids started crying.

He turned around, still holding his gun.

They stood with their arms straight at their sides, their hands clenched into fists, their faces screwed tight as they wailed, their eyes on the dog.

Ernie came in, towering behind them as he assessed the scene. He took a kid under each arm and carried them screaming and kicking back through the dark to the sunshine outside.

Devon spotted a phone by the bed. He used his handkerchief to pick it up and call headquarters. After requesting a coroner and forensics team, a social worker from Child Protective Services, and an officer from Animal Control, he broke the connection and called Dreyfus at home. The lieutenant's wife answered.

While he waited, he looked at the dresser and saw a spilled bottle of perfume, its contents running across to drip on the floor. Still flowing, so either the dog had knocked it over, or the killer had. Its name was Heart Throb, its scent cloying with musk.

"Devon!" Dreyfus shouted happily. "Where the hell are you?"

"At work. I need an APB on Bobby Tutts."

He was quiet a moment. "You weren't supposed to start 'til Monday."

"I'm standing in a room full of shit, a dead dog, and a woman with a second mouth under her chin. You want me to go home?"

He sighed. "What're the stats on Bobby Tutts?"

With the Lexus idling roughly at the curb, Ernie said, "Thanks for a fun afternoon, Devon."

He smiled. "Anytime."

"Problem is, you mean that. Don't you ever take a day off?"

"I've just come from two weeks' leave."

Ernie snorted. "I heard you spent part of it working for Sergio Tierrasantas."

"Have you met him?"

He shook his head. "You know what's gonna happen if you don't let up? You're gonna be walking down a dark alley some night and take a bullet in the back."

Devon wondered if that was a friendly warning or a veiled threat.

"You oughta listen to me," Ernie said, sounding more angry than worried. "You act like you're fighting a war against evil all on your own, but the Lone Ranger only wins in the movies."

"I don't always work alone," Devon said, remembering Sergio had once called him the Lone Ranger. "You were a big help today."

"Yeah, I carried the kids outta the shit." He shook his head. "I think they were more upset by the death of their dog than their mother."

"The dog probably gave 'em more affection."

Ernie snorted again, opened the door and got out, then

leaned back in. "I hope the next time you call, I'm not home."

Devon watched him walk away, then pulled a U and drove back to Mesa to catch Sunland Park to I-10 South. He took the downtown exit to the county jail and parked in a space reserved for cops. On the women's floor, he wrote a request to see Alma Rose, then waited in an interrogation room.

When she came in, he stood up and said gently, "Sit down, Alma."

She did, placing both hands on the table and picking at a torn cuticle.

Sitting across from her, he reached out and caught her fingers. "You'll only make it worse."

She met his eyes, holding tight to his hand.

He smiled. "How you doing?"

She shrugged.

He let go and leaned back, sliding his hands into his pockets. "Bobby's last name is Tutts. He was living with a woman named Sabrina, but by the time I got there, he was gone."

Alma's amber eyes were so sad, he wanted to comfort her but forced himself to keep his distance.

"I know a psychologist who works with hypnosis. Would you be willing to let her try'n help you remember what Bobby and Steve were talking about that night?"

"Will you stay with me when she does it?"

"If you want."

She sighed. "I should've never let Steve do this to me."

"Do what?"

"Put me on the street. Put me in jail. Now I might go to prison for killing him, when all I ever wanted was to make him happy."

He nodded.

She smiled weakly. "You're going way out of your way to

help me and I can't figure out why. You picked me up three times, wanting nothing more'n what you could get from any girl on the street. What'd I do to you?"

"The thing to remember is I picked you up, not the other way around."

"Why are you helping me?"

"I like you."

"Me?"

"Yeah. You, Alma."

Slowly a smile curled the ends of her mouth. "I like you, too, Devon."

"That's all there is to it."

She laughed, though her eyes were still sad.

He took out one of his cards and slid it across the table. "If you need anything, let me know."

"Thanks," she whispered.

He stood up. "I'll call that doctor and ask if she'll see you. Hopefully, she can do it today or tomorrow."

"Tomorrow's Sunday."

"Yeah, well, she's Jewish, so that shouldn't matter."

"Are you?"

He shook his head, his hand on the doorknob. "Catholic."

"I was raised Catholic, but I don't feel like much of anything anymore."

"Don't believe that."

"That I'm not Catholic?"

"Think about it," he said, opening the door.

He went back to the desk and wrote an order for her to be tested for HIV. At headquarters he instigated a search of the books for a mug shot of Bobby Tutts, then looked up Dr. Szold's home address.

She lived in a gated community at the north end of Stanton. After giving his name to the guard, Devon waited, wondering if she would see him, but in less than a minute, the guard opened the gate and waved him through.

The complex was expensive, its manicured lawns just beginning to green up in the warmth of spring. The visitors' parking was a good ways from her door. By the time he got there, she had it open but wasn't in sight, so he rang the bell.

Rene came from the hall, dressed to go out. "Detective Gray. This is a surprise. I'm sorry, but I have a date."

"I'll only stay a minute."

She gestured him in, then closed the door. Her apartment was tastefully decorated with antiques. Oval portraits of European-looking men and women, a Victorian settee beneath a gold-framed mirror, a glass étagère displaying porcelain figurines that could have come from turn-of-the-century Vienna. He walked across to stand in front of the balcony's sliding glass door and look at her view of the mountains: a barren, craggy ridge stretching north.

From behind him, she asked, "Would you like a drink?"

"No thanks," he said, turning around. "I've got a murder suspect who claims she didn't do it. She says the man who did was talking with her husband just before it happened, but she wasn't paying attention. If I could get her to remember that conversation, I might get a lead on where the killer is now. Do you think you could help her remember through hypnosis?"

She sat down on her gold brocade sofa and crossed her legs. Her dress was a mellow green, silk from the way it slithered away from the smooth sheen of her stockings. "I might."

"Are you willing to try?"

"For my usual fee."

"How much is that?"

"A hundred dollars an hour."

He stared hard. "Do you know my brother's supporting four people on three hundred a week?"

She didn't bat an eye. "I have an arrangement with the school board to work with their students at a reduced rate."

"How reduced?"

"Half."

"So he's paying you fifty dollars an hour to tell us Misty's scared."

"There's more to it than that."

"Not much."

"Misty's parents are happy with the progress I'm making. Do you have a problem with it?"

"I can't see any progress. She's still crawling into my bed every night."

"My impression is you like women crawling in your bed."

Astounded, he asked, "Is that why you nailed me to the wall yesterday?"

"I'm sorry. But being as you're a large part of Misty's problems, I didn't think it wise to respond to your flirtation."

"I wasn't flirting with you."

"As you say you have no intention of sleeping with your niece, yet she continues to come to your bed with undaunted hope. Obviously your approach has confused Misty, and probably every other woman you associate with."

They stared at each other across the Old World air of the room. Finally he asked, "Do you ever toy with the idea you might be wrong?"

"Occasionally," she conceded, "but my psychological specialty is sexual behavior."

Her doorbell rang. "My date," she said.

"Is it a man?"

She stared at him so long, he said, "You better let him in."

She rose and walked across to open the door, then said hello in a strained, formal tone.

The man who came in was Hunter Jones, a defense

attorney specializing in high-profile criminals.

"Evening, Hunter," Devon said.

"Detective," he answered in an unfriendly tone, looking at Rene.

"I'm here on police business," Devon explained. "Came to ask Dr. Szold if she'd help me with a case I'm working on."

"So you're off suspension?"

"Much to your clients' displeasure."

Hunter chuckled and asked Rene, "Has he convinced you to donate your talents?"

She met Devon's eyes. "Yes, he has."

He smiled. "Can we do it tomorrow?"

"Where?"

"The county jail. Want me to pick you up?"

"Please. I'll be free at two."

He walked out and drove back to headquarters, where he found a copy of Bobby Tutts' mug shot in his mailbox. Accompanying the photo was the information that Tutts had served five years in Huntsville for possession with intent. Devon took the photo to the county jail. Twenty minutes later, the matron brought Alma to the interrogation room, closed the door, and left them alone.

Devon was leaning against the wall opposite the door. He nodded at the photo on the table. "Do you know him?"

She took a few steps closer and studied the picture without touching it. Finally she said, "Yeah, that's Bobby."

"What's your hesitation?"

She shrugged, her eyes still on the photo. "He's older now. His hairline's higher. And his face's harder, more mean."

"But you're sure that's him?"

Still looking at the photo, she nodded.

"Okay. The psychologist's coming at two tomorrow. Maybe you'll remember something that'll give me a lead."

They stared at each other across the cold room. Then she said, "Tell me something."

"What?"

"Anything."

He sorted through his mind. "A priest says Mass in jail on Sunday. You could go."

She smiled sadly, then looked at the closed, solid wooden door. "Is there anything I can do for you?"

"Like what?" Though he knew what she meant.

"What I did before."

"I don't have a condom. Do you?"

She shook her head, not smiling at his joke.

"Did you use 'em with your husband?"

"No."

"Even though you knew he was unfaithful?"

She pulled a chair out and sat down.

"I've ordered a test. Maybe you're clean."

She shook her head. "There's a word for this, isn't there?"

"For what?"

"That I'm in prison for killing him, when he's the one who killed me. Isn't there a word for that?"

"Irony."

"I knew you'd know that word." She smiled sadly, then stood up and walked out to where the matron was waiting in the hall.

Devon started hitting the bars close to the border, showing the photo discreetly, trying to find a trail. Though some of the bartenders obviously knew Bobby Tutts, none would admit it. Devon figured the word was on the street that Tutts was wanted for two murders, both low-life victims no one was likely to stick their neck out to avenge. He also figured Bobby was long gone, maybe in Mexico, for sure out of Texas. Unless Tutts was stupid. There was always that chance.

When the bars closed, Devon drove home, so tired he fore-went his usual nightcap and walked through the dark to his room, where he stripped himself naked and slid into bed. He had barely closed his eyes when he opened them again to watch Misty come in. She was crying. Without thinking, he pulled her down beside him and held her close, only the covers between them.

Chapter Nineteen

"What's happening, Misty?"

"I'm scared."

"Of what?"

"The man who wants to hurt me."

"That's over. Didn't anyone tell you?"

"Daddy did, but I didn't believe him."

"Why not?"

"He lies to Mom when he doesn't want her to worry, so I figured he was doing the same thing to me."

"He wasn't. I gave the man what he wanted and he called it even between us."

"What did he want?"

Devon sighed, moving away from her to lie on his back. He remembered Dr. Szold had said Misty could handle the truth better than being kept in the dark, so he told her. As she listened, she slipped under the covers to snuggle against his chest. When he finished, she asked, "And Elise isn't mad about having to give the jewelry back?"

He shook his head.

"So she won't tell what you did for Eric last year?"

"Did your father tell you about that?"

"Mom did."

"We should've told you at the time," he said, turning to face her, "but we thought you were still a child and better off not knowing."

"I'm not a child."

He nodded. "You know you shouldn't be here."

"I want to be with you," she pleaded, her voice breaking with new tears. "Please don't make me leave."

He pulled her close and buried his face in the perfume of her hair, thinking to be so deeply desired was a blessing. But despite the fragrance he now realized she had doused on herself before coming in, she smelled like a child. He met her eyes. "One of us has to leave. I guess it should be me."

"No!"

"Then go back to your room." He brushed her hair away from her sweet urchin face. "Will you do that for me?"

She sighed. "I guess."

He watched her walk out, leaving the door open as if he might change his mind.

He closed it and turned on the light, got dressed and began packing the small brown suitcase he had been carrying around since leaving Samantha, the same one he had thrown everything into the night he left Prairie's in anger. It was a pathetically small leather box holding a minimum of necessities, the last of which was his whiskey. He snapped the locks shut, turned off the light, and walked through the dark to his car.

When he stopped in the street to shift into drive, he saw Misty on the porch, her white cotton nightgown clinging to her elfin body in the wind. He accelerated away from her, having no idea where he was going.

At Rim Road, he turned right, then left again on Mesa, following it downhill toward the heart of the city. On the corner of River Street, he saw the Travelodge with its red vacancy sign still lit. He parked in front of the office, went in and rang the bell. The clock on the wall said two-twenty-three. Finally the desk clerk came in wearing a bathrobe. He looked Devon over, glanced out at the Lexus: an expensive car, a man alone, conservatively dressed in a sports coat over clean jeans and a neatly-ironed shirt, the car not his and the shirt ironed by his sister-in-law though the clerk had no way of knowing that. Seeing a man of means offering an American Express card to pay the bill, the clerk gave him a room.

Devon parked in the space numbered the same as his key, took his suitcase off the backseat, and walked up the stairs. The room was number thirty-five, the same as his age. He opened the door, then turned around and looked at the city stretching into the dark prairie of west Texas. He turned his back and walked into the room. It was brown, drapes and carpet chocolate, walls beige, the bed covered with a dusty rose spread.

A flower for a flower, he thought, lying down and covering his eyes with his elbow, wondering why he felt so bad when he had done the right thing. Maybe a tad late but, unlike with Prairie and Samantha, before the damage was irrevocable.

The interrogation room was a cubicle eight feet square with no windows, one door, and a fluorescent light in the ceiling. A sad room permeated with the dread of inmates meeting with cops or lawyers, trying to salvage a future after jail. When Alma was brought in, it was obvious she didn't believe she had a future. Devon could see it in her slack posture, the downturn of her mouth. He leaned against the wall as she sat with her eyes closed, her hands clasped in the hands of Dr. Szold across the table, a tape recorder running beside them.

"You're in the kitchen," Rene said, her voice a non-threatening drone. "What are you doing?"

"Looking in the refrigerator," Alma mumbled from within the trance, "trying to find something for supper."

"What do you see?"

"A six-pack of Coors. Steve must've just bought it, only two cans are gone. A bottle of ketchup, a squeeze bottle of mustard, an almost empty jar of salsa, some moldy cheese."

"What do you decide?"

"To make goulash. There's a pound of burger in the freezer, egg noodles in the cupboard, an onion and some paprika. I'll make goulash. Steve likes it."

"What are you doing now?"

"I take the burger out of the freezer and put it on the stove. I should wash my hands. I've just come from work and I didn't have a chance to wash. Took the condoms off and threw 'em out the window, wiped my hands with Kleenex, that's all."

Devon remembered when she had done the same things with him. He had given her a handkerchief to clean up with, that was the only difference. And maybe that he felt some affection for her, but he didn't know the others hadn't felt the same.

"Where are Steve and Bobby?" Rene asked.

"In the living room."

"Doing what?"

"Talking."

"What are they saying?"

"I'm not listening."

"What are you doing?"

"I turn on the water, lather my hands with soap. I'm careful to clean them good, running a fingernail under my nails, getting all the crud out, all the scum off."

"What do you hear?"

"The water."

"What else?"

"The men's voices."

"What are they saying?"

"I don't know."

"Listen harder, Alma."

She frowned, trying to hear the voice of a dead man talking to the man who had killed him. "Yago," she whispered.

"Yago?"

"Yago's got it. That's Steve. The fuck he does, Bobby says. Steve says, I'm not shitting you, man. Yago's got it." Alma jerked, yanking at her hands held by Rene.

"What is it?" she asked, holding on.

"Cops at the door. OPEN UP, POLICE! Let Steve deal with 'em. He was the one doing all the yelling. I'm not gonna open the goddamned door. Shit! What the fuck was that?"

"What?"

Alma moaned. "Where's the goddamned towel? Steve's always taking the towel, walking away drying his hands, putting it someplace stupid, I never know where. God-damned cop! What's he doing walking in here like he owns the place? Ow! He's hurting my arm. Won't even let me dry my hands. Jesus, God! Steve! All that blood, he's gotta be dead. Jesus! God in Heaven! No! I didn't! Bobby! The window! No, no!" She was crying, gasping sobs ripping her breath. Suddenly she stopped, then whispered, "Devon?"

"Who's Devon?"

"Just a trick. Prob'ly doesn't remember me. Nice guy, though. Nice smile." She half-laughed. "Asked me to dinner. I should've gone. Then I wouldn't be here with a stupid dead husband who wanted me in those movies that rich creep makes. But there're some lines you can't cross. I *told* Steve stuff like that won't go away. Shit like that snowballs. He didn't listen. Now he's dead 'cause of those dirty movies. I should've gone with Devon. He was so nice! Touched me so gentle. Fancy car, plenty of money, handed over my twenty like it was nothing. Guess he's as gone as my dead husband. God, I'm so stupid!" She was crying again, her face bare of makeup, naked in the light, an open wound.

"It's all right, Alma," Rene coaxed. "Devon's here. He wants you to stop crying, to leave that night behind and come back to now. Everything's all right. I want you to remember that, nothing else. When I count to three, you'll wake up. One, two, three."

Alma pulled her hands free as she tossed her head and laughed. "I told you it wouldn't work."

Rene turned her eyes on Devon, with accusation, he thought. He smiled at Alma. "Remember Yago?"

She shook her head.

"Steve and Bobby were talking about him that night."

"Did I tell you that?"

"Yeah. And about a rich creep who makes dirty movies."

"Do you know *his* name?"

Devon nodded. "And I'm gonna nail him."

Rene was quiet as they walked to his car. He held the door for her, and she met his eyes as she got in, but neither of them spoke until they were following the curve of Stanton up the mountain. Then she said, "Alma didn't kill her husband."

"I know," Devon said, stopping at the gate. To the guard he said, "Dr. Szold lives in number forty-six."

The guard bent down and looked at her, nodded, and opened the gate.

Parking in a visitor's space, Devon said, "Let me walk you." He went around to open her door.

"You're such a gentleman," she said, getting out. "It's surprising in this day and age."

He smiled. "I'm a good Catholic boy, raised the old way."

She looked up at him as they walked toward her condo. "You learned your lessons well."

"So did you. That was quite a performance."

"Do you think she'll be convicted?"

"Unless I can find Bobby."

"What about this Yago?"

"Street name. Prob'ly not written down anywhere. Steve moved in mean company. I haven't found anybody willing to admit they knew him or Bobby. It'll be the same with Yago."

Rene sighed. "How much time will she get?"

"Depends on her lawyer."

"What's your guess?"

"Ten to twenty."

She stopped and met his eyes. "For a murder she didn't commit?"

"I'm doing everything I can to help her, Rene."

She started walking again. "Maybe a good lawyer can help more than you can."

"Why don't you ask your friend Hunter? Might heal his soul to defend someone who's innocent."

Climbing the stairs. "You don't like him, do you?"

"No."

"He likes you. Admires you, at least."

He watched her search for her keys.

She found them and opened her door. "Would you like to come in?"

He shook his head.

"I'm sorry if I misjudged you. It's just that you're so . . ."

"What?"

"I sense a great deal of anger just under the surface of your professionalism. Am I wrong?"

He shrugged. "Thanks for your help today."

"You're welcome." Still she made no move to go in. "Will you call me sometime? If you just want to talk, or whatever."

He smiled. "If I call, it'll be both."

She blushed, making him laugh.

"For an expert on sex, you don't seem very experienced."

"I'm not."

"Not at all?"

She shook her head. "Do you think that makes me a bad therapist?"

He gave her a gentle, chaste kiss. "I think you're just what Misty needs."

He descended the stairs without looking back, though he could feel her watching until he turned a corner and left her behind.

In his motel room, he called Ernie Minos at home.

Ernie groaned. "This is Sunday, Devon."

"You ever hear of anyone named Yago?"

"Yago Stallone, sure. Known on the street as the Stallion."

"Know where I can find him?"

"The county morgue. I checked him in on Friday night."

Devon broke the seal on a new bottle of Old Crow. "What'd he die of?"

"A vein full of smack so pure it'd kill an elephant."

"Where'd he get it?"

"Who knows?"

"Come on, Ernie. You know who's selling what on the street."

After a moment, he muttered, "Word is he got it from Bobby Tutts."

"Who gave it to Bobby?"

"Let it go, Devon."

He stood up and walked to the window where he looked down on his Lexus, its color barely discernable under a thick coat of dust, the hood still pockmarked from Carl Lowdy's shotgun, the engine badly in need of an overhaul. "Where is he?"

Ernie's laugh sounded sick. "Prob'ly Acapulco, spending his money."

"Who paid him?"

"To do what?"

"In the last forty-eight hours, he's killed three people."

"They were all low-lifes. Nobody'll miss 'em."

"Who wanted 'em dead?"

"Don't do this."

"Give me a name, Ernie. I'll keep you out of it."

"You can't."

"Meet me in Jaxson's, fifteen minutes. If you're not there, I'm going to Dreyfus."

"You're killing yourself to save a whore!"

"I'm doing my job."

Ernie sighed. "Fifteen minutes."

Devon looked at his bottle of whiskey, left it unopened, and walked out.

Jaxson's was an up-scale restaurant on the corner of Mesa and Castellano. From outside it looked like an adobe hacienda. Inside were muted lights, paintings of Navajos with horses, and the quiet hush of private conversations. At a back booth in the bar, Devon and Ernie sat watching each other as they waited for their double bourbons on the rocks. When the waitress had come and gone, Devon said, "Give me a name."

"I got one should ring a bell: Tierrasantas."

"Keep talking."

"Sergio makes movies. You know what kind I'm talking about?"

Devon nodded.

Ernie sipped his whiskey. "He's got a scout picks girls out of barrios in Juárez. Girls nobody'll miss. He likes 'em young. Twelve, thirteen. You know what happens to 'em."

"They die."

Ernie shrugged. "Most of 'em are half-starved anyway. All that's ahead of 'em is turning tricks for two bucks a roll. It's not like they're missing out on any kind of future."

"Who's the scout?"

"It was Yago. He'd go down there and find 'em, promise to bring 'em to America and set 'em up in the good life. But where they went was Sabrina's. She'd put 'em up 'til the film crew was ready. Bobby'd take 'em to a studio in Ojinaga." Ernie finished his drink.

"How'd Steve figure into it?"

He shook the ice down. "Steve'd fuck the girls on camera, then they'd send him outta the room and Bobby'd finish it. Steve caught on to what was happening. His last job, he filched the film." Ernie drained his melted ice.

Devon pushed his full glass across the table.

Ernie sipped at the fresh drink. "Yago made a mistake picking the girl for that film. Her family had enough money to raise a stink. So he got scared and went along with Steve, trying to blackmail Sergio into trading the film for a hundred grand. They were out of their league. Bobby offed Yago for betraying the organization. Then he went to Steve, trying to get the film back. Steve said he'd given it to Yago. Bobby knew Yago didn't have it."

"Who did?"

"Sabrina. She was tired of playing hostess. Sick, too. With AIDS, you know? Trying to cut herself in so she could quit hustling, get off the street and her kids outta that dump. That's what she told me, but it never would've happened. She would've snorted her share, then come crawling back, wanting in again."

"Back to you?"

"Yeah, but it wasn't my decision. I handle payroll, that's all." Ernie emptied the glass.

Devon snapped his fingers at the waitress walking by. "Another round."

He and Ernie stared at each other until she brought the drinks. Watching Ernie gulp half of his down, Devon asked, "Did Bobby get the film from Sabrina?"

Ernie nodded.

"Did you call and tip him off we were coming?"

Ernie slumped back in his seat. "I didn't know he'd kill her."

Devon picked up his glass and sipped at the whiskey until it numbed him just enough that he could restrain himself from flooring Ernie.

"It all worked out," Ernie hissed. "Sergio called this morning to say everything's back where it belongs."

Devon set his empty glass down. "Where's Bobby?"

"I already told you. Acapulco. Maybe Bogotá. Maybe Río. In a few weeks, Sergio'll be back in business and there's nothing you can do about it."

"We could set up a sting, bring in the Mexican authorities, bust the operation in Ojinaga."

"This kinda shit's gonna happen whether you know about it or not."

"We're cops, Ernie. It's our job to stop it."

"It can't be stopped! Sergio's got enough money to buy whatever he wants." He emptied his glass. "All I want is a little oasis to keep my family safe."

"Is that what you think you've got?"

He nodded. "And I'll keep it if you get off your high-horse and let me ride. I'm not doing nothing but looking the other way. You should, too."

"You're doing more'n that, Ernie."

He smacked his empty glass on the table. "My daughter's graduating from Lourdes Academy in June. You think I could've sent her there on a cop's salary? Next year she's going to St. Mary's. You know what the tuition is? Twenty grand a year. I've got two more daughters at Lourdes. They're living like the Kennedys, and me a cop on the beat. I'll look the other way to give 'em that. Don't judge me."

Devon caught the eye of the waitress, held up two fingers for another round. When the drinks came, he slugged half of his down, feeling it melt the chill in his heart.

"What about the girls from Juárez? You think their fathers didn't love 'em as much?"

Ernie stabbed his ice with his stir stick. "Most of 'em sold their daughters to Yago. Don't tell me they loved 'em."

"Okay. Maybe nobody loved 'em. Does that make 'em fair game for Sergio to slaughter so he can get his rocks off?"

"The street's hot with word you're poking into this, but you're only coming off suspension 'cause Escobar dropped the charges. Sergio made that happen." He drank half his whiskey and set the glass down. "He can make a lot more happen for you, Devon."

"Help me nail him, Ernie."

"It can't be done! He owns the law in Presidio and Ojinaga, even the fucking D.A. here."

"D.A.'s can be busted like anyone else."

Ernie shook his head. "Even if you pull off a sting, you'll never get it in front of a grand jury. Sergio didn't spend four years at Harvard Law for nothing."

Devon finished his drink, watching Ernie over the rim of the glass. "How many girls has he run through that studio?" He set his empty glass down. "We can put him on death row where he belongs, give you full immunity for testifying against him."

Ernie leaned close, his eyes fierce. "I'll be dead if I open my mouth. So will you. But we won't get the mercy of a bullet. His thugs'll kidnap us along with one of my daughters and your niece, put 'em in a movie and make us watch the filming, *then* he'll have someone like Bobby cut our throats on sheets already wet with the blood of the virgins we hold most dear. Even after that, nothing'll change 'cause he'll buy the cops who replace us. We got only one choice, and that's to accept his money and use it to do whatever good we can."

The waitress came back. Devon waved her away.

Ernie lifted his glass and drained it dry. "Now you know all this, it's one or the other. You know that, don't you?"

Devon nodded.

"Can I call Sergio and tell him you're with us?"

"You gonna call him from here?"

"No, I always do it from home so I can look at my daughters' pictures while I'm talking to the fucker."

Devon reached for his wallet and took out a twenty, the same amount he had given Alma for what at the time felt dirty. He put another twenty on top of it.

Ernie laughed. "Next time I'll pick up the tab. What the hell, once you pay the initiation, it's all Sergio's money."

Walking out of the snug restaurant, they hunched their jackets closer against the chill of a windy night. The parking lot sloped downhill with a view of Juárez in the distance. Devon thought of the girls growing up with one good dress and worn-out shoes, how they must have smiled at the rich *gringo* who promised them heaven while hiding a knife up his sleeve.

Ernie unlocked his car, a Ford Taurus, beige on beige. "This is how the world turns, Devon. You won't regret it."

"I hope you're right."

As Ernie bent over to get in, Devon pulled the gun from the back of Ernie's belt. Ernie sat down hard, having felt the loss. Devon nudged the barrel behind Ernie's ear and pulled the trigger. He shut the door, walked to his own car and started the engine, used his handkerchief to wipe the gun clean of prints, and tossed it in the Dumpster as he drove out of the lot.

In his room, he opened the bottle of Old Crow, slugged down a drink, then sat staring at the phone as he sipped at another. His first thought was to call Prairie and tell her to get the hell out of Sergio's reach. Then he realized she would come to El Paso expecting his protection, something he couldn't give because he had no intention of cutting Sergio slack. Wondering if he had been too quick, if maybe Ernie might have buckled under more pressure, he thought of calling Dreyfus. He could couple his confession with an offer to run the sting alone, infiltrate Sergio's organization and bring him down.

Dreyfus wouldn't go for it. Unwilling to publicize a crooked cop in a department on the take, he would sweep the killing under the rug, veto the sting because it wasn't their jurisdiction, slap Devon on the back and tell him to stick to investigating homicides, not committing them. But Dreyfus wouldn't forget; he'd pull it out every time Devon bucked protocol.

The phone rang. Expecting the desk clerk, maybe asking how long he planned on staying, Devon picked it up. "Yeah?"

"How smooth you are, Detective," Sergio said, his voice oily with ego. "A man to my liking in all respects."

His mind reeling to figure how Sergio had found him, Devon muttered, "It's not mutual."

"The benefits are. In one moment of decisive action, you eliminated a rotten apple in your organization and the last threat to mine."

"What're you talking about?"

"Bobby followed you from the restaurant. He's in Juárez now and called only a moment ago." Sergio chuckled. "Don't bother to say anything, Detective. As useful as I find your talents, I'm afraid I couldn't believe your sincerity if at this point you offered your assistance. Neither will I forego the pleasures of watching you maneuver against me. As an aid to your fortitude, I give my word never to harm anyone you hold dear. The only life you'll risk is your own."

Devon stood up. "Why didn't you make this pact before Prairie was raped?"

"Sodomized, Detective. There's no doubt the child is yours."

"You sonofabitch."

"I assure you I had nothing to do with her misfortune."

"Yeah? I haven't talked to Greco yet, but after I do he'll say different."

"I'm afraid you're too late. He hanged himself in jail last night. It seems someone neglected to take his belt away."

"That someone being your partner."

Sergio laughed. "I sincerely wish you luck in your maneuvers, Detective, and look forward to our next encounter." He hung up.

Devon yanked the cord out of its jack and threw the phone against the wall. The bell jangled as if in mockery as it bounced on the carpet. He lifted his whiskey bottle, ready to throw it too, then set it back down and leaned with both hands on the table as he tried to clear his mind.

Ernie had known all along where Bobby was. They had probably arranged a signal for outside of Jaxson's. Ernie hadn't given it, thinking he had pulled Devon into their pocket, assuming Bobby was ready to kill the cop they couldn't corrupt, not the one they already had.

Devon saved Bobby the trouble and delivered the death

Sergio wanted. Because of Sergio Tierrasantas, he had now killed two men, been tricked into eroding his already shaky moral ground, and manipulated into defeating himself. He had to admit the tactic was brilliant.

He crossed the room and opened the door. Looking at the lake of lights seeping into the desert, he thought of Prairie in the dark that was business as usual in Presidio County. She was safe, Misty too, because Sergio wanted Devon's opposition. So even in that, he had won; the only way Devon could was to quit.

Hearing the distant wail of a freight pulling its way north out of Texas, he felt a great emptiness left behind. More than his integrity had been lost. By killing the last remaining witness, he had eliminated the only opposition capable of bringing Tierrasantas down. A yawning fissure of despair threatened to suck Devon, too, into the paralyzing prelude of death. He kicked it shut and numbed his soul by swallowing whiskey straight from the bottle until finally, through the amber haze of liquor against the light, he saw the truth: his derailment may have been accelerated by outside forces, but he had jumped track way back when he let Eric skate from murder.

Mistakes snowball. How many times had he told himself that in his years working homicide? Lately all he'd made were mistakes, ricocheting off that misstep last year. The realignment, too, was his to make.

Tonight he would finish his whiskey. Tomorrow, tender his resignation, turn in the Lexus, and buy himself some wheels. Then, on the first day of his sobriety, head north in search of someplace to heal.